REDEMPTION LANE

REDEMPTION LANE

rachel blaufeld

Paperback ISBN: 978-0-9915928-5-2

Edited by Pam Berehulke
www.bulletproofediting.com
Cover design by © Sarah Hansen, Okay Creations, LLC
www.okaycreations.com
Images © 4X6, © Vadim Kozlovsky
Formatted by Tianne Samson with E.M. Tippetts Book Designs
www.emtippetsbookdesigns.com

Warning:
Content contains explicit sexual content and crude language, and is intended for mature audiences. Parental/reader discretion advised.

DEDICATION

At twenty-three years old, I was a young woman smitten with a somewhat reformed bad boy. Wearing leggings, a tank top, and ankle boots, I danced on tables while he mountain-biked like a wild man through the woods, and watched sporting events. I went to school during the day and worked as a counselor at night; he worked days. But somehow we found the time to fall in love.

Seventeen years later, we both work days. Our nights, we spend with our kids. I still wear leggings, but with cardigan sweaters and slippers. He still rides his bike, but more cautiously.

Life never stops, but I'm still smitten with the man sleeping next to me at the end of the day. I love staying in to watch sports, and he chuckles about the clubs I create in my mind—where there is dancing and so much more.

This is for my husband, who makes sure we don't run out of coffee—ever—and brings me doughnuts and supports me in all my big, giant, colossal dreams.

I love you ~ Author Puma

AUTHOR'S NOTE

Alcohol and/or drug addiction is a serious matter. If you or a loved one believe they may have a problem, please contact a local AA for meeting or support information.

Alcoholics Anonymous is an international fellowship of men and women who have had a drinking problem. It is nonprofessional, self-supporting, multiracial, apolitical, and available almost everywhere. There are no age or education requirements. Membership is open to anyone who wants to do something about his or her drinking problem.

www.aa.org/pages/en_US/find-aa-resources

CHAPTER ONE

bess

Back then...

"UGH, shit. God damn," I mumbled to myself as I stood up, holding my hand to my forehead while I stumbled toward the kitchen.

I'd woken up curled in a ball on the floor, my cheek resting in a tiny puddle of drool on the rug immediately inside my front door. Nipples peeking through my tiny white crop top, skinny jeans stuck to my body, and knee-high black leather boots completed my look.

I know, not a very glamorous situation for a twenty-one-year-old coed. But pretty much my daily ritual.

Standing, I held my palm to my forehead, running it over my cheek as I tugged cobwebs of hair out of my mouth. Memories of the night before flooded my brain as my feet tried to remain steady on the floor.

"Ouch," I said to myself.

If I concentrated hard, I could remember being high last night, dancing on the makeshift bar until a guy lifted me off and took me somewhere else for another hit of something even better. Things were hazy after that.

Finally reaching my destination, I gently leaned my clammy forehead against the cool vibrations of the fridge/freezer combo, willing its chilled touch to drag the pain and awful thoughts away. It didn't.

Oh well, I'd come to prefer my current state of pain to the one I'd lived in as a little girl, and later as a misguided teenager left alone to her own devices. Yes, I would take dry mouth, a wicked hangover, and incessant jonesing for my next hit over watching my mom walk out or being left with an emotionally absent father.

Any day, hands down.

Speaking of hands, my fingers drifted back to the rat's nest that was currently in my hair, my thick long waves twisted in a million different clumps only a bottle of conditioner and a tearful comb-out would solve. That was what I got for sleeping on the floor, resting my head on a burlap mat instead of a fluffy down-filled pillow in my bed.

After taking a small step backward, I opened the fridge door and grabbed the bottle of orange juice, then poured some into the dirty mug sitting next to where my bony hip was resting against the counter. I sipped it slowly, trying to avoid it sloshing in my stomach, and willed it not to come back up, which was no easy feat.

Take a tiny sip, Bess, then a big breath in through your nose and out.

I repeated this mantra until my eyes no longer watered. The natural sugar eased only the smallest pinch of pain, but just enough to make it so I could move.

When I turned a little too fast, the juice became a brutal rolling storm in my belly, threatening to come back up. Slowing my pace, I made my way to the bathroom for some useless ibuprofen and to pee.

With my butt on the ice-cold toilet seat, I looked at my watch. One o'clock in the afternoon. Okay, so it wasn't exactly morning, but it was Friday, the one day I didn't have any classes. Nothing missed, nothing lost.

I'd wiped and moved on wobbly legs to wash my hands and get the pills when I heard my phone beeping. Geez, that fucker was so loud. Where the hell was it? I leaned down, resting my hands on the vanity and thought hard, then felt it vibrate in my back pocket.

Bingo. Score one for Bess. I found my phone without running upstairs to use the Find My iPhone app on my neighbor's phone, which might have happened more times than I cared to admit.

I cupped some water in my hands and brought them up to my face, although most of it dribbled down my chin before I swallowed the tiny iridescent blue over-the-counter capsules that would bring little to no relief.

But who really wanted that?

Actual relief meant covering up the real pain that burned in the pit of my stomach, the empty ache I desperately tried to fill with boys or pills or booze. Or all of the above.

Turning and resting my butt on the sink to check out my text message, I rolled my eyes.

CAMPER: Yoga with hot DJ & blacklight. 5:30 p.m.

With stiff fingers, I typed out a response that turned into a conversation.

ME: Seriously? Happy hour instead?

CAMPER: Nope. Yoga, then margs at Texi Mexi in our sweaty yoga gear.

ME: Say pretty please.

CAMPER: Pretty please! Be ready at 5.

I didn't respond; I knew there was no talking Camper out of it. Besides, she lived one floor up, and she and her long legs and big curly head would show up at five o'clock whether I said yes or no.

Whipping around sixty-five miles an hour too fast for my current state, I faced the medicine cabinet again and pulled out the tiny first aid kit covered in pink and purple kitty stickers, opening the stupidly concealed container with caution. That box, proof of my stunted childhood, held everything that was precious and sacred to me. Carefully, I took stock of its contents: two extra-lush joints, five tabs of Molly, and a few oxy.

Shit, I was low on pharmaceuticals. I made a mental note to call my "guy" before plucking a pretty little Molly or two out of the box. I needed to dim the pain slowly seeping from my heart, and while I was at it, enhance the upcoming yoga experience a touch.

I wasn't sure how Camper did it; that girl raged as hard as I did. Didn't she?

We'd been friends since freshman year, immediately bonding when we'd found ourselves in a nearby tattoo parlor during orientation week. We were both taking the first bold move of our college lives, establishing our independence with a permanent reminder on our fresh and creamy young skin.

Despite her bubbly nature and peppy white smile that often clashed with my somber demeanor, we'd been inseparable ever since. Living the last two years in the same apartment building, taking identical courses, covering for each other, and most importantly, avoiding Friday classes so we could live it up Thursday through Sunday.

Setting my magic pills on the dresser, I stripped out of my smelly clothes from the night before. As they fluttered to the floor, I watched their descent, remembering moments of my own extremely real downward spiral.

Then I crawled naked between my cool sheets, shutting my eyes for a moment or three hours.

CHAPTER TWO

lane

G OD, I was fucking going to kill my brother with just my bare hands. I should have done it years ago, but had never found the balls to actually follow through with it. At the moment, I couldn't even begin to understand what the fuck was wrong with me. Or him.

How the hell does he talk me into this shit?

I was becoming successful in my own right, running my own business, but I might as well have still been the little boy staring out my bedroom window, wondering how I was going to fix Jake's current mess.

How was it that I couldn't take charge of my own identical twin brother?

Oh, right, I was four and a half minutes older and technically had been in charge of cleaning up his fuck-ups since we were nine when our parents died in a car crash. We'd been sent to our grandparents, and they did their best, but they had zero clue what to do with a wild child like Jake.

Neither did I.

Throughout our childhood and adolescence, I was consumed by worry that our last living family members would give up on him. And that would have been worse than the alternative—telling the truth.

With my shoulders held high, wearing a fake smile and a polite demeanor to hide my broken soul, I spent the majority of my teen years sacrificing anything I might have wanted for the sake of my brother.

Like college. I was accepted to Vanderbilt; my brother wasn't. So we stayed close to home and went to the University of Pittsburgh where my brother got to play D-1 baseball. I got an undergrad business degree, an MBA, and an education in sleeping with my brother's hand-me-downs.

Except, all I ever wanted was to get the heck out of Dodge. I hated being close to home or anywhere that resembled that gray, colorless, craptastic place. And by home, I meant anywhere in the Northeast; any-fucking-where there was a change of season. Fall, with its leaves dropping casually all over the place, like they didn't have a care in the world. Those pesky little pieces of life and their flitting to the ground were only followed by an icy chill, snowflakes in the air, and cold wind in my face—a constant reminder of the jagged ache of our loss and my mistakes.

But I went to Pitt and slogged through the shitty weather like a good and devoted brother, and I even stayed on afterward. Apparently I found some sick satisfaction in handling my brother's dirty work and prolonging my own suffering.

Like now. My brother was casually sleeping with the yoga instructor at his gym, Fizzle Fitness. And she was teaching a five-thirty class he couldn't make, so he sent me, his identical twin, to take his place.

"Practice in the back row, she'll never know, Lane," he insisted over lunch.

"Seriously?" I asked. "Jake, we're twenty-five years old and you still want to play the bait-and-switch routine like when we were kids?"

Brushing aside my objections like he always did, he said, "I'm just in a bad spot, and I gotta do something for the gym. You understand putting work first, right? Still, we all need to get laid, bro, so do me this one favor. Yeah?"

And like that, I gave in to my asshole brother.

I did like yoga, but I preferred the quiet kind. The type where I could actually allow my mind to run free from responsibility. I didn't need the flashing, thumping, party-scene class version.

But there I was, positioned in downward dog on my thick black mat, stretching out my tendons in the last row just like Jake suggested, trying to keep Lexie, the instructor and his current main squeeze, from coming over. I was flashing my brother's girl a smirk like he would—should—have been doing, when two college girls walked in right as class was about to start. One chick set up her mat in the front row, and the other one dropped down right beside me.

I couldn't be upset; the girl next to me was smoking hot. Intrigued, I took in her long wavy brown hair that she was twisting into a messy bun, small tits in a bright blue halter top, and tight hips and a round ass poured into tight black yoga pants. The disappointing thing was she fucking stank, and my eyes began to water from the stench wafting my way, like booze and stale sweat. This girl smelled like a bar after a long Saturday night.

Was she drunk? Was she even legal?

Slightly turning my head the other direction as I concentrated on Lexie's instructions, I breathed the air coming from the too-skinny, nondescript blonde on my left.

Some punk, new-age, rap combo blared through the speakers, and I took in the absolute ridiculousness of my surroundings—the DJ with big cans on his ears was jamming to his own tunes completing the picture.

Welcome to Crazy Town.

The lights dimmed further and beams of black light swirled around the room as if we were in a dance club, giving everyone some spots of neon glow in the darkness. Which made this the least likely place to unwind, in my opinion. To actually relax, I looked forward to the beer or two I planned to have after class.

We were jetting through sun As and Bs, hopping back to chatarunga, and jumping up to our hands faster than I could even take one breath. I was pretty sure I was getting whiplash when all of a sudden something landed on my hip, knocking me forward right onto my stomach, and it didn't move, just lay there heavily on top of me, pinning my hip bone to my mat.

"What the hell?" I said as I turned over, instantly holding my mouth closed because the foul odor from earlier enveloped me.

"Bess!" The girl's friend from the front came running back, a blur of bright pink Spandex with her huge ponytail of curls whipping around her face, paying no mind to Lexie still trying to conduct class. "Bess! What happened?" she screamed at the brown-haired young woman sprawled across my mat.

We were both met with silence. I was still on the floor where I'd slid over on my knees, so I gently nudged the young girl, but she didn't respond. Her friend dropped down next to me and violently shook the still body in front of us. As I watched, my gaze fell on the unusual tattoo on the unconscious girl's arm, a crying eye that looked as if it were begging me to help.

"Bess, honey, Bess, wake up!" she yelled to her friend before whispering, "Oh my God, she's dead."

I moved my hand to the smelly but beautiful girl I had come to know as "Bess," and felt her wrist for a pulse. When I felt a thready beat, I said to the woman whose name I didn't know, "She's alive."

We were causing a scene with the unconscious girl on my mat and her friend slumped to the floor next to her, the friend shaking and quivering, almost turning blue herself, yet Lexie kept right on teaching.

What the hell is wrong with her? Why isn't she handling this?

And then I remembered. I was supposed to be the owner of the club we were in, so naturally, I'd be handling this situation. On my own. As Jake.

Like I said, I was going to kill my brother.

CHAPTER THREE

lane

Four years later

Fuck, it was cold up in the mountains. The damp air hung all around me, its cold moistness winding its way through my suit jacket and seeping into my bones. Either I was a pussy or my blood had drastically thinned after only a few years of living in Florida. Growing up in this shit up north, I thought I'd be prepared—at least physically—for a quick business trip close to home in the fall weather.

Mentally, I still despised what the weather represented, but this was going to be an in-and-out straightforward meeting with a medium-sized account.

I can do it.

After landing at Pittsburgh International Airport, I rented a car and went straight to the cemetery. Being the responsible grandson, I made a quick visit to my grandparents' graves before hightailing it out of the city to my destination.

No, I didn't bother to see my brother. He was up to his usual shenanigans, sleeping with countless women, searching for something that didn't exist, fucking up in his business over and over again, and hiding behind being the poor little boy who grew up without a mommy and daddy.

Unlike me, he wore his mixed emotions proudly, flaunting his highs and lows, and his ambivalence to the meaning of life. I kept mine cloaked in a facade of success and purposefulness.

As I pulled up to my hotel and stepped out of the car, the temperature felt like it dropped twenty degrees since leaving the city. Running my hand through my thick hair, I took in the palatial edifice looming over me, a crown jewel in the middle of cow country with enormous cathedral towers.

They will make me a pretty penny.

Pretending not to be affected by the cutting wind, I stood tall, motioning for the valet. Taking my keys, he asked, "Checking in or just here for dinner?"

My hair blew in the breeze, and I was forced to push it back once again with my cold fingers.

I wanted to reply to the stupid valet, *No, I'm checking out and heading back to my big house in sunny Florida, complete with a revolving door of plastic women*, but that would have been out of character for the revered Lane Wrigley—if you believed my reputation in this business.

Keeping my cynical thoughts to myself, I simply said, "Checking in," and headed to the front desk.

At reception, I didn't have to announce myself. They were waiting with bated breath for me, fully expecting the man who was reportedly changing the hotel industry with an advanced software tracking system for guests, supplies, payroll, and purchase orders. My software package was a "hotel manager's best friend and a hospitality franchise's knight in shining armor," according to the latest review in the hospitality industry rags.

I wondered why the valet hadn't been put on alert, but realized he probably expected me to arrive in a limo rather than a rented SUV.

Once I entered the business world, I kept my personal life to myself and rarely revealed anything about my past to my clients. I never saw a reason to drop clues as to where I grew up—either before or after my parents died. They were almost one and the same, both with their gray, downright depressing climate and nature. And both were in the past.

I didn't need anyone's sympathy or pity. I'd moved on, learned to live with my regret and sins by omission, but not with the changing weather. It was and always would be a trigger for my depression and guilt, and just admitting that stole my man card from me.

The lanky blonde with a big smile at the front desk yanked me out of my reverie when she greeted me by name. "Good evening, Mr. Wrigley. Welcome to the WildFlower," she said as she pulled her shoulders back, practically shoving her oversized tits in my face.

All I gave her back was a curt, "Thanks," while maintaining my distance.

"We have the Sunflower Suite all ready for you, sir." She'd continued to smile, but it dimmed somewhat as she processed that I wasn't in the mood for small talk.

"Sounds good. Can I still order dinner at this time of night?" I inquired politely like the gentleman I'd been raised to be.

"You sure can." More pearly white teeth were displayed, along with a small flip of her hair added for good measure. Just in case I wasn't getting the message.

So not going there.

I took the key card from her hand and once again said, "Thanks."

"My pleasure. Is there anything else I can get you?" she asked, leaning forward slightly to give me a better view of her tits.

Oh, dear God.

"No, thanks. Good evening."

I refused any help with my bags and headed to the Sunflower Suite for what was sure to be anything but a bright and sunny evening. Not only did memories of my childhood plague me, but every time I came back north, I thought about *her*. The brunette, gorgeous from a distance, but toxic to herself and the world around her. The girl I could have, *should have* stayed and helped, but deserted in a fog of fear. After all, who was she to me? Nobody.

Bess—that was her name.

Somehow I continued to feel enormous guilt related to that day, which was practically ancient history by now. I should have forgotten all about it, but it haunted me.

She was nothing. Yet she'd become somewhat epic in my mind over the last few years.

Had she been the one chance for me to redeem myself? Was that why she'd literally fallen at my feet? Rather than taking the chance to explore why she picked me, I'd run—sprinting away from anyone who even remotely reeked of needing someone else.

It was one of my biggest regrets—messing with Jake's sleeping arrangements rather than helping Bess—which only served to underscore how totally fucked up my priorities were. It was yet another example of bad judgment calls on my part that added to the well-hidden list buried deep in the recesses of my mind.

I didn't know what I would have done had I followed my instincts, but the girl clearly needed help. Unfortunately I was more preoccupied with my silly sibling rivalry, and sick of being Mr. Nice Guy to my brother. It was high-fucking-time Jake learned a lesson, that his behavior had consequences. Lord knows, he'd gotten away with murder over the years.

Although I'd spent months—years—obsessing over leaving a young girl who was crying out for help, the last thing I wanted in my life was a needy chick. I already had a long list of those types in my life, namely Jake, Jake, and Jake. Thanks to my brother, neediness was a major red flag for me.

At least I had waited for the ambulance to arrive before bolting. And as I'd hoped, Jake didn't get to screw Lexie that night after she caught on to his little ruse. In fact, she'd come to fuck me, and while I didn't think I would have enjoyed it, I did in some sick, twisted way. I'd come hard as she pulled on my hair, yelling *my* name and screaming in delight.

On paper, I might have been the good brother, but that didn't mean I was a saint. I knew my way around the curves and slopes of a woman's body the way a NASCAR driver knows their way around a track. It was the only trait we had in common. Jake and I both liked women, and we knew how to pleasure them.

But after a few days of Lexie lingering beyond her welcome, I grew bored with her dumb smile and barren brain. The offer to merge my company with one based in Florida came at the right time. I accepted it immediately, and never looked back on my days in Pittsburgh.

Except for thoughts of *her*. Bess.

Arriving at the Sunflower Suite, I slammed the hotel door shut behind me with my foot, kicked off my shoes in the corner, then stalked toward the bed, hoping this little Northeast jaunt came and went quickly.

CHAPTER
FOUR

bess

I TURNED to run my hand along his forehead, making my way to rub his ear, searching for tranquility in the warmth of his dark brown eyes. "Oh, Brooks, baby, we gotta get up," I told my bed partner, but he looked apprehensive. Burrowed deep in my covers, I didn't want to get out of bed either. A chill had come over the mountains.

But we had to start our day, so with a quick kiss to his furry brow, I nudged my ninety-pound black Labrador, Brooks Bailey, out of bed and through the door to do his business while I ran to do the same in my small powder room. It wasn't long before I heard a paw scratch on the front door, and let the only man I had kept intimate company with in the last few years walk through the door. Of course, he was looking for breakfast.

The coffeemaker sputtered over the sound of my dog crunching his chow as I lifted the tiny blind above my sink and surveyed the day outside. A thick layer of fog had come over the mountains, enveloping my porch and limiting my already darkened view of the tiny brook that ran along the bottom of the hillside. Fall was officially here.

I poured myself a big mug of java and headed to my bedroom to get ready for my day, taking solace in the quiet I once despised. Nowadays, the calm serenity of rural living was the salve on my ever-present wounds, coffee the only drug in my house.

Not really a house or home, but a refuge from my past, I lived in a small two-bedroom cabin overlooking a rambling brook in rural Pennsylvania. It was a gift from my dad when I got out of rehab and decided to stay in the quiet rolling hills and lush forestry of Ligonier, close to the treatment facility. It was a crutch I didn't use, but its presence nearby was comforting nonetheless.

I also didn't want to go home to Pittsburgh and face whatever reputation I left behind. My past could stay right where it was. In the past.

As for my dad, he didn't really owe me anything. I'd come to understand he did the best he could and we'd forgiven each other as I tackled the steps of recovery. But I took the house he offered me.

I owned all of my actions and indiscretions, and had learned not to place blame on others. But the man felt guilty enough over his shortcomings as a single dad—a little too late—and giving me the house provided him some peace of mind.

Turning on the shower, I let the water heat up. Steam filled the bathroom and funneled its way around me, allowing me to undress without catching a cold. After spending too long under the spraying water, I dressed in my usual worn-in and frayed skinny jeans, layered long-sleeved T-shirts to cover my mistake of a tat on my bicep, and Nike Air Force Ones. I'd traded in my go-go party boots and crop tops for a more practical wardrobe the day I left treatment.

These shoes reminded me of when I was happy, playing kickball in the alley with the boys around the neighborhood before I was old enough to feel the effects of not having a mom. In other words, before I fucked up everything. Before I substituted the lack of a mother's affection with cheap beer and robotic teenage sex in the backseat of a car or in the twin bed of my youth.

But that was all back then, when I was constantly seeking to feel anything other than pain and discontent. Now I just felt nothing.

I survived on little to no emotion, a baseline of honest work, the company of my dog, and the relaxing sounds of nature.

After applying a light layer of lip gloss in the hallway mirror, I let Brooks pee once more, throwing the ball down the hill a few times so he blew off some steam before I left him for the day.

And then I was out the door.

"Hey, May," I called out to the head of housekeeping as I walked in through the back employee entrance to the WildFlower Resort and Spa.

"Hiya, Bess! How was the driving out there in the fog? Been here all night, but I'm gonna leave soon," she responded.

"Oh, fine. You know, I'm a tough city girl. No fog is going to bring me down," I yelled back, more for my benefit than May's peace of mind.

As I shoved my stuff in my assigned locker, I had started to change into my uniform when a thought occurred to me. *Actually, the tiniest thing could crack me in half.* With my usual fatalistic attitude, I knew it was only a matter of time before my carefully constructed world would come falling down.

Although I used the staff locker room, I wasn't a housekeeper at the WildFlower like the others who used it. One of my small circle of friends, May allowed me to use the locker room. The woman double my age was reliving her youth and had high hopes I would find myself a gentleman—her words, not mine. *You're certainly not going to do that in your waitress uniform*, she'd said, so she encouraged me not to travel to and from work in that crappy outfit.

"What you got on there, girl? More of those ugly basketball shoes and ripped jeans?" May called after me.

"You know it, May," I shouted back from the locker area, glancing back at her. Even in the ugly WildFlower housekeeping uniform, May looked beautiful. She was curvy in all the right places, her black hair cut in a short bob around her round face, and she was always smiling.

"Hope you didn't come through the main hotel looking like that. You're never gonna catch Mr. Right wearing that!"

It was the same daily banter we'd been having for years.

"Well, that's good because I'm not searching for him," I said as I walked out of the locker room and made my way into the staff corridor.

For the last three years, I'd worked in the resort's fine dining restaurant, serving breakfast and lunch six days a week. The job kept my hands and feet and fingers and toes busy, and especially my mind.

I did finish my marketing degree via correspondence after rehab, but sitting behind a desk scared the living shit out of me. Too much idle time. So I got a job slinging dishes, and I liked it just fine. I made good tips and paid my bills.

Mostly, my coworkers had come to expect little more from me than small talk over coffee, a walk with our dogs, or grabbing a movie together. No late-night drinks or parties, never a suggested jaunt to an after-hours club, and definitely not a chance in hell for yoga with a DJ and a strobing black light.

Not that there was any of that in small-town Ligonier, another reason why I stayed on in Podunk, USA, after a sixty-day stint of drying out, getting clean, and learning basic survival techniques.

Garbed in my navy slacks and tight striped vest over a pressed white blouse, with my hair pulled into a ponytail and a few loose strands falling around my face, I tucked a pencil behind my ear and went over the specials on the blackboard in the kitchen. My stomach rumbled, so I grabbed a scone and a cup of coffee to enjoy while I chatted with Ernesto, the resort's pastry chef, as I waited for the breakfast rush to start.

We might be in the middle of nowhere, but the WildFlower served as a major stomping ground for luxury conferences, executives visiting the booming factories nearby, and women looking for a mountain retreat or, as we laughingly called it, "glamping."

Swallowing my last bite as the big hand hit twelve and the little hand six, I was out the kitchen doors. I took in the few people already lined up, waiting to be seated for breakfast. Shelby, the hostess, was struggling as usual to make it happen, so I decided to wade in.

I went over and started directing suits and a few spa ladies where to sit. At the end of the line was a tall guy with a full head of mussed jet-black hair. He was wearing a gray pinstripe suit and brown wingtips, and had his head buried in a newspaper, his wild hair such a contradiction to the rest of his expensively clad, well-heeled body.

"Excuse me? Do you want a table," I asked.

He flipped the paper down, peering over the top of it, and his crystal-blue eyes sharpened. A series of expressions flitted over his face, first hurt or sadness, then morphing into what looked suspiciously like lust. In the end the man continued to stand there, saying nothing and looking bewildered.

Weird.

Unnerved, I stared back at him for much too long, but his gaze mesmerized me, capturing my body, mind, and soul in a way I wasn't familiar with. It left me wanting to stare forever.

What the eff, Bess? Stare forever? Just seat the damn guy.

"Are you ready to sit for breakfast," I asked, using my professional tone as a shield. I wasn't on the menu, and definitely wasn't one of the specials.

He cleared his throat and said, "Yes. Table for one." Then he added, "Please."

"Right this way."

In the end, I didn't seat him in my section. I had no desire to deal with his stuffy weirdness.

CHAPTER
FIVE

bess

G EEZ, that guy was a little bit creepy, but mostly intriguing, if I were completely honest with myself. He sat in his corner booth, never taking his gaze off his morning paper, folding and creasing it with precision.

I served my tables but couldn't resist keeping an eye on him; there was something about the way he wasn't looking at the scenery like most people did. Not once did he turn his head toward the scenic windows to take in the large trees that were turning vibrant shades of orange, and the bunnies scampering across the wet grass.

He barely glanced at the menu before I heard him curtly asking Joe, the other waiter on duty, for coffee and eggs with toast. And then after devouring everything on his plate, washing it down with a second cup of coffee, he slipped out of the restaurant without even lifting his eyes to the room.

That was it. He was gone, and I felt some strange draw to this man who was sexy, yet all business, which made absolutely no sense. By lunchtime, I'd forced myself to put the guy way out of my mind.

I was leaving for the day when my supervisor, Maddie, called me into her office. Tripping over my own feet, I stepped over the threshold, but didn't sit down. "Is everything okay, Maddie?" I asked as I stood behind the enormous dark green club chair opposite her desk.

"Everything is fine, Bess," Maddie said with a dismissive wave of her hand. "Never any problems with you, honey. But today I had a visit from a gentleman staying at the hotel with a very strange request. He wants you to join him for dinner tomorrow. In fact, he extended his stay by one night to make time for you."

I felt my brow furrow in confusion. "I don't understand. I didn't even talk to anyone today. Who would want to have dinner with me?"

Maddie motioned for me to sit and leaned forward. "His name is Lane Wrigley. Apparently he's some hotel industry big shot here on official business. Do you know who he is? Did you ever meet him before? Hear of him?"

Sliding into the seat, I shook my head. "No. I've never heard of him before. Ever. I've been living here in this small town since I left college—you know that. How would I know some hotel biz guy?"

Maddie narrowed her eyes. "I didn't think you did, but I went to upper management with his request, and they want you to go. They want to know what the man wants. Maybe he's looking into the inside of operations here."

I blew out a breath and said, "I don't even know who you're talking about, Maddie. You know I keep to myself. This is nuts. I'm a waitress, and now the boss guys want me to play corporate espionage?"

Completely ignoring my protests, Maggie rattled off, "Tall guy, black hair, blue eyes, wearing a suit. He ate with us today. Maybe you saw him in the restaurant?"

Surprised, I sat up straighter and said, "Oh, him. Yeah, he was all spooky. At first he stared at me, then he just ignored me. I don't think so, Maddie." I stood up, prepared to leave for the day, but Maddie pulled out all the stops.

My supervisor stood up and walked around the desk toward me with wide eyes. "Listen, Bess, just go and see what he wants. It will reflect well on me, with my bosses. The top brass apparently want to hire him, they feel like they need him." Her tone turned pleading as she added, "I'll even give you a paid day off the next day."

I rose out of the chair. "I don't want a paid day off. I don't like being off, you know that. But fine, I'll do it, but it has to be early. Like five o'clock tomorrow, because I *will* be at work the day after."

As I walked out of her office, I heard Maddie yelling, "Swing by tomorrow and I'll confirm the details. Thank you, Bess."

I didn't even bother to change as I was leaving. Instead, I went straight home, let Brooks out, ate a lonely dinner for one, and did something I hadn't done in a long while.

Later that night, I pulled into the mostly vacant church parking lot and sat in the driver's seat with the car idling. I was early, eager to get somewhere I never wanted to go, and I was sweating. A cold, nervous chill overtook me, sending fine tremors over my entire body. Beads of perspiration dripped down my sides, lined the nape of my neck under my long and heavy hair, and slid uncomfortably down my back and into my ass crack as I watched other cars pull in alongside mine.

Allowing everyone else to exit their cars first, I waited. I wanted to slip into the basement meeting room unobtrusively, to be invisible; I wanted my long absence from the meetings to go unnoticed.

I pulled a ball cap over my hair, tugging the bill of it low, and glanced at my reflection in the rearview mirror before I finally opened the door of my SUV. Then I forced myself to turn and threw my jeans-clad legs out of the vehicle, planted both my feet on the ground, and willed them to walk toward my destination.

Move, Bess.

I did. Slowly at first, before eating up the concrete in my comfy, reassuring Nikes, hurrying to do what I needed to do before I chickened out.

When I tugged the door open, it creaked and clanged loudly,

drawing unwanted attention to me as I stood hesitantly in the doorway. My eyes stung and I started to turn back around before I felt a large hand on my arm.

"Stay, Bess. It's okay. You'll be okay. No hard feelings," said a gravelly voice, raspy from cigarettes, warm from coffee, and soothing like a blanket in front of a fire on a cold night.

I nodded my head, unable to form the words, and finally sputtered, "Thanks, AJ."

My sponsor wrapped his arm around me and guided me to a seat next to him. Big and strong, with his shirt and jeans smelling of the outdoors and his latest construction job, AJ's comforting presence quieted my jangling nerves.

Sitting on my hands, squelching my need to fidget or pick at my dark red nail polish, I listened intently to the others' stories of perseverance and strength while wrapped tight in the soft embrace of my sweater.

I didn't share or talk, only absorbed the stories of others' struggles, finding some inspiration in their strength. And then I went home to my cabin, crawled into bed still wearing my clothes, and held my dog.

CHAPTER SIX

lane

On my second night at the resort, I took the front desk girl up on her unspoken offer to have a drink together. Clearly I was having some sort of existential breakdown after changing my flight, asking a waitress to dinner, and basically rescheduling twenty-four hours of my busy life for an absolute nobody.

Well, not really a nobody if I were honest with myself. Which I rarely was anymore.

She was the woman—the girl—I dreamed about nightly, along with the tattoo of a crying eye. That image lurked in the back of my mind, judging me when my own two eyes closed at night.

Still, these weren't risks I took on a day-to-day basis. Or ever, for that matter.

My outer shell formed the day I became an orphan. It hardened as I matured until it became impermeable, and my professional persona as a businessman was locked into place. I was smart—the one widely known fact was I turned down Vanderbilt, the Harvard of the South, choosing instead to enroll in an "accelerated program" at the University of Pittsburgh. At least, that was what my bio read.

I didn't wheel and deal or make concessions. I was stubborn and formidable, determined and tough as nails.

Don't let my wild hair and trendy appearance fool you.

The women who were in and out of my bedroom weren't needy; they knew the score. Sex, dinner, companionship, and that was it. I traveled, worked, and fucked. I didn't take phone calls, and I didn't respond to texts when pets died or friends fought or there was a sad movie on TV.

In an effort to appear as though I interacted with employees low on the totem pole at all the establishments I did business with, I met Cara, the bubbly, all-too-cheerful, and way-too-willing blond receptionist for a nightcap.

Of course, I didn't mean to take her to bed. But I did.

Ever since I'd screwed Lexie's brains out, sex had become nothing more than another challenge to me, a presumed competition to be the best lover, a man who knew his way around every inch of flesh on a woman. I wanted to be a gentleman in a suit by day, a lion in the bedroom by night.

After a few beverages in a dark corner of the bar, I stood to escort Cara to the elevator, my hand drifting to the small of her back as she stood from her chair.

She leaned in and whispered close to my ear, "Let's be discreet. You go up first and I'll follow behind. I know your room number."

Ignoring what she said, since it was ridiculous, I never let go of her back.

Once we were upstairs, she slowly stripped for me, revealing black thigh-highs and ample breasts. I spent some time licking and sucking those tits, not allowing my mouth to wander up to her lips.

That was not something I did with regularity. Mouth on mouth reeked of feelings and intimacy. Something else I didn't do.

She kept making these awful fake moans. "Ooh, Lane, or should I call you sir? Ooh, ah, ooh. You are a naughty CEO." She sounded like a dying cat, and I could almost see her counting my money in her head.

I knew that look well from the ladies back home. The women who never got a call back—they also made those money-hungry faces masked as lust.

My hand slipped between her thighs and the wide-eyed, bushy-tailed small-town girl was sopping wet for me.

"Ooh-ooh—ooh."

I kept thinking, *Please shut up. I'm going to lose my hard-on.*

Too bad. Not all of the lionesses could meet my prowess, and Cara was a poor match for me. The woman might be competent working behind a desk, but she truly lacked dick-sucking skills, not to mention the ridiculous noises she made.

A brand spanking new fantasy rolled through my head—visions of a lonely, yet seductive waitress dressed in navy slacks and a little matching vest, her long hair spread down around her neck—and I came silently.

Is she in the building?

With nothing else to do with my newly found day off, I stayed confined to my suite, ordering both breakfast and lunch from room service. I'd already made up my mind to do business with the WildFlower. They were a legitimate resort despite being in a rural cesspool, and I could make a good bit of cash from their contract, so I had absolutely no reason to stay other than my dinner date.

I wasted my day alternating between banging on my laptop, doing push-ups and sit-ups, and contemplating what I would say to Bess. My mind ran through a million and one scenarios including lies and half truths, but the whole truth was the only one that sat well with me.

Except somehow, I knew I wouldn't do it. I wasn't even sure if I knew the truth anymore.

Yeah, I'd made myself into some type of ice-cold, unfeeling, all-business machine over the years, but when it came to this girl, I had a little soft spot that grew wider by the minute. Over the years, I'd contemplated what she'd been doing, and if she'd even survived. If she had, I wondered if her friend ever told her about the random guy who semi-helped and yet semi-ditched her.

After I'd taken Lexie to bed that ill-fated evening, I'd sneaked into the bathroom and called the emergency room, pretending to be a cousin when I asked after someone I had no business inquiring about. "I'm calling about a young woman, Bess, brought in after almost overdosing?"

They'd only said, "I'm sorry, sir, but we really can't give you any information."

And I'd begged, "Please, I just need to know she's alive, that's all." I'd added, "Our family is so worried, we haven't heard anything yet and we just need to know that she's still . . . with us."

I'd known nothing about the young woman or her family, but I'd been desperate to know she survived. "Please," I'd said again, this time my voice raspy.

"I shouldn't say anything," the woman finally said in a low voice, "but she is alive. She was discharged with her father an hour or so ago. Hope she makes it." Then the line had gone dead. With a quick click, that had been the last I'd heard or known about Bess.

And here she was—waiting tables in a fine resort in the middle of absolutely nowhere, working for what happened to be a potential client of mine.

Not able to dwell anymore, I grabbed the phone and dialed the spa.

"Good afternoon, Mr. Wrigley. How can I assist you today?"

"I would like a massage in my room. Can you accommodate me on such short notice?"

"Certainly. Let's see, how is half past two? I can send someone up then."

"Good. That works. A female, please."

"My pleasure, Mr. Wrigley."

"Thanks," I said before slipping the handset back into the cradle.

With only twenty-two minutes left to waste before my brief respite arrived, I texted my brother.

ME: Hey, what's up? I'm in PA. Saw Grandma and Grandpa's graves before heading to the mountains for a meeting. You good?

It took about five minutes before my phone beeped with a response.

JAKE: Hey there, you responsible little fuck. Good for you, you visited. I don't do fucking cemeteries. They don't know you visited. You could have seen me instead.

ME: Yeah, I know. My bad. Listen, I'll call you from home and we'll set something up. OK?

JAKE: OK, fuckface.

On that endnote, I powered the phone down and waited for the masseuse to arrive with her table and, hopefully, her magic hands. Hands that would help me stop obsessing over the past and the unknown future for at least an hour.

Which they somewhat did—until it was time for me to jump in the shower and clean up for dinner.

I was a man obsessed, a completely new brand of Lane Wrigley. All because a girl I had never formally met, whose name I only knew from hearing her friend screaming it, had broken through my shell and touched my soul. In my head, I knew it was all wrong, and that I should get in my rental and leave the state of Pennsylvania faster than I came, but I couldn't.

In a pair of jeans and a freshly pressed designer long-sleeved T-shirt, I made my way to the quiet tavern for dinner at a quarter after five. Management had insisted dinner be early, and I didn't want to argue. But it did feel a bit strange to eat hours before I normally even finished working.

None of it mattered because there she sat, hands in her lap, semi-watching the television behind the bar, her hair down, drifting around her shoulders, hiding her long lashes and profile. I took a moment to watch, trying to convince myself to turn and walk away. To run, like I originally had to Florida. I should just hurry back home to the beach and my lonely diet of work and women—women who needed nothing from me.

Bess. The girl I'd harbored an ongoing fascination for since the night we met, and since then had carried a borderline mental obsession with the exact episode that led to meeting her.

The girl who so obviously was a mess and needed help, the young woman I left in the care of a belligerent EMT who was annoyed to be called out on a Friday night to help a strung-out, presumably spoiled college girl. While I went home and screwed my brother's flavor of the week.

Bess, the girl I had abandoned, was my one chance at redeeming myself. No longer a girl, she was now a grown-up woman who clearly had no recollection of ever meeting me, now waited tables in Pennsylvania for a living, and had just lifted her head and caught me staring at her.

I moved toward her with purpose and authority; after all, I'd called this business dinner. Approaching the table with my hand out, offering to shake hers, I said, "Hi, I'm Lane Wrigley."

Clearly apprehensive, she stood and warily brought her small palm to meet mine, and shook my hand while saying, "Bess. Bess Williams."

A small tingle ran between her hand and mine. Not love at first sight or any of that crap, not a burning desire that ran straight to my dick. It was more an electric current, a familiar one—at least for me. I remembered checking her for a pulse with her girlfriend screaming in my ear, her small palm limp and lifeless in my hand.

Now her hand was warm and once again tucked inside my own. Irrationally, I felt as if she held my heart within her hand, the heart that beat life into my body, and that I might arrest if I let her hand go.

I should have been telling her, *No, please, don't stand. Have a seat.* But I was so transfixed with our fingers touching, with her natural scent—neither stale nor perfumed, but fresh—affecting me. So I stood there for a heartbeat too long, simply holding her hand as I enjoyed the moment.

Her head tilted a bit to the side as she studied me, silently asking with her eyes why she was here. She was obviously not entertained or the slightest bit excited by my dinner request, let alone with my inability to release her hand.

When I finally let go, her arm dropped back to her side, and she gazed down at the tiny pulse beating in her wrist. Perhaps she felt it too? Then she sat back down.

Sitting down across from the woman of my obsessions, I leaned in and spoke. "Bess, it's so nice to meet you. I'm sure you're curious as to why I invited you here."

This was where I meant to tell her the truth. At the very least, the part that related to her. Not everything; not even the most well-equipped, overly trained shrink was prepared to handle that news.

I should know. I had one of those back home.

After finally being in the obviously confused girl's presence for a few moments, I gathered she'd become a private, self-contained person. No longer the wild coed reeking of booze and all-night partying, this was a young lady who would not appreciate me bringing up the sordid details of the past.

Clearing my throat, I continued. "Well, Bess, I run a fairly large hotel management company. We provide software that monitors and graphs all functions of the hotel from occupancy to profit to soaps used, and then my staff interprets that information in a million different ways for management. The WildFlower would like to do business with me, and I want to really get to know their operations and staff first."

"Oh." She relaxed slightly, sitting back more comfortably in her chair as she out let a sigh of what appeared to be relief. "Nice to meet you, Mr. Wrigley," she said, her hands still clasped in her lap.

I leaned forward in my chair, keeping eye contact as I added, "Lane, please. I hope it's okay I call you Bess?"

"Yes. That's fine. So, what can I tell you about the WildFlower?"

My pulse rate ramped up at the idea of her wanting to get right down to business and hurry up with our dinner. Wanting to slow things down a bit, I changed tactics.

"How about we order a drink?" I suggested. "Something to eat? And then we can get to the nitty-gritty? Sound good?"

She nodded her head but made no move to pick up a menu. I waved for the server, who rushed over and gave Bess a big smile and quick greeting before asking what he could bring us.

"Water with lemon, please," Bess answered.

"I'll take a beer on draft, whatever you have that's local. And how about something to eat?" I said to the waiter and then turned to face Bess. "Do you like fried pickles? I have to admit, they're a weakness of mine," I asked her with a wink.

"Sounds great," she answered with a small smile, and our server rushed off to pound our order into the computer.

"You know, it feels good to be back around here. I went to U of Pitt and from time to time, my fraternity would come up to the country and cause havoc. Hayrides and bonfires . . . Crap, it feels like forever ago," I said, spewing off shit I never really discussed. Sitting up straight, I apologized for my walk down memory lane.

Bess sat there quietly, not offering much. She definitely didn't mention going to Pitt herself.

"Well, there isn't much to do around here," she finally said softly. "So I can only imagine what a bunch of bored college guys could get into."

"It is quiet. Do you like that?" I asked her while leaning in.

She opened her mouth to answer but was interrupted by the arrival of our drinks.

I watched as she thanked our server, gifting him a big smile of gratitude, and I wasn't sure if it was for bringing the drinks or for interrupting our conversation.

As the waiter turned to leave, I said to Bess, "Go on, you were going to say something."

Focused on squeezing her lemon into her water, she kept her eyes on the glass when she said, "Yeah, I guess I kind of like it now.

Actually, I took some classes at Pitt too. But I think this area suits me better." She kept her gaze trained on the table, watching her own hand lift her water before taking a drink.

I took a long swig of my beer before answering. We were heading into the twilight zone, only Bess didn't know it. I knew she went to Pitt and what happened when she lived on the college campus, but she didn't know I knew, and that made me uncomfortable. My insides began to burn with anxiety, causing heat to travel up my throat, and I nearly sighed aloud with relief as the beer cooled the flames of embarrassment inching up my neck.

"Really?" I asked as nonchalantly as possible.

"Uh-huh," she said with a nod.

"What a coincidence. Small world," was what I said next. Why? I had no fucking idea. Maybe because I liked feeling uncomfortable and shitty? After all, that was my norm—feeling crappy.

I decided to move the conversation along and carry us out of dangerous territory. "Well, I have to say, I was dreading being here in the damp weather, but the good news is that it's grounded me to my room. I'm getting a ton of work done without the distractions of living on the beach."

"Oh, fun, I didn't know." Once again interrupted by a delivery, this time it was the pickles, Bess reeled herself in. "That must be nice being near a beach," she offered as we helped ourselves to food.

Remembering why I was supposed to be here, I tilted my head toward the retreating waiter and asked, "So, are most of the servers friends? Do you all hang out outside work? What's it like when you're not at work? Are you a big happy gang?"

I took in the way her chest rose and fell beneath her long-sleeved black shirt. The outline of her bra was lace, her skin was creamy, and her breath was raspy when she answered. "Some of us. I'm actually close with a few girls on the housekeeping staff, but not many of the dinner servers because I'm usually gone by then."

"Right. Thanks, by the way, for staying to join me," I said with a full smile, leaning back in my chair and smoothing my hair out of my face.

I would never part with my longer, shaggier style. It was the only feature that said "bad boy" about me. Except I was never a rule-breaker growing up, other than when it came to my hair. Probably because my dad kept his hair long and I remembered playing with it as a kid.

My mane.

Lane the lion, Bess the lamb.

Pulling out of my memories, I focused back on the subject of my last thousand nights' fantasy. "I guess you get in pretty early in the morning? I feel bad to have kept you here," I said, then mumbled mostly to myself, "The request for an early dinner time now makes sense." Mentally, I kicked myself in the ass for not realizing this woman had been at the hotel since before dawn.

"Yeah, I do," she said after she took a sip of her water. "I get up pretty early to head over here. I guess that's why I know most of the housekeeping girls. I never used to be a morning person, but I kind of like it now." Her expression grew wistful as she added, "It's peaceful waking up before everyone else, taking in the dew while walking my dog outside."

Enthused at the prospect of something else we could chat about before pretending to talk about more hotel logistics, I leaned forward. "So you have a dog? What kind?"

"A Lab."

Our server came back to clear the pickles and refill our drinks. While he was there I ordered a burger, and Bess went with a salad.

"Your dog must love running around in this cool weather," I said when we were alone again.

"He does. Keeps me exercised," she said, her features relaxing and softening when she spoke about her four-legged friend.

And that was the way the evening passed . . . with bullshit small talk about weather and morning dew, dogs, and hotel scheduling.

By telling a lie, I was on the dullest date ever with the only girl I ever wanted to win over. Except, it wasn't a date. Starting with my little "business dinner" fib, I began a brand new bad habit of my own—deceiving young women. A habit I couldn't change because I'd appear to be even a bigger asshole.

But I had no choice, so I spent the dinner perfecting Lane Wrigley, the overly involved businessman, getting to know Bess Williams, the unimpressed, fragile, mysteriously beautiful waitress, whose rapid breathing and racing pulse took my breath away.

CHAPTER
SEVEN

aj

CAREFULLY maneuvering my truck through the slick mud, I left my construction site. After pumping up the volume on the rock music, I jammed the heat on full blast, my hands still cold from standing outside as I checked on the guys and went over plans with my foreman. I waved my hands in front of the vent, letting them warm a little, then waited a second to crack the window and light up before pulling out.

As I took a long draw on my Marlboro Red, I glanced back at the shopping center. It was going to be the biggest one in the area, and we couldn't fuck up one square inch of it. It was a huge contract for me at thirty years old.

Fucking A.

It was nothing my company couldn't handle. My fragile psyche was a different story, but no one would guess that by looking at me. To the casual onlooker, I was all brawn and rough flannel around the edges.

My pickup barreled out from the dirt road and I picked up speed as I hit the main highway, pulling into the diner for a quick cup of coffee a few moments later.

"Hey, Shirl, babe! How you doing today?" I called out over the bells ringing on the door.

"Hiya, AJ, honey!" she said back with a smile, tiny creases forming around her light green eyes, her laugh lines exaggerated. For a married middle-aged woman, she was still pretty smoking, even though she kept it all toned down. With her red hair tied back in a bun and a pencil stuck over her ear, she screamed *small town.* Although I knew there was more to her story, I just didn't know what.

"You good?" I asked her with a knowing nod, reminding her that each day sober was a freaking God-given blessing. Despite all my outer bulk and glory, I was a sap on the inside, and the waitress with at least a decade on me knew it.

She gave me a soft, "Yeah," as I sat down at the counter, smelling bacon from the fryer and cinnamon wafting from the pie case.

"Two coffees, okay, doll?"

"Two?" she asked with her eyebrow raised.

"I'm making a life change today," I said with a wink.

Shirley turned toward the coffee machine, shaking her head and her tiny ass. "Oh, you are?" She turned back toward me, placing the two Styrofoam cups in front of me before leaning back on the counter separating the dining area from the kitchen with her arms crossed over her ample chest.

"Yep, so how much do I owe you? I gotta get the hell out of here." I didn't want to get into any more of it with her.

"In this case, it's on me, buddy."

I threw a few bucks on the lime-green counter and hightailed it out of there, two cups of steaming coffee in my hands. But not without noticing the strange look pass over Shirley's face. I sure as fuck didn't have time to worry about that, though.

Driving past the WildFlower on my left, I glanced at the barren land on my right. Soon all that land would be scooped up with the little micro-economy the resort created around here. My mind wandered, imagining dollar bill signs, anticipating all the work I could bid on.

And then I thought about *her*. Bess had started coming to meetings again more regularly, and I knew there had to be something up, more than she was admitting, but I wasn't going to push. It was my time to get a little closer to the brown-haired beauty, and that was exactly what I was going to do.

Blowing smoke out the window, watching it fade into the cold air, I thought that the rehab center should have known years ago that introducing me to Bess would be problematic. She was gorgeous, vulnerable, alone, and shit—gorgeous. With big round brown eyes framed with long, full chestnut hair, fear and vibrancy rolling off her in equal waves, she became mine that day.

She'd been sitting in the bay window, her long hair falling down over her thin arms, nearly hiding her tattoo. It was the last time I'd seen her wear a tank top. I couldn't help but stare that afternoon at her soft eyes and weak smile, which were such a contradiction to the large eye inked on her arm with two teardrops falling from it.

For the last four years, I'd watched silently and patiently, waiting for the right moment to approach her, to make her aware that she was most definitely mine. And that she didn't need to shed tears anymore.

Throwing the truck in park next to her house, I stepped out and waited for Bess to roll home from her shift. She was going through something and needed someone, and that someone was going to be me—like it had been every other time for the last four years. Except this go round, it would be with me as something more than just her sponsor, more than just a friend.

When the coffees were cold, I decided Bess wasn't coming home after work, so I texted her.

> ME: Hey, how you doing? I popped over to see you with coffee. You okay?

After waiting another ten minutes and getting no response, I left. When I got home, not really remembering how I drove or parking the car, I paced the hardwood floorboards of my house.

It wasn't until after eight o'clock that night that my phone finally chimed.

> BESS: Hey, sorry. Actually had something at work this evening. :(

> ME: Work? What? You don't work dinner. I was fucking worried.

> BESS: Some stupid thing for management—nothing to worry about. Back to my regular routine tomorrow. Thanks for worrying, though. Night.

And just like that I was dismissed. Well, too fucking bad. I'd been waiting a long time to take the opportunity to claim what was mine, and it was in the palm of my calloused hands. No way I was going to let it slip away.

CHAPTER EIGHT

bess

AFTER tossing and turning for what felt like a million hours, I got up and walked a very disgruntled Brooks Bailey. My dog liked his rest. He'd been giving me dirty looks every time my knee made contact with his rib cage as I wrestled with the covers, and my emotions.

The moonlight lit my way down the hill to the lake. Brooks trailed along, sniffing, stopping to pee, rubbing up against my leg, welcoming a pat on the head. We didn't need a leash. We had rescued each other and neither of us were going anywhere. Neither loyal owner nor adoring pet were in any position to ditch the life we'd made together. I was resurrected from the past; Brooks from the pound.

I was no stranger to insomnia. It had become a way of life for me in rehab without the aid of anything to lull my overactive brain to sleep, but this was a new brand of sleeplessness. A man had crawled beneath a layer of my skin, burrowed somewhere underneath my hardened shell of indifference, and I had no clue what to do with that.

Were there meetings for this sort of thing? If it were drugs or alcohol tempting me, I could call AJ or go to a meeting.

Ugh, AJ. What's up with his popping by and bringing coffee?

But I didn't have time to worry about him. Nor did I think there were support groups for dealing with being smitten with Lane Wrigley. Although, I was sure there was a very long string of us—women—probably each and every one of us a random, lowly hotel employee wishing and praying that *he* would take more than just a professional interest in us.

Coming to a stop, I settled on an old tree log about thirty feet from the stream and allowed the soothing sound of the rippling water to wash over me. It was chilly out today, and even tucked into an old sweatshirt with Sherpa-lined boots on my feet, a chill traveled up my spine. I felt coarse hair brush along my cheek as I lowered my head into my hands, and sensed my faithful friend sit down beside me.

At twenty-five and unattached, it wasn't unusual that I was having these feelings—an inappropriate attraction to a man with power and money at work. After all, there was real blood running through my veins. My core heated at just the thought of the man and his ridiculously out-of-place messy black hair. And like that, my boots felt way too hot and my sweatshirt confining.

Tilting my head to the side, I leaned my cheek on my dog's head and whispered my secrets in his ear. I couldn't even say them out loud to an animal.

"Ugh, Brooks, why didn't I think about this when I left rehab? Making a life beyond this meager existence? A life with love and men and sex?"

A lone tear made its way down my cheek, disappearing in black fur, but Brooks didn't have any answers for me.

"It's no biggie, Brooksie. He'll be gone tomorrow, and we'll be back to life as we know it. Just you and me and nobody else," I said, more for my own peace of mind as I got up and walked home.

Feeling very much like my former hungover, tired, and strung-out self, I entered the WildFlower already dressed in my waitress uniform. In no mood to face May or anyone else who knew about my dinner meeting, I hurried to the kitchen and ducked my head to avoid chitchat with any of the other employees, certain the rumor mill was alive and well.

They were all staring at me.

Rushing into the kitchen, wishing for a quiet cup of joe and a buttery scone with Ernesto, I ran smack into a hard wall. A wall that went by the name Lane Wrigley, standing front and center in the middle of the kitchen, all wrapped up tight in a suit and tie with a big grin on his face.

"I'm sorry, Mr. Wrigley," I muttered. Unsettled, I straightened my clothes and smoothed my hair from our collision, my body still burning from the briefest moment of contact. My emotions were a mangled car in a five-car pile-up or worse.

"It's Lane, and no worries," he said with playfulness flitting through his blue eyes. "I didn't mean to scare you. I was actually getting ready to leave and wanted to thank you for your time."

This was yet another version of Lane Wrigley, neither the ice-cold, all-business man I first saw at breakfast two days ago, nor the warm but consummate professional I had dinner with, but a more fun version disguised in another perfectly pressed suit.

"Um, it was nothing." I waved my hand in the air while backing up a few inches, trying hard not to breathe in the masculine scent surrounding me. It was a high I didn't think I could afford to enjoy.

Already turning and heading through the kitchen door toward freedom—the dining area—I skidded to a halt when Ernesto called out, "Um, Miss Bess, the restaurant isn't busy at all. Why don't you take a few of my fresh treats and coffee in the back for you and Mr. Wrigley? He can learn more about the hotel and how we operate in the restaurant." He motioned toward the overflowing baking sheets on the counter filled with fresh muffins, elaborately iced pastries, and mouth-watering scones.

"He probably doesn't have time for that, Ern, but thanks," I said, feeling my cheeks heat and knowing they were probably a bright shade of red, deeper than the cranberry filling oozing from the Danishes lining the baking sheet.

"Actually, I do," Lane said. "I had to make some changes to my travel plans, so I'm flying a private charter home. They can leave when I want, and a pastry sounds great." He walked toward the large tray of goodies set on the stainless counter, pretending to examine the sweets, but held my gaze in his peripheral vision.

"Good!" my meddling coworker interjected, then shoved a plate at Lane and me, instructing, "Take what you want and go."

So, with a scone and a to-go cup of coffee in my hand, I led Lane back to the break room. I didn't dare take a whiff of the cinnamon Danish in front of me for fear that Lane's heady scent would fill my senses instead.

"Well, this is an unexpected surprise," he said as he sat down at the large round table in the center of the room. He pulled out another seat and insisted, "Here, this one is for you."

"I really shouldn't be doing this," I said. "They're paying me to wait tables." I took a quick sip of my coffee as I stood there, uncertain what I should do.

Lane took a deep swallow of his coffee and shook his head. "Ah, that's some good coffee. Come on, I don't bite. Sit."

I did, setting my plate in front of me, unsure of where my appetite flew away to. The only hunger I felt was for the man in front of me. Watching his mouth, staring at him taking a large bite of his blueberry muffin, my own mouth watered, and it wasn't because of the fluffy pastry.

When he finished chewing, he leaned in. "You're still working right now, Bess, so relax. We'll call this business—again." He took another bite and added, "Shit, this is good! I haven't had one of these in a long time. I wonder where I can get something like this in South Beach?"

I let out a little laugh. "I don't know much about South Beach, but I'm pretty sure that's where the South Beach diet originated. I'm also pretty sure you can't eat sugar-filled, butter-laden muffins on that diet."

"I guess not. Maybe I'll have to come back here for another one soon," he said with a smirk.

"Umm, not sure a muffin is reason enough to come back here," I said as I pinched off a tiny nibble of my own treat.

"Well, it would only be one of them, although I may have to wait until spring. This weather here, it leaves a lot to be desired," he said and for a moment, he got a faraway look in his eyes, as if he went somewhere else for a second or two. The pain—so palpable—I'd sensed a few days before when I'd seated him at the restaurant, seemed to ice over the bright blue of his eyes, dimming them for a moment. And then, just like that, his eyes sharpened and focused on me, exuding warmth again.

"I guess I'm just used to it," I said with a shrug. "What's the temp now at home for you?"

Weather is a safe subject, unlike him coming back to the WildFlower.

"Gorgeous, warm, but not stifling. You should come see for yourself." He finished his muffin, then drained his coffee cup.

I had to remind myself to breathe. "I'm not sure that's in my budget for right now, but someday, maybe I will." My skin was prickly with nerves at what he was suggesting, itchy with how much I actually wanted to do that. Visit Florida . . . and see him again.

Taking the last few sips of my own coffee, I stood up and said, "I'm going to get back to work now. I mean, my actual job, but this has been really nice of you to take the time to meet me and get to know me. I'm sure management appreciates it." Then I stuck out my hand and said, "Nice to meet you, Mr. Wrigley."

"Once again, it's Lane," he said, "and I really appreciate it." But he didn't shake my hand. Grasping my fingers with his larger ones, he brought my hand to his lips and placed a light kiss right above my knuckles, his lips lingering and torturing my senses.

"Umm, well, it's been a pleasure doing this." I stumbled over my words, working my hand free and waving it around since I had no freaking clue what else to do with it.

"No, the pleasure's been all mine. Meeting you hasn't felt like work at all."

The spot where his lips had made contact tingled; the small patch of skin, on the bone and near a vein, must have been singed or burned. I expected to look at my hand and find a hole.

"'Bye, Lane," I said, rushing out as fast as I could.

Does he kiss all hotel employees on the hand?

I couldn't wait to leave work that day. Despite my best intentions, I'd fueled the employee gossip mill, a position I didn't like hoding and wanted to desperately shed. As I was hightailing it out of the building, Maddie stopped me again.

Shit.

Standing in front of me with a gift-wrapped box blocking half her face, she called, "Bess, one sec!"

Seriously, what now?

I stopped moving but didn't speak.

"Thank you so much for taking one for the team and graciously meeting Mr. Wrigley. Apparently the hotel got the deal with him, and management is tickled," she said while bopping back and forth from foot to foot in her sensible flats.

"No thanks needed. I did it, and Mr. Wrigley already came to thank me in person, as I'm sure you heard, so the whole thing can be put to bed now. I gotta go," I said as I started moving down the hallway, leaving in my ugly work clothes again.

"Wait!" Maddie called for me again.

I turned on my heel and looked at her with one eyebrow arched.

"This. This is for you," she said while shoving the gift toward me.

"Oh, that's not necessary." I shrugged and turned on my heel for the second time.

"Bess! It's not from me," Maddie yelled.

This got my attention.

"Who's it from?" I asked as I whipped back around, afraid of what she might say.

"Mr. Wrigley, of course."

"Of course," I repeated, grabbing the package and walking straight to my car, not stopping to say hello to anyone else. Then I threw it—not gently—into the trunk, where it taunted me the whole drive home.

CHAPTER NINE

lane

M Y sweaty hair fell in my face as beads of perspiration rained down my forehead, running into my eyes and dripping off my nose as I ran along the beach. I'd been back in Florida for a week, and since then I'd either been working my ass off or exercising like I was training for the Olympics.

Unable to get *her* out of my head, feeling fucking ridiculous for my whole silly and foolishly elaborate good-bye scene, and raging an internal war over whether to contact her or not, I was unrecognizable to myself.

I basically asked the girl to visit me after pondering another trip back to that shitty weather. Unable to stop thinking about the sheer insanity of it all, and wondering what the hell was happening to me, I continued to punish myself with my brutal workout.

"Hey, Lane! How are you?" I heard someone say from behind me, then felt a pat on my ass.

Turning, I took in the redheaded beauty and said, "Hey, Christie, how's your run?"

Although I didn't slow down, she lengthened her stride to pace me and kept up. "Better now that I caught you! Where you been?" she asked with a salacious smile, her words coming out winded and breathy.

A few weeks ago, I would have gotten hard over the combination of her tone and her meaning, but not today.

"Working, honey," I said, barely needing to overexert myself with my own words.

"Well, you look good," she said, holding her line.

"You too!" Nodding my chin toward the road, I said, "There's my ride. Time for me to cool down. See you around, Christie."

With another grab of my ass, she was gone. "Hope so. 'Bye, Lane."

Needing to cool down, I slowed my pace. Without considering why, I moved my hand back to my ass, brushing off the memory of Christie's unwanted touch. I pulled out my earbuds and hit the Stop button on my pacer watch while I caught my breath. Typically, I alternated running with yoga.

Yoga, of course.

Bess, my head screamed as loud as my muscles. Yoga only reminded me more of the woman I'd now officially met under false pretenses, yet still hadn't been able to dislodge from my brain.

Of course, for the last seven days, yoga wasn't possible for me. There was no way I could slow my thoughts enough to relax into the poses, let alone wrap my head around what the whole damn class symbolized.

Inner peace, of which I had none. Because of her.

Well, maybe not just her. My shell was starting to crumble. I was alone. No parents or grandparents, just a brother who was a full-time babysitting gig. And a stable full of girls with names like Candie or Missy who wanted nothing more than to be seen with one of Florida's most eligible bachelors.

As I walked in circles with my hands on my hips, taking deep gulps of air while I came down from my runner's high, I couldn't help but glance at the Florida sun setting, its light reflecting off the water. But I couldn't enjoy the sight.

Why did I have to lie to Bess? I should have told her the truth. This wasn't me; I wasn't a liar. The lie was eating me alive, but I didn't see any way out of it. All those years I'd duped girls for my brother made me despise lying, yet here I was doing it again. This was probably some kind of sick payback for playing the bait-and-switch routine for Jake, as well as everything else I did for him that I never wanted to do in the first fucking place.

Stopping and stretching for a second, opening my quads, I contemplated if there was any way of righting this mess I'd made for myself.

No.

The WildFlower deal was done. My lawyers had just signed off this morning on the final paperwork. There was no longer the cover of checking into the inner workings of the resort; I had no reason to stay in touch. The only clients I ever kept an eye on were the ones in major cities, the ones I liked to visit—Vegas, Chicago in the summer, Los Angeles. Not the middle of freaking nowhere.

My chance was gone.

Kicking up sand, I made a beeline for my car and my life as I knew it.

"Hey, Randi, how are you?" I asked into the phone stuck in the crook of my neck as I toweled off from my shower.

"Hey, baby, I'm great. Just back from an assignment in the Bahamas, a swimsuit shoot. You?"

Dry now, I paced my massive bathroom. "All good. Wish I'd been somewhere warm, but I just got back from the wet wilderness of Pennsylvania."

"Ooh, you poor baby," Randi purred into the phone, and her voice affected me like nails dragged across a chalkboard. A shiver ran up my spine, and I had to lean on the counter.

Staring at my despicable self in the mirror, I asked, "Want to grab some sushi?"

"Sure! I'd love to. When?"

"Now." I didn't want to leave myself room to change my mind. Randi was a smart choice for distraction. The control was always in my hands with her.

"Oh, cool. I need a little time to freshen up. Do you want to pick me up or should I meet you?"

Staring down at the black countertop, unable to watch my own actions anymore, I said, "I'll grab you in an hour?"

"Perfect. 'Bye, Lane. See you soon, hon."

I swiped my finger across End Call without another word, sealing my evening's fate.

CHAPTER TEN

bess
Two months later

IT was a cold and brisk Sunday. Small snowflakes flitted through the air before sticking to the almost bare branches and settling to rest on Brooks's block-shaped head as we took a walk down the hill.

I bet it's warm and sunny in Florida.

Christmas was upon us! *Yippee*! The entire resort was fully decorated and in full-on happy-holidays mode, churning out cookies and hot chocolate, building a different gingerbread replica daily and touting the benefits of the eggnog facial for women and peppermint back scrub for men.

I found myself feeling more alone than usual, taking solace in thirty or forty too many cookies, and avoiding May's constant nagging about whether I'd heard from *him*.

Why would I hear from Lane? He'd been a man doing his job, securing another million-dollar client for his company. He wasn't a living, breathing human being interested in me.

And why should he be? I was just a reformed druggie—although currently clean and sober—a waitress who survived by living each day in the same boring, compartmentalized way.

But I wanted him to be. Something about the way Lane reached for my hand that night to greet me, or placed the gentle kiss above my fingers the next day, it felt familiar somehow, as if we'd done that before.

It didn't feel electric or like blazing fireworks, but more like milk and cookies after a long day at school. Comforting and homey, which was all a little hokey considering my mom wasn't waiting with a snack when I got home from school.

I grew up in a two-bedroom on the second floor of our apartment building. After my mom left, the neighbor watched me after school. When I got older, I let myself in to be greeted by my pet—a purple-ish beta fish—and made instant noodles for my dinner.

So the idea that some man's hand felt like home was absolutely ridiculous, and I shoved the whole concept to the back of my mind while I swept snow off my face and coat.

It was only mid-afternoon and I was already miserable. I hated my days off with a passion. If I could, I'd work every day. The monotonous routine of work kept me sane, despite my solo existence. The dull routine of waiting tables clung to my soul, embedding a sense of security in its predictability and ordinariness, and left me with a false confidence that I actually had a life. Other than just me and my Lab. Waitressing gave me a concrete purpose, a task to perform, like taking a pet out to relieve himself.

I stared down at the red leather leash in my hands. I didn't even put it on my damn dog, but brought it with me on each and every walk since I received it two months ago in that ridiculous gift box— from him.

It had been an informal large box from the hotel's gift shop, a bunch of stuff picked out at the last minute, yet nothing was haphazard. Each item demonstrated that he'd heard every word I'd said the night before. In addition to the leash for my dog, there were cashmere gloves for cold mornings, a package of Pitt decals, and a lemon juicer, presumably for my lemon water.

Not sure of what to make of the presents, I shoved any hope of

Lane like-liking me to the back of my head and filed the dinner as an odd but good memory.

The thought of gifts brought me back to the present and the looming holidays. I was so desolate this year, I'd even considered a visit to my dad on Christmas Day, but then quickly signed myself up to work for double pay. Ernesto had invited me to join his family, and of course, there was May with her open invitation to join her anytime, any day, anywhere she went.

But I would probably work a double and come home and eat by the fire with Brooks.

My negative energy swirled around me like the weather settling in the area, an isolated numbness traveling my veins and old desires surfacing, trying to bubble to the top.

Deciding it was time to do something about it, I pushed the temptations down as I trekked up the hill in my boots, then let my dog back in the house, changed my shoes, and jumped in my SUV.

I pulled into the church parking lot and parked quickly, not hesitating to get out of my car. I hoofed it to the door that led to the basement, covering my mouth with my fleece scarf as I braced against the wind. As usual, the door slapped open faster and harder than I wanted, but I hadn't been as much of a stranger since last time, so no one paid me any mind.

I'd been coming to AA meetings twice a week or more since I fell back into the fold a couple of months back, after my dinner with Lane. My recent regular attendance was less about the temptation of watching Lane enjoy a beer during our meal, and more about what he symbolized.

Living.

Which was something I wasn't really doing, and didn't feel was mine to expect.

Except AJ kept trying to make me think I should. It felt dirty to me—both the suggestion of living and AJ saying it. But I tossed it aside because what the hell did I know?

Taking my seat, sandwiched between my sponsor and a relatively new girl who worked at the bank, I sat on my hands and looked at my feet. Conversations swirled around me and I listened, passively enjoying the camaraderie of the people who were closer to me than family. As I took it all in, it occurred to me that what these people were doing—the nodding, encouraging, smiling, being brave for someone else, and drinking coffee—all of it helped the mind and body thaw.

But with the warmth came wants, desires, and deeply stashed dreams. No wonder I chose to spend my life in the middle of the mountains where the cold seeps through you at least eight months of the year.

I fidgeted in my seat, twisting my ankles in my athletic shoes, squirming on top of my hands as they called the meeting to order. And that was when AJ nudged me.

"Go, speak, share. It'll be good for you," he whispered in my ear.

"Shh," I hissed, but my body betrayed me and lifted me from my seat, then walked me toward the front.

I stood at the front of the long room, my hands shoved into my pockets, swaying back and forth on my feet as I faced the audience and stared at my hands resting on top of the podium.

"Hi, I'm Bess," I said, my voice cracking, then continued a little louder. "And I'm a junkie. I liked—loved—it all. Alcohol, pills, the harder stuff."

Shit. I mumbled to myself, struggling to form the words needed.

"Like I said, I'm Bess. Sorry for being rude. It's been a while since I've spoken in front of a group. I'm an alcoholic and drug addict. I've been one since I was eighteen years old. Before that I dabbled in a little of everything, but it wasn't until I went to college that I truly lost myself, and drugs and alcohol took over my life."

"Hi, Bess. Welcome," the group chimed in as one.

"Well, let's see," I said, shifting from foot to foot. "I grew up with my dad—just the two of us. My mom up and left when I was a little girl. I remember standing in the doorway of our second-story apartment and watching her walk down the steps, dragging her huge suitcase. She never even turned around. Not once. So, with her gone, my dad did the best he could, and he really did a good job until I went to high school. When I was still young, he would toss a ball to me or take me to his auto shop with him. But he didn't know what to do with me when I started to become a woman. He had no clue what to say to me about boys or friendships. He's just an average blue-collar mechanic. Yeah, he's done well, owns his own shop, and I didn't ever really want or need for anything, but someone to talk to. So, yeah, he could have done a little better in the talking department."

I took a deep breath. Still bouncing back and forth on my feet, I cracked my neck, refusing to look out to the crowd as I continued.

"I was sort of a small-chested tomboy. I liked hanging at the Y, playing ball when I was younger, and back then the boys were my friends. Until the other girls developed, and I didn't know what to make of my own development. The little I grew, I hid under hooded sweatshirts and jeans with holes in the knees. My appearance, my attitude . . . let's just say, I never really learned how to navigate boys or a big circle of friends, and I ended up allowing boys to take advantage of me, which started a vicious cycle. I'd let the neighborhood kids use me, get incredibly sad, and repeat. I know—poor me. But that's what happened, so I have to own it."

I took a deep breath, still staring at my hands as I continued. "College was different. There was so much freedom, and a chance to try on so many personalities, make new friends, and start a different life. Unfortunately, party girl felt best. There were so many pills and parties and joints and drinks. It became a way of life. When I was having fun, I couldn't remember how lonely I'd always been, so I kept going until I was 'having fun' all the time."

Looking up for the briefest of moments, I saw that everyone in the crowd had their eyes trained on me. I lowered my gaze, unable to face them in this moment.

"It was all fun until I collapsed. I had gone to a yoga class high and stoned, all hungover and dehydrated, and as soon as I turned upside down, I was done. That's all I remember. Apparently, I passed out cold. The owner of the gym called an ambulance in time, and I made it to the hospital for them to pump my stomach and help me dry out. That was the easy part in comparison to what came after. And now."

Once again, lifting my eyes slowly, I checked in to see if I should continue. Scanning the faces in front of me, I was relieved to see that they were overwhelmingly open, their expressions merely curious and supportive. Finally steady on my own two feet, I felt goose bumps break out on my skin as I prepared to finish.

"I had one really close friend back then, and I haven't seen her since I left the hospital. It's not like she didn't try, but I refused to add her name to the list of people who were allowed to visit me in rehab. It was too painful to think about her seeing the non-fun version of myself, so I locked her out, and I've been alone ever since. The relationship with my dad never got better, his guilt making it even harder to try, and without a good friend who really knew me, it was just me against the world. Problem is, the thought of living life this way for the next few decades is starting to scare me, pushing me to want to be the 'fun me' all over again, and I can't do that either. So I'm stuck between a rock and a hard place. Alone."

I stepped down from the front to applause from the audience, receiving affirmations from the people I passed on the way back to my seat. One lady stopped me and grasped my hands, urging me to not regret the past, and told me she'd pray for me.

AJ was waiting for me. "It looks like you could use a shoulder or a flannel shirt to cry into, Bess," he said as we walked toward the door.

"I just hate being a burden to anyone. I guess it's been way too many years on my own," I answered.

"A cup of coffee is not a burden," AJ said as he held the heavy door open with his broad shoulder for the two of us.

"I know." I looked away, swiping a stray tear from my cheek.

"Come on, let's go." He nodded to the cars.

"Poor Brooks is alone all week. Why don't you come over and I'll make coffee, okay?" I asked, knowing he would agree.

AJ winked at me as he said, "I'll follow you home, pretty girl," and we jumped in our cars.

CHAPTER
ELEVEN

bess

WITH the radio on and Brooks lounging by the fire AJ built in my fireplace, we drank coffee and talked. It wasn't odd; at least, it didn't feel that way. AJ had spent plenty of time over at my place in the early days of my being out on my own, holding my hand while I got my life in order, allowing me to go through all the stages of recovery, and the emotions that went with them.

His sponsor did much of the same for him when he first left rehab. Lucky for AJ, he didn't need his sponsor that often. At least, not anymore.

Like I needed AJ now.

He wasn't that much older than me, but he was much wiser when it came to life. He hadn't wasted time on college because he had been in the throes of using since high school. After cleaning up, he started a construction business and made a life for himself close to where his grandparents used to live, finding peace in a simpler life.

Finished with my mug, the scent of coffee and campfire hanging in the air, I leaned my head back, letting it rest on the back of the sofa as I closed my eyes. I'd been crying about how lonely I was, questioning, "Is it always going to be this way?" when I felt AJ's hot breath move closer. It smelled like coffee and mint with the faintest trace of tobacco.

His mouth lit a path of heat along my collarbone, and the sleeve of his flannel shirt grazed my wrist as he brought his hand up to caress my cheek. This did feel odd. My sponsor, the gentle but demanding man in front of me, had never touched me other than enveloping me in friendly bear hugs. This was a gentler touch, his rough and calloused fingers sending a message in their soft path.

I lifted my head slowly, opening my eyes and taking in his inviting ones before dropping my gaze. I focused on his light brown five o'clock shadow as he spoke.

"It doesn't have to be that way, Bess. You don't have to be alone. You're not alone. You have friends, and you have me."

His eyes searched mine, begging me to understand the hidden meaning behind his words. I didn't really have *friends*. And we were nothing more than sponsor and sponsee.

I didn't really have him. Or did I?

"AJ . . ." I breathed out his name slowly, looking up but hesitating to meet his eyes.

"Bess, don't. I know this isn't the best idea, but we know what each other has been through. I care for you, and I'm pretty sure you care for me. We could be good for each other. Let me be there for you. I don't want you to feel alone."

Another tear made its way down my cheek as my heart pounded a frightfully fast rhythm in my chest. AJ was soothing and strong—a rock for me—and I felt something deep for him, but wasn't totally sure what the feeling was. But as he looked at me with his clear sea-green eyes and his messy, dark blond hair falling over his forehead, while holding me tightly in his cozy flannel embrace, my body relented and my head nodded. I felt it moving up and down, small unsure movements, but a definite affirmative.

I'm not alone.

His hand reached down and squeezed mine while the other stayed steady on my cheek. My breath quickened and my heart doubled its already rapid pace, but I didn't move. I stayed the course, waited for what was to come next, and then his mouth was on mine. Chapped yet tender lips took over my own, learning the feel and taste of mine.

AJ was there for me. He was showing me; I felt it as our clothes slowly made their way to the floor—followed by us.

I wasn't a virgin, but I hadn't been touched by a man in at least five years. The last encounter I remembered was following a long night out with some guy I met at a bar. There hadn't been anyone since I became sober; this was all brand new. My hands shook as I tried to wrap my arms around the naked man on top of me.

AJ held his weight up on one elbow and whispered, "Hey, it's okay. We can take our time. Shh, relax."

And then he trailed kisses down my neck until he reached my cleavage where he alternated between my breasts, kissing, nipping, and sucking. I relaxed into the rug beneath me, the fire roaring to my left, nightfall filling the windows on my right. His hand made its way down my abdomen, only hesitating for a second while waiting for my nod, before dipping inside me.

His lingering mouth finally joined forces with his masterful hand, and my core began to blaze as big as the flames lighting our silhouettes. Then the dam broke and I shattered, my own wetness only cooling me for a moment.

I nudged AJ to make his way back up to kiss me. God, the flavors and sensations were all so vibrant. This was nothing like the muted lust of being high or drunk. I tasted myself on his tongue, smelled my orgasm swirling through the room, and felt his hardness pressing into me—igniting my heat once again.

"You doing okay? Bess?" he asked me.

"Yes." It was quiet and breathy, but I definitely said *yes*.

As he leaned back to grab his jeans, I felt AJ's absence immediately. Silently wondering what he was doing, if he was leaving—if he didn't want me anymore—I wondered if anyone could ever truly want me. Then I watched him pull a condom wrapper from his pocket, and breathed a sigh of relief.

Pathetic.

He was back on me in a minute, searching with his eyes once again, waiting patiently yet asking me to hurry at the same time.

I took the package, hoping I remembered what to do, then ripped it open and slid it on him—committing a major no-no in the recovery world—before he slid deep inside me, taking his time until we both had exhausted any worries of being alone on this night.

CHAPTER TWELVE

bess

AJ and I fell into a routine that meshed with my usual steady, less-than-exciting life—early evenings spent by the fire, then dark and sweaty nights rolling together between the sheets before parting ways in the early hours of the morning. The air grew colder outside, snow falling daily on my little side of the mountain, but our passion burned bright inside my cabin. A few days turned into two weeks, and all of a sudden we were a couple.

He cooked for me, took me back to his house—the one he built with his own hands—and showed me all the rooms designed to hold a big family someday. I smiled and murmured my praise of his handiwork, but it all seemed presumptuous on his part.

We went to AA meetings and sat separately, hurrying home to reconnect physically as soon as they were over. It was a relationship based in convenience, but didn't feel exactly that way when we were in the moment.

It felt passionate when we were together, but truthfully, who else wanted me?

Lane invited me to Florida. No, he didn't. Not really. He was just being polite.

Was I settling? Was I confusing the first display of any physical attention in close to half a decade with passion and heat?

And what really gnawed at me was that I imagined somewhere deep down inside AJ, he felt guilt or some responsibility to see this through with me. He was my sponsor first and my lover second.

But it had been so long since I'd experienced affection of any kind. It was truly the first time my body responded so vibrantly to a man's touch, I couldn't stop whatever crazy train we were riding.

Our newly formed relationship met head-on with its first obstacle today, Christmas Day, December twenty-fifth. It was a day for family, friends, lovers, prayers, wishes and peace, and I was driving my usual route to work as dusk colored the sky pale pink and gray in anything but peace.

My warm breath created a smoky fog when it hit the cold air in the car, my gloved yet still-cold fingers fanned out over the wheel, my stomach tied in knots over my choice, but I had to do what I felt I had to do.

I was working. AJ wasn't.

He wanted me to go to the dinner he was hosting for friends at his home. I wanted to work.

It was an argument that began in the middle of the night last week. AJ slid out of me, taking care to wrap me tight in the blanket as he went to dispose of the condom, and came back with a warm cloth to clean me up. Always the caring, thoughtful one, he turned to me and tucked a stray hair behind my ear as he whispered, "Christmas is just a few days away, Bess."

"Really?" I said, somewhat teasing and a tiny bit sarcastic.

"Yeah, babe," he said, his voice cracking with something I didn't quite recognize.

I decided to try to lighten the odd tension I sensed building between us. "I got you a little gift!" I said while batting my eyelashes.

AJ threw his leg over mine, careful to not lay all his weight on me, and gripped my hip firmly, letting me know he wasn't in the mood for joking. "Got you something too, but that's not the point. I want you to come to my place for dinner. A bunch of us from the meetings, we all get together every year to avoid big boozing-up type parties. We cook and relax by the fire, and I need you there."

"I'm working," I whispered as I tucked my head under his chin, then placed a small kiss on his chest.

"Get out of it," he murmured as he kissed the top of my head.

"I can't, AJ. I work every year. You deal with the holidays your way, and I deal with them in mine." I felt his body stiffen, and didn't have the strength to look up and meet his eyes.

"Bess, that's not fair. We're together. I'm there for you, and I want you to be there for me. I want us to be together for the holiday, under the mistletoe." He tucked his finger under my chin and brought my face up to meet his.

I shook my head. "I can't, AJ. Please don't push, but I need to work. It's how I deal. I'm sorry, I know I'm letting you down, but I just can't be with you on Christmas Day. I can come over for a little while when I finish up work, though."

At this, he moved to get out of bed and slipped back into his jeans and flannel shirt. "Well, that sucks and I can't accept that, Bess. You're not my booty call. I have feelings for you beyond you stopping by at night."

And then he left, just like that. The odd thing is, I didn't even get up to watch him pull away.

Yet as I drove to work this morning, images of his truck pulling away kept blending with memories of my mom walking down the stairs and never glancing back.

It made me wonder—did he turn around and look behind him as he drove away?

Lucky for both my drab mood and myself, my shift started as soon as I changed at the WildFlower. The line for Christmas brunch snaked down the hallway from the restaurant. We were full with reservations, but there was no way we would turn away the families who showed up at the last minute—we would just hustle even harder.

Better for me. My mind will stay occupied.

The crisp white tablecloths were dusted with glittery fake snow, and candles glowed inside the poinsettia centerpieces. The room smelled like fresh pine thanks to the dozen or so fresh trees lining the perimeter of the dining room, decorated with shiny baubles and wide gauzy ribbon shot through with gold thread, and every so often I caught a whiff of eggnog from the special French toast on the buffet.

As Christmas carols piped through the speakers, I worked my tables with a smile and a red bow pinned to my vest. From a distance, I watched other families celebrating, sharing and experiencing a special day together. I tucked the notion in the back of my mind that this was how families were supposed to be—spending time together, tossing back champagne and clinking their glasses, then tossing back some more. Little boys and girls clanked mugs of hot cocoa filled with marshmallows, high on their own drug—sugar.

Festivity cloaked the room like a heavy winter parka; there was no escaping it. Although the alcohol-infused orange juice in the room didn't bother me, I was rattled by the sentimentality of it all. I couldn't escape the pinch of pain in my chest while bearing witness to something I'd never had nor probably ever would. The occasional children's laughter that rang out was the only salve to my pain. After all, how could anyone deny a child the experience of Christmas Day?

After cleaning up and resetting the room from brunch, I was able to take a short break. I hid in the kitchen, having a bite to eat before dinner service began. Ernesto went home after the last pan of French toast made its way out. Before he left, he kissed me on the cheek and wished me a merry Christmas. It was one of the nicest gestures I'd ever experienced.

It wasn't like we didn't celebrate as I was growing up; we did. After mom left, Dad would send his current secretary out to buy me a few "girl things" for Christmas. There were nameless Barbies, cardigans with tiny crystals sewn on the collars, and vanity sets. After Christmas, I would throw them all in the corner. I didn't really know what to do with any of that junk since I didn't have a mom. But I always pretended to be excited and sought comfort in my dad's hug following my attempt at a heartfelt reaction. After all, it was my one chance at affection all year long.

Dad didn't cook, so we always were invited over to that secretary's house for dinner. Every year it was someone different; he'd go through a few of them from one holiday to the next. We would eat, and then I would watch my dad and his secretary celebrate under the mistletoe.

At some point in my mid-teens, I opted to work holidays for time-and-a-half at the local drugstore, which ironically, was how I funded my first bad habit—booze—a much better way to forget my lack of a mother than work. And an easy way to lure a fumbling yet warm teenage boy into my arms to give me the affection I craved.

Caffeinated and nourished, I made my way out to the restaurant for the dinner service. The buffet had been taken away and the elaborately set tables arranged for us to serve a five-course holiday meal. More families dressed in their Christmas outfits filed in, different from the ones we'd served breakfast to. But like the breakfast crowd, they oohed and aahed at the festive decor and ambience.

After wishing each and every table a happy holiday and taking beverage orders, I went to collect drinks from the bar. This was the reason why I tried not to work too many dinners. The back and forth to the bar, the anxiety over the smells and seduction of the many burgundy and amber-hued liquids, and the guilt of being an innocent participant in someone else's problem, all of it meant I normally stuck to serving breakfast and lunch. But I made an exception for a holiday.

Sidling up to the bar where the drinks for the restaurant came out, I pulled out my tablet to take a quick peek at the menu. Without looking up, I said, "Hey, Robbie. What's up?" The bar area was quiet; after all, who opted to spend Christmas alone other than me?

I heard, "Happy holidays, Bess. Not much. Nice to see you on a dinner shift," over the clinking of glasses.

Yeah, I guess.

Then I had the strangest feeling as an indescribable warmth coated me. It started in the center of my chest, radiating its way outward until I was fully covered in a fine sheen of sweat.

And then I heard it.

"Hi, Bess. Merry Christmas."

The heat source had come closer. It was now sitting on the end stool, its breath so close, I could feel it on my skin, singeing me. But it wasn't an *it*. It was a he.

I looked up and my eyes met his. "Merry Christmas, Mr. Wrigley."

"Lane," he quickly corrected me.

"Merry Christmas, Lane. What are you doing here?" I asked rudely with no regard for his feelings, or the fact that I was at work and he did business with my employer.

"Well, that's a bit complicated," he said right before Robbie interrupted him, shoving a large tray of drinks my way.

God bless Robbie.

"Oh well, happy holidays again," I said quickly. "I'm sorry, but I have to get back to work." Averting my eyes, I picked up my tray and walked away as his heated gaze burned my back. I didn't dare turn and look, but with every step, I felt like I was running away from home.

And then the smell of whiskey raced up my nose, chasing any warm and fuzzy feelings I might have away. Desperate to get away from the temptation—of both kinds—I hurried to deliver the beverages.

CHAPTER THIRTEEN

lane

For the first time in five years, I went home for the holidays. Not really home, but to the five-star William Penn Hotel in downtown Pittsburgh. Why the hell did I leave the sun and sand to make a trek back to the ice and snow? I knew damn well why, but I wasn't about to admit it aloud.

I needed to be saved from myself. I needed redemption.

With one more small lie, my life had turned sour. I carried the guilt of that dinner with Bess around with me, and it weighed me down like a trunk full of bricks. Our shared breakfast the morning after was my additional carry-on, a briefcase of evidence that I couldn't do anything right. That baggage piled up with other suitcases full of indiscretions on my back, staying with me whether I was eating sushi with Randi, going for a punishing run, or conducting business meetings. They were with me always, weighing me down like a European traveler on a six-month tour.

My life was beginning to look like an empty movie set, and I had to save myself from becoming a poor excuse of a person like Jake.

Mostly, I obsessed over fixing things with Bess. Problem was, there were no *things*. It was a great big nothing built up in my head, so there was nothing to fix.

The halfhearted greeting I got from my brother should have been my first clue to the lunacy of my plan. I'd landed at dinnertime in Pittsburgh on December twenty-third, and had decided to give my brother a ring before I rented a car.

After selecting Jake's contact info from my phone's screen, I'd stuck in my earbud so I didn't have to hold the phone to my ear while walking to the rental counter. He answered right before it went to voice mail, and by his tone, he'd apparently debated answering at all.

"What?" he barked into the phone.

"Hey, Jake! Merry Christmas to you too," I said, laying it on thick.

"Merry fucking Christmas to you, Lane."

I paced the waiting area in front of the rental counter. "I'm here. In Pittsburgh. Thought I'd see you in person for the holiday."

"Is that so?"

"Yeah. You around?"

"I am now, but getting out of Dodge tomorrow. Got a sweet little honey I'm taking to the mountains. Sorry, my man, you shoulda called me sooner."

"Now that you say it, I guess so. Well, I'm here, so you want to grab a beer tonight?"

"Sure. Where you staying? Oh, never mind. I know where. Only the best for Mr. Hotel Software."

"Drop it, Jake," I grumbled.

"Take it easy, dude. So, the Tap Room? Eight?"

"Fine. See you then."

I disconnected and got my car, thinking I should have taken a flight back to Florida.

Later that night, over drinks with Jake and his "honey" named Courtney, I learned they were heading up to the mountains to ski. As luck would have it, they were staying at the WildFlower. Like a fool with a winning lottery ticket, I'd exclaimed, "Cool! They're my client, so I should have no problem getting a room. I could come up and have dinner with you two!"

Jake looked at me like I'd completely lost it, but Courtney got me. She was ecstatic to meet her beau's brother, and even more excited at the prospect of spending Christmas with his family.

It was decided. I would drive up the next day and have Christmas Eve dinner with Jake and "Court" before they spent Christmas Day skiing. Then I would drive back to the airport and get on a first-class flight back to Florida.

I was counting the minutes.

At least, I told myself so.

But I didn't get on a flight. I spent Christmas morning pacing the carpet in my suite—the one management had on hold in case a VIP like me wanted to stay at the last minute—debating what to do.

Was Bess downstairs? How could I tell her the truth? Did she take the holiday off?

After wasting the day worrying over it, I threw on a suit and went down to the bar for a drink and something to eat.

Spending Christmas alone was nothing new for me. I was used to it, so I settled into the cushy bar stool and ordered a Lagavulin straight up. After throwing back the scotch, experiencing the slow burn that came with it, I opened the menu to see what I would be eating for my holiday dinner when I felt the tingle.

Yes, an actual tingle ran up my spine, and before I could consider what the fuck was happening and when exactly I'd turned into a giant wuss, I heard Bess's voice.

Sneaking a quick glance, I saw she was preoccupied and talking with her head stuck in her notebook, so I hurried up and made my way over to her. The tingle ramped up into a full-blown electric shock with every inch closer I got to the source.

When I said hello, she asked what I was doing there. I wanted to come clean, I really did, but before I could, she brushed me off and went on her way to do her job. Like an idiot, I thought there would be another chance, so I waited.

It finally dawned on me she wasn't coming back when she sent runners to get her drinks. So I ordered a steak and moved back to my original seat, where I had a better view of the restaurant floor. I always planned better on a full stomach.

No way was I leaving now.

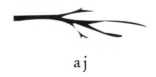

aj

I paced my kitchen until the oven timer rang, signaling the turkey was done.

Thank fucking God. Now these asses can eat and go.

My Christmas was sucking big-time. I wanted Bess to be with me, but she wasn't.

I kept picturing her bursting through my door, all bundled up for the cold and apologizing for being late, but there was nothing. No random noises or car lights outside. Just my recovery gang and me shooting the breeze around the fire, avoiding bellying up to the bar, and killing time until December twenty-sixth when this miserable holiday was officially over.

"That smells fucking great," my buddy Pete yelled from the other room.

I'd rather smell pussy; Bess's tight one, to be exact. Once I got a taste of that sweet cunt-sugar, I didn't want any other. And I wanted her now. By my side.

My mind was in overdrive, unable to slow or halt the continual loop of Bess. Somewhere, the rational side of me knew it was my addictive personality. The addict in me didn't care. I wanted my next hit. *Now.*

"Damn right! I know what to do with a bird," I shouted back to my room full of guests, sliding my poker face on. I'd perfected that shit when I was using, and refined it more when I got sober and started giving construction estimates.

I was a master of disguise. Thank fuck because no one outside this kitchen could know what drug I'd traded up for—a brown-haired one with legs that went on for miles.

Slapping the turkey onto a platter, I called out, "I'm gonna grab a quick smoke outside and then I'll serve dinner." But I couldn't even think about eating.

CHAPTER FOURTEEN

bess

LANE sat all night at the end of the bar. He made small talk with Robbie, ate his dinner, ordered dessert, and occasionally looked up and spotted me. I caught quick glimpses of him, never meeting his eye, but I knew every single time he turned his eyes on me. My cheeks burned, fire licked up my back, and embarrassingly enough, my panties got wet.

I asked Paul to do my bar runs for the evening; he knew my background. After I blamed it on the booze getting to me, he was gracious enough to do that favor for me.

But it wasn't totally the alcohol. It was mostly the hot-blooded male at the far corner.

Now the end of another holiday had come, and my feet were at war with my heart. My body longed to crawl into bed and go to sleep. Unfortunately, the muscle beating furiously in my chest screamed for more Lane.

I wound my way around the back hall of the hotel to the housekeeping locker room in an effort to avoid any temptation to talk with him by walking through the restaurant. Beating back desire the whole way, I tried desperately to lose myself in the sterile ivory decor, a stark contrast to the opulence of the hotel's front areas. Christmas carols were still piping through the speakers, and "Rudolph the Red-Nosed Reindeer" did little to calm my nerves.

Opening my locker, I checked my phone and found I had two voice mails and thirty-two texts. Quickly scrolling through the texts, I realized they were all from AJ. They started out benignly enough, wishing me a merry Christmas and asking about my day, before they sank into a pathetic slump, begging me to text him and hurrying me to finish work.

After packing up my bag, I hit Listen To Messages and held the phone between my ear and neck.

> *Hi, honey. It's Dad. Merry Christmas. I was hoping to hear from you, thinking you probably worked a double, but wishing you spent some time with friends. I know I didn't say it enough when you were growing up, but I love you. Come see me sometime, Bess-baby. Okay, happy holidays. 'Bye.*

After the beep came my next message.

> *Bess! It's me, AJ. Where the hell are you? I was hoping to at least wish you a merry Christmas in person. I know we left on bad terms the other day—well, I did, and I'm sorry, but I have to see you. It's Christmas, and I don't want today to end without seeing you. Come on, Bess, answer the phone or text me back. Shit . . . please?*

I shoved on my jeans and sweater, slammed my locker shut, deleted my dad's message, and walked to the door. Completely lost in thought over AJ—picturing him pacing and taking drags on his cigarette while leaving me that message—I was trying to dig deep and find some inner resolve over his current freak-out as I swung the door open.

"Ouch!"

"Shit! Sorry," I said as I looked up into blue eyes, a little red-rimmed, and shadowed behind dark hair.

"No, it's my fault. I shouldn't have snuck up on you, Bess," Lane said, his hands held high in mock surrender.

"What are you doing back here?" I leaned against the locker room door, taking in the fact that even under the harsh bright light of the staff hallway, Lane looked lickable. I knew that underneath his perfectly pressed Italian suit of armor he was toned and fit, based on the times I'd collided with him. Both times I'd practically bounced off his muscles.

And that hair; it was such a contradiction to his proper and business-like appearance. It was wild and always mussed, and I wanted to dig my hands in it and use it to pull him close before melding my lips to his.

Hot damn. I was a hormonal puddle ever since sleeping with AJ. It was like the power was back on and all my sexual fuses were burning brightly.

AJ. The man waiting for me, texting and calling nonstop. The guy who doesn't want me to be a booty call.

"You okay?" Lane asked, pulling me out of my heated moment.

Was I flushed? I brought my hand up to touch my cheek, and sure enough, it was hot to the touch.

"Yeah, I'm fine. Tired. I worked brunch and dinner today, so I'm just really tired." I stumbled over my words. Collecting myself, I asked again, "What are you doing back here?"

This was when my world tilted because Lane leaned in with a smirk and a wink and whispered, "Checking on my favorite WildFlower employee, and wishing her a very merry holiday."

If I were a kite floating through the sky when he leaned close, I was a jumbo jet at thirty thousand feet when he mentioned "favorite employee."

He brought two fingers up to his lips and said, "Shh. Keep the favorite part on the down low, because I don't want to offend anyone."

Afraid to speak, I stayed quiet, but he didn't.

"Happy holidays, Bess," he said as he moved closer and tucked a strand of my hair behind my ear.

When did this totally inappropriate flirting and touching start?

"Umm, Mr. Wrigley, I'm not sure I'm understanding you exactly. What are you really doing here? In Pennsylvania? Back at the WildFlower after your deal was closed? On Christmas by yourself? And who let you back here?" The pitch of my voice rose a little with each question until I was practically squeaking as I flailed a bit, waving my hand up and down the staff corridor.

But I wasn't quite finished because then, boldly and out of left field, I asked, "Why me? Why are you back here talking to me?"

He leaned back on his heels, a tiny glint in his eye as he said, "Let's see. I came back to Pennsylvania to see my brother for the holiday, except he had plans to go skiing up here. So, I came up with him and his lady friend. We had dinner last night, but today was their day on the slopes, which left me all alone."

Licking his lips, he ran his hand through his dark hair and leaned close once more. "As for why I'm back here with you, I can't really say. I only know I haven't been able to get you out of my head since our unbelievably boring dinner in the tavern, or the coffee we shared in the back room the morning after."

His expression softened. "There's just something about you, Bess. You're sweeter than the aroma of the blueberry muffin I devoured with you, prettier than the sun setting over the ocean back home, and tangier than the lemons you squeeze into your water. Something I can't put my finger on pulls me in and makes me want to be close to you, probably the same thing that makes you want to run. Hell, it makes me want to flee so fucking fast, but I'm not. So, just don't."

He stopped talking and looked intently in my eyes. I stared back, studying the blue of his irises. They were so blue, but more a cornflower shade than ocean. There was something untouched and innocent about them, which was probably misguided to think on my part, considering that standing in front of me was an extremely successful, well-traveled, worldly, and probably well-fucked man.

My throat dry, I choked out, "I'm not sure what to say. Actually, I don't think any of this is appropriate, and we should probably just part ways." Completely unnerved, I pinned my lower lip between my teeth, and could almost taste a tinge of coppery blood as I bit down on it.

And then I got lost in his eyes, like blue skies floating above me. My mind drifted, barely registering the arms that reached out and framed me against the door. The sky came closer. It was so, so blue, not a cloud in it. And then he kissed me. Lane's lips touched mine softly, and I braced myself against the wall. I was falling or floating, I didn't know which.

His mouth was warm, his tongue probing my troublesome bottom lip, looking for entrance. I gave it, and my own tongue found its way over to his side. He tasted like scotch and some other smoky flavor mixed with gingerbread.

What did he have for dessert? Maybe gingerbread cheesecake?

I sought the sweet and ignored the bitter, not one bit tempted by the essence of alcohol, only the man. In my mind, I was an innocent girl without a past, and definitely not a past that included cocaine and ecstasy and months of inpatient drug and alcohol rehab. Just a young woman entranced with a gorgeous, brilliant, smart man, one I assumed was very rich and worldly.

Lane broke away first, but didn't step back. Instead he reached one hand behind my neck and released my ponytail. My hair fell all around my shoulders, giving me a false sense of protection. And then he invaded my space once again while muttering, "Need another taste." His lips feathered along mine cautiously before his tongue swept along my bottom lip, forcing itself inside. No longer gentle, Lane was now fucking my mouth, and with every stroke of his tongue, I visualized other body parts delving long and luxuriously inside me.

I wanted his dick in my mouth, deep and choking. I was like a fiend, tapping a vein, tying a handmade tourniquet, seeking the fastest, quickest way to feel my high.

My body was hot and sweaty, desperate to intertwine with his. My hips were drawn forward, reaching for something they didn't know but wanted to—intimately. I'd fallen down the rabbit hole, lost in everything Lane, searching for the way in or out from this brand new sensation. Behind closed eyes, I could almost feel him pulsing inside my vagina, holding my hips steady while he rammed inside me, pulling out all the way and then doing it again.

I was so wired I was practically hallucinating. I didn't know who or what I was.

And then he broke away. My eyes wide, I watched him catching his breath, the rapid pulse fluttering in the hollow of his throat matching mine beat for beat.

Stepping close again, he leaned in, his lips lingering on my temple before grazing my ear. "Now it's a very happy holiday, Bess," he said as his breath fanned along my cheek.

I needed space, air, room to breathe. Sliding to the side, I hitched my bag higher on my shoulder, just now realizing I was still holding it despite my descent to the dark side. Rational thought finally returning to me, I found my words.

"Happy holidays, Mr. Wrigley. I'm not sure what just happened, but I don't think it was meant to, especially between you and me. I trust you can find your way out of here since you figured your way back. Good night," I said, and walked straight down the hall to the rear exit.

It took every single fiber in each and every muscle of my body to keep from turning around and rushing back to the party known as Lane Wrigley.

CHAPTER
FIFTEEN

bess

TWISTED in the covers, Brooks hot and heavy on top of the comforter, I was in the middle of a very graphic dream when the sound of my phone ringing dragged me back to reality. I swiped the Call button without looking and murmured hello as I rubbed my eyes, then pushed up to lean against the headboard.

"Bess! Thank fucking God you answered. I was about to bang down your door."

"AJ, hi," was all I could muster, my voice sounding breathy and guilty. I felt like I'd been caught with my hand in the cookie jar.

"Hi, you okay? Where've you been? Was work okay? I tried to get a hold of you all day yesterday. I thought you mighta come over after your shift."

As if I could do that . . . after the kiss.

I rubbed my hand over my face, then slid it down and gave Brooks a scratch on the head as I said, "Yeah, everything is fine. It was just a long day and I was exhausted. All I did was come home and collapse into my bed."

"Well, Christ fucking almighty, I was worried. I'm outside. I've got your gift, and some coffee," he said, and I could hear the snow crunching under his boots in the background.

"Oh. Well, one sec. Let me throw on a sweatshirt and I'll be right there."

I disconnected the call and grabbed a ratty old Pitt hoodie, throwing it on over my tank and my tattoo. After sliding into my boots, I opened the door and shoved my hands in the big front pocket of my sweatshirt as I stepped out onto the porch with Brooks in tow, my pajama pants billowing in the wind.

My dog abandoned me, running down the hill to a tree to relieve himself at the same time AJ pulled me into his arms and breathed in my scent deeply.

"I'm sorry, Bess. So sorry, I was hard on you. I pushed too much, too hard. I know. Can you forgive me?" His hand dug into my arm, locking me in his embrace as he continued to inhale me.

After wrestling loose a bit, I looked up and caught the fever in AJ's eyes. They were searing with passion and need—for me. A shiver ran right through me. I'd never been so desired as now. And last night.

By two different men.

I swallowed my feelings and spoke. "It's okay, AJ. I'm fine—we're fine—but I just can't go as fast as you. I need my space, and I need to work. It calms me."

His scruff from the day before grazed my forehead, his nicotine smell tickling my nose as he pulled me close again. "Yeah, I get it, baby. Like I said, I pushed too hard."

"And all those texts? You can't do that, AJ," I said into his broad chest.

He stepped back and stared me down. "I know."

He turned back to the steps and went to his truck, grabbing two coffees off the hood before saying, "Forgive me?" while looking at me with puppy-dog eyes.

I nodded and wrapped my arms around myself, trying to stay warm. Done with his business, Brooks stood on the porch next to me, looking up at me with his own big brown eyes, trying to will me to feed him.

"Come on." I opened the door and let AJ in, taking one of the coffees from him as we crossed the threshold. Brooks trotted in behind us, his tail wagging.

I took a long sip before putting some food in Brooks's bowl. As my dog began to munch away, AJ sidled close again. I was leaning against the counter, drinking my coffee, and he came right up to me and caged me in while setting his cup down behind me. He ran his nose along mine and whispered, "Merry Christmas, Bess," and then he kissed me. He kissed me hard, his lips closed, as if he was sealing us together.

It was such a déjà vu feeling, framed the same way I'd been the evening before against the locker room door. But this time I wasn't falling or floating; this time I simply felt trapped.

Yanking myself back to reality, I took a deep breath or twenty. I was having trouble filling my lungs with oxygen.

"I'm sorry, AJ. I'm not myself. It must be the holidays and everything. I had to serve a lot of booze last night at dinner, and I guess it got to me." There I went again, using my addiction as an excuse.

Actually, a blue-eyed, dark-haired guy got to me.

"Oh shit. I should've figured or asked." AJ cradled his head in his palms, looking up at the ceiling as he murmured, "Shit, shit, shit." Then he turned to face me and said, "We should get you a new sponsor. I'm too close to everything now."

"No!" I yelled. I didn't want anyone else in my life. I had enough issues, and had no desire to get close with another stranger.

"Shh, calm down," he said as he leaned in and kissed my cheek. "It's gonna be okay, sugar baby."

What was with the sugar?

I didn't have time to dwell on anything because with those words, he dipped his hand in his pocket and came out with a little gift box.

"Here, open this." He opened my palm, placing the gift there as he spoke.

My hand trembled. What was it? Jewelry?

I mumbled, "You didn't have to," and pulled the ribbon off in a swoop. It went fluttering to the floor like my heart had done less than twenty-four hours ago.

Carefully, I opened the box to find a silver key ring inside. It was a large circle with a few charms hanging off of it—a Labrador, a B, a snowflake—and an unknown key.

"It's beautiful," I said with a lump in my throat.

I leaned against the counter and AJ moved in again, but this time he didn't cage me in. He stood in front of me, keeping his arms at his sides, and leaned in so he could speak in a hushed tone by my ear.

"I got it at the mall," he said. "Picked the charms by myself. That's the key for my place, so you can come by anytime you want. Morning, noon, or night, because you never have to ask. I always want to see you."

The breath whooshed out from my lungs. It was the most beautiful thing anyone had ever said to me, and I felt slightly tingly, but more prickly from guilt than happiness—guilt over feeling more tingly last night with Lane.

And not melting at the words just spoken to me.

I told myself I had to do something sweet in return, so I grabbed AJ and pulled him in for a hug, sealing my lips with his. Asking for open passage with my tongue, I swept it through his mouth and hoped to feel those melty feelings I thought I should be feeling.

Then my doorbell rang, and Brooks immediately went nuts. My quiet corner of the country had never been so busy.

I yelled, "Who is it?"

From the other side of the door, I heard, "It's Oscar from the resort, Bess. I have a delivery."

"What?" I mumbled to myself, and then called Brooks away from the door.

When I pulled the door open, Oscar from shipping and receiving stood out in the cold with a medium-sized box in his hands.

"Hey, Oscar. What's this?" I asked while beckoning him to come in from the cold.

"I don't know," he said as he stepped inside. "Management asked me to run it over." With a shrug, he handed the box to me.

Taking the package, I noticed the red ribbon dusted with silver sparkles and the small gift card on top. As I turned it over in my hands, assessing its weight and trying desperately not to shake it, I said, "Oh. This is strange, but thanks."

Oscar stepped back, opened the door, and crossed the threshold as he called out, "'Bye," but I didn't really notice or care.

Because I was pretty certain I knew who the box was from, and I was equal parts scared to death . . . and dying to open it.

CHAPTER
SIXTEEN

bess

L ATER that evening as dusk fell, I sat at my kitchen table. A candle burning in front of me created the only light in the room as I twisted the tiny piece of paper in front of me, catching random letters and numbers in the flickers of candlelight. Afraid to stand and see my reflection, I stayed in my seat.

I was a horrible person.

After the package arrived, I dropped it onto the counter and asked AJ if he wanted to walk Brooks with me. We'd strolled down the hill, holding hands. With my right hand nestled inside his big left one, I'd carried the leash in my left.

We made it all the way down to the frozen stream, where AJ grabbed me with a sudden fierceness and pulled me into his arms for a kiss. I refused to let go of his lips, deepening the kiss until we were ready to strip naked in the freezing temperature.

It was greedy on my part; I know. But I'd been shaken by the gift box and the waves of emotion still swimming in my stomach from the night before, and I needed to feel content—fulfilled and comforted. Because there was no way Lane could want any of that with me. I was a phase to him; he was slumming it or something.

So I used AJ.

This was exactly why people in recovery didn't get involved with their sponsors, or often—with anyone. There were too many lines to cross, and I crossed them all when I dragged AJ back up the hill and into my bed.

My panties had been soaking wet and my heart racing. Neither response was for him, but that didn't stop me from ripping his clothes off before pushing him back onto the mattress and straddling his muscular body. As I'd leaned in to kiss him, his hand wound its way down to my core and his fingers slipped easily inside me.

"You're so wet," he'd said before finger-fucking me—it was nothing more than that.

"Oh." I gasped, throwing my head back in ecstasy, my eyes glued shut, my core tightening for someone who was not even close to being in the room.

Sex and lust swirled in the air as AJ removed his hand and curved it around my back, pulling me in again.

"Sweet baby, I love seeing you let go like that," he whispered before tucking my hair behind my ear.

I wanted my hair back. It was my shield. I couldn't look into his eyes without seeing the absolute horrid truth of the scenario, so I didn't. Squeezing my eyes tighter, I reached across the bed, grabbed a condom, and after slipping it on him, rode AJ like a stallion, leaving nothing behind.

He held my hips in place, giving himself purchase to push up and deep inside me, and I clenched my legs around his massive thighs, picking up speed with every thrust. Sweat beaded on his chest and I slowed for moment, leaning over and licking the tiny salty trail before making my way to his nipple.

As I swirled my tongue around the sensitive nub, I picked up speed again with my hips until I finally had to sit up. Placing my hands on his chest, I went buck wild, chasing another orgasm, or some kind of relief from the heat I was feeling.

All the while, my stomach dropped like I was on a carnival ride. Regret threatened to rise up in my throat as I treated AJ like my own stud dog. I shoved the emotion back every time I slammed my pelvis down on his, until we both were satiated physically.

But only one of us was fulfilled emotionally. And it wasn't me.

Now as I stared into the open flame in front of me, scanning the piece of paper in my hand, determined to find some reason to let it drop into the fire and watch it burn—I couldn't.

The paper had been sealed in an envelope in the bottom of the box, covered by a bag of lemons, a fancy beach towel, and a dog collar to match my recently acquired leash.

Feigning tiredness, I'd let AJ down easy. I'd been nice enough to wait for him to pull his pants back up, head out to his car and light a cigarette, then drive down the road before I ran to the box.

As soon as he was out of sight, I grabbed the package, set it on the table, and ripped it open. When I saw the towel, I'd scratched my head in confusion . . . until I opened the long envelope.

I stood stock-still, staring in shock at the single piece of paper until it fluttered to the floor—the way my body felt like it wanted to.

Overwhelmed and unsure about what any of it meant, I decided I should at least open the card still taped to the outside of the box. Inside was a piece of WildFlower stationery with the name and address of the hotel crossed out in dark blue ink.

Dear Bess –

I wish I could say I'm sorry for my behavior in the hallway last night, but I can't. I have some inexplicable draw to you, Bess Williams, and it doesn't seem to be going away. After our last meeting, I tried to let it be and get back to life, but there was always a nagging desire to see you again.

I promise you this last meet-up was

somewhat coincidental. My original intentions were to see my brother, since I hadn't seen him in a while, but when he said he was going to the WildFlower for the holidays . . . well, I couldn't resist the temptation of going too.

I have to head back to Florida to work, but want to see you again soon. Please don't presume the gifts inside are too much. They're not. I hope the towel lures you out of the cold temperatures to come and see me where there is sun year round.

I've taken the chance you will say yes and included a ticket with no date restrictions. Use it whenever you can escape work.

We also have plenty of water and lemons in Florida, but this will keep you until then. I also included something for your pup. I don't want him to feel left out.

I'm leaving my number at the bottom of this note. Please call me when you get this, and any other time you wish.

And to let me know when you can come and visit.

~ Lane

P.S. If you have trouble with management taking off work, I'm sure I could pull a few strings.

This time the card flitted to the floor, joining the ticket, and I slumped down next to both of them. I wasn't really sure how much time I wasted there, but it was dark when I finally got up, and that was mostly due to Brooks pacing by the door, needing to go to the bathroom.

Standing on the dark porch as I waited for Brooks, I watched the stars and dreamed of Florida, tanned skin, and ocean air. And in my daydream, there wasn't the faintest whiff of evergreen or nicotine anywhere.

CHAPTER
SEVENTEEN

a j
Six weeks later

SOMETHING was up with Bess, and it wasn't just recovery bullshit. It was more, and I knew it since the day after Christmas when she fucked me like I was nothing but a hard cock, then pretended to be exhausted afterward, putting off spending time together.

Since then, she'd asked me to "slow things down." She rattled off some bullshit like, "I care about you, AJ, but I don't want to take advantage of you. We're better off as friends, I think. Either way, we need to slow things down. Think about what we want. Blah, blah, blah."

What the fuck? Slow what down?

She'd never used the key I'd given her to my place, she picked up all kinds of extra shifts at work, including dinner, and she'd started going to the morning meeting on her day off. She knew damn well I couldn't go to morning meetings. That was when I checked on my crew, and if I didn't show up, they goofed off.

Fuck! I punched the air as I paced my large wraparound deck. It was nearly Valentine's Day, and this had been going on for too fucking long.

I'd just come home from a meeting, one that Bess said she would try to attend. But she texted and said she took someone's dinner shift and added, *I don't think we should go to the same meetings. Too much hidden baggage and not good for the group.*

Why not? We weren't *together* anymore. We'd done nothing but hug since the day she used me and tossed me out. I'd made a proclamation, given her a key, and apologized. She'd been dismissive of everything—except the thorough fucking. And now she was worried about the group.

Fuck the rest of everyone else.

And I still loved her. I'd been infatuated with the dumb girl since she stepped foot out of the treatment facility and opened the passenger door to my car. I'd be damned if I didn't make this work. She needed me.

I decided to do something about it and stomped down off the deck, heading straight for my truck. I threw the door open so hard, it almost fell off the hinges, then I climbed in and sped off.

As I entered the bottom of the very long and pretentious driveway leading to the WildFlower, I experienced a single moment of regret. Perhaps I was acting irrational? But then I tossed that thought aside and climbed the steep drive up to the main hotel in my four-by-four, pulling right up to the valet circle.

"Hey, man, I'm just stopping in to see someone who works here. Want to leave it out front?" I asked the young dude.

"We're not supposed to do that, but as long as you're quick, no problem, sir," he answered, all professional in his little valet vest.

I tossed him the keys and walked toward the entrance.

"Who're you visiting?" he called after me.

I hesitated, not wanting to answer, but felt like the asshole was doing me a favor.

"Bess Williams," I called behind me.

"Sorry, man, but I think she just headed out. She needed another one of the staff to do a favor for her, and they left about five minutes ago. I was on break, so I saw them leaving out the rear entrance."

He tossed my keys back, dismissing me.

"What favor?" I demanded to know.

He shrugged. "Don't know, buddy."

I wasn't his buddy, but I let it go.

"Do you know which direction they were heading?"

"Listen, I shouldn't have even got involved. I'm not supposed to discuss staff comings and goings."

"Yeah, I got you," I bit out, before jumping back in the cab of my truck.

My tires crunched along the wet gravel as I pulled up in front of Bess's place. The porch was backlit from the house, and I could make out Bess leashing Brooks and handing him off to another woman.

What the hell?

Brooks never went on a leash. Who was the other woman? What was Bess doing with her precious dog? So many questions ran through my mind as I jumped out of my truck and stomped toward the two women. They both were staring at me like two does caught in the headlights and it was hunting season.

Actually, they were, but I didn't have a gun. Just lethal anger pumping through my veins.

"AJ, what are you doing here?" Bess called from the porch.

"Oh, I don't know, maybe looking for you? After all, we were dating, getting to know each other real well, and then you dropped me like a hot potato. Kind of like it looks you're about to do with your dog."

My words dripped with venom, and my muscles were tense from anger. A thick cloud of negative energy circled me that even I could sense.

"Um, I don't know what you mean. I'm not dropping Brooks and I didn't drop you. And I have company, so I don't feel comfortable discussing this right now," she answered back.

I'd made it up the front steps by now, and I didn't care that she had *company.*

"Hey, I'm AJ." I stuck my hand out to the other woman, who was much older than Bess. Probably mid-fifties, and wearing a WildFlower housekeeping uniform.

"May," she said quietly, holding Brooks on his leash.

The dog's butt wriggled on the porch as his tail wagged for me. At least someone was happy to see me. I bent over and scratched him on top of his head.

Clearing my throat, trying to dislodge the lump that had formed, I said, "May, would you mind giving Bess and me a sec?"

She nodded as I took Bess by the arm, only just noticing she was in her waitress uniform and not her usual jeans and sweater. Breathing deeply, I noted she smelled like potatoes au gratin and whiskey. I should have realized this woman had been at work since six o'clock this morning serving food to less-than-appreciative people.

But I didn't. I couldn't.

After pulling her aside, I said, "Bess, what the hell are you doing? Why are you avoiding me? What are you doing with your dog?"

"AJ, I told you. This was going too quick for me. I'm overwhelmed, and it's all too hard to figure out. Balancing who we are as friends and lovers—with you being my sponsor—it doesn't work for me. I needed you as a support, and now I'm feeling that loss. Since I need some space, I'm going away for a few days, and May is watching Brooks."

She waved her hands between the two of us the whole time she talked about that balancing bullshit, finally letting them fall at her side before dropping the real bomb.

"Away?" I roared into the night.

Now I'd gone and done it. She backed up a step.

"You're scaring me, AJ."

Reining in my emotions, I reached out with a gentle touch to her arm. "I'm sorry, Bess, but you caught me by surprise. Where are you going? When were you going to tell me?"

She focused her brown eyes on me, soft with emotion, and said, "Florida, for a few days of rest and relaxation. I was going to text you tonight. I apologize, AJ, but I need this. I need to get my head on straight."

I spun around, stamping my foot on the ground, finally landing back face-to-face with her and replied, "This is fucked, and you know it. If you're holding a grudge about Christmas Day, I said I was sorry. You said you accepted that! Now, you're hauling off to Florida? By yourself?"

"It's not that. I just need to figure some stuff out."

She averted her eyes and slipped past me as she said, "I have to go say good-bye to my dog and pack. I'll call you when I get back, and we can talk, okay?"

It didn't escape me that she'd completely ignored my question about whether she was traveling solo. My temper popped another notch higher.

"No, that's not okay, but you don't leave me much choice," I said before walking back to my truck and kicking the door before opening it.

I sped away for the second time from Bess, wondering if she ever watched me drive away.

Even once.

CHAPTER
EIGHTEEN

bess

M$_Y$ hands shook as I removed my watch, my slim bangle bracelets, and my belt. And not without a small tremor.

My jitters were blatantly obvious to the naked eye, which was probably why I was relegated to the extra-long search and pat down in the security line. Little did they know, I wasn't trying to sneak any contraband on the plane.

The truth was, I was trying to reconcile putting myself onboard.

My whole body shook as they instructed me to take off my cardigan, revealing skin that had not seen the sun in years and a tattoo I tried to keep hidden. Both now peeked out from my tank top, hence the sweater.

"Please put your feet here and raise your arms in the air," the TSA officer instructed me, waving his detector wand as he spoke.

I stood as he told me before letting my thoughts consume me once again.

In a weak moment, I'd called Lane two weeks ago. The package had been looming in my kitchen for a month at that point. The ticket continued to haunt me, infiltrating every one of my thoughts until I realized I wasn't going to be able to let it go. I hated myself for calling, but I despised myself even more for what I did to AJ.

Blanketed in self-loathing much like my porch was covered in snow, I was like a self-destructive missile, burning down bridges and ruining relationships.

I'd never been vindictive. I'd spent years hurting myself instead of disappointing others, and then I used AJ in a way I couldn't even think about. Just the thought alone caused my heart to drop into my gut.

Of course, I'd cooled it off right away, but without much of an explanation.

Worst of all, I'd not been able to say "I'm sorry," and that fact was plaguing me. Apologies became a way of life in the twelve-step world, and I needed to take responsibility for what I'd done. Even though I felt strongly he never should have encouraged us being more than friends, I had to own my behavior.

Rather than calling AJ and apologizing like I should have done, I went on to make a further mess of my life with my phone in one hand and a sheet of paper in another.

"Okay, ma'am. You're free to go to the gate," I heard before snapping back to reality. After shoving my carry-on bag back together and zipping it, I moved toward the gate, tentatively putting one foot in front of the other.

I was working through some of my current shit with my new sponsor, so I tried to conjure up some of her wisdom as I stepped onto the moving walkway, struggling to envision her face and hear her words.

I'd met Shirley at the morning meetings; she'd been in recovery for twenty years and was a waitress at the local diner. Shirl, as everyone called her, had been married to Wayne for sixteen years, and she said she saw a lot of herself in me. Over the course of the last month, I'd become close to the forty-five-year-old woman after pouring my heart out one morning over a cup of coffee while sitting at the diner counter. Revealing all my dark secrets for the first time in years, I'd let it all loose on Shirley. And she hadn't batted an eyelash.

Rather than pass judgment, she'd simply said, "Aw, honey, don't make yourself sick over this. You're too young for that. So you made a mistake and thought you liked AJ. But you didn't. You found yourself a Prince Charming, and it's about time you go for it. Do it for me!"

Seemed that was all the encouragement I had needed, because that night I picked up the phone and dialed . . .

"Lane Wrigley," he'd said upon answering.

"Hi, Mr. Wrigley, I mean Lane. It's Bess Williams. I know it's a bit belated, but thank you for the holiday gifts."

"Bess, hey! How are you? Hold on one sec."

I'd heard a door close and he was back. "Good to hear from you, Bess. Seriously, no thanks needed. Actually more than good, it's great to hear from you. Hope you're calling to say you're going to take me up on my offer for a visit?" I could almost see him winking on that note, the teasing nature of his words traveling through the phone.

"Well, I wasn't sure if the offer still stood," I'd said quietly.

"Why? Of course it does. I made it," he answered. I could hear him moving, the sound of his pacing on what sounded like a hardwood floor coming through the phone.

"Okay. Well, I think I'd like to come."

"Great. When? Actually, I'm in Denver right now, working at a ski resort. I'll be here through next Tuesday. How about next weekend?"

Again, I went with, "Okay."

Then I heard a knock on the door and a muffled, "Excuse me, Mr. Wrigley?"

"It sounds like you're busy," I said, stating the obvious as I mentally cursed myself for my stupidity.

"It's no problem. There's a time difference, so we're still working here, but they can wait. So, next weekend, yeah?"

"Yeah."

"Cool. What's your e-mail? I can forward you an updated itinerary after it's ready. In fact, why don't you text it to me when we hang up?"

"Mm-hmm." I was speaking in murmurs, afraid to make words

or phrases, forgetting how to speak in full sentences.

"And don't worry about any of the details. I'll take care of everything. I gotta go now. Okay?"

"Okay."

"Call or text with any questions, Bess. I'm already looking forward to spending time together."

That was two weeks ago, and I'd never called or texted with anything but my e-mail address, and now I was getting ready to board a plane to see him.

Was there some type of rule book for this type of relationship?

I rushed by lonely souls sitting in airport bars and society women browsing in newsstands on my way to the gate, only stopping for a small cup of coffee. Stumbling over my own feet, I made my way to B4 where I would get on a flying death trap to perhaps an even more fiery death, otherwise known as Lane Wrigley.

As I rode the down escalator after I arrived, the Florida sun streaming brightly through the large windows in front of me, I squinted at the group of people waiting at the bottom. Standing tall, dead center, his black hair a disheveled mess, was Lane. When I neared the bottom of the moving staircase, I patted my hip to reassure myself. Tucked in the pocket of my light pink cardigan was a piece of paper with an address.

Not for family, friends, or even a hotel, but for an AA meeting. Just in case.

No, I hadn't divulged any of this to my host, but Shirley thought I should have it with me, so she called around and found a meeting for me. They met every night at six o'clock in the basement of a church.

Isn't that where everyone dreams about going when they visit the Sunshine State?

CHAPTER NINETEEN

lane

I'D stood like a fool waiting for my guest to make her way toward me, my feet practically glued to the tacky tile floor as I watched her ride the escalator like it was a red carpet. Once she stepped off, the craziness of what I'd done settled over me like a dark storm cloud.

Then she smiled. It was tentative and soft, like her quiet personality, yet it pushed all the storm clouds out of the way.

More happy than I should be to see her, I stepped forward and said, "Hi! Welcome to Florida!" I gestured toward the window, certain I was wearing a cheesy grin, and pretty damn happy my eyes were safely hidden behind dark aviator shades.

"Hi," she said in a low voice, tilting her head shyly so her hair fell in a curtain over her face.

"Do you have other luggage?" I asked, grabbing her small carry-on case.

She shook her head and murmured no.

Low maintenance; not what I'm used to.

"Well, let's roll. How was your flight?" I lifted her small piece of luggage with one hand, rather than rolling it like a wimp, and placed my other hand on her lower back, guiding her toward the exit.

"It was good, I guess. It's only my second time on a plane, so as far as I know, it was all right," she answered.

I stopped and raised an eyebrow, pushing my hair out of the way. "Get out. No way."

"Uh-huh. The only other time I was on a plane was spring break in college. A bunch of us went down to Panama City, here in Florida." She lowered her gaze, allowing her hair to once again fall in front of her face.

Who would have thought that a girl who was so fucking intoxicated that she passed out on me during a yoga class was this sheltered.

And I'm lying to her.

The thought caused a cold sweat to break out on my skin, even though I was in the air-conditioning. Standing in the middle of the airport, I gently lifted her chin and took in her natural beauty as I said, "Hey, that's cool. I was just shocked. I travel week in and week out for work. Sometimes I forget that's not normal."

She nodded.

I moved my hand back to settle on her lower back. She was warm, heat seeping through her sweater and singeing my hand. "Well, Bess Williams, let's go and have some fun."

And, God help me, find a way to come clean.

Sadly, I knew only too well what lies festering did to someone.

Once settled in my convertible, I took Bess to an outdoor café for dinner. We made small talk in the car, but mostly I watched Bess take in her surroundings. She stared out of the car with wide eyes and amusement at all the joggers and sunbathers in miniscule bikinis walking around South Beach.

"We're a long way from Pennsylvania," I said, teasing her.

"I can see that," she jabbed back in her shy way, and I couldn't help but wonder what the hell happened to this woman. She was so different from that day she fell on my mat.

Was this what she was like before? Or only after?

I wanted all the answers to the Bess puzzle. After solving it, I would gently put it back on the shelf so someone else could have it for keeps. Except I was starting to think that could be next to impossible. As I watched her hair whipping and blowing, her delicate features taking in the glow of the Florida sunshine, and her brown eyes wide with excitement—or nerves—I thought, *Who the hell would put this girl back on the shelf?*

We went to a small Mexican place I typically frequented with friends or the occasional coworker. It wasn't a see-or-be-seen type of place. It was more the no-frills, pitchers of beer or sangria, and chips with guacamole type of establishment.

After being seated on the back patio, I said, "So, I take it the weather is better here than back home?"

"A little bit," Bess replied.

"Some days, I can't believe I grew up in the cold weather. Life is so much better when the sun is shining. I know that makes me sound like a baby, but I don't care."

A likely story. Not once had I ever shared the truth behind my aversion to the changing of the leaves or the bare tree limbs that heralded cold weather.

"I kind of like the seasons," she said as her smile grew. "I mean, I know the cold sucks, but I think it makes me appreciate the good-weather days more."

"Guilty as charged," I said, raising my hands in the air in surrender. "I'm a big pussy—excuse my French—who doesn't like the snow."

My conscience pricked at the fibbing, the tiny alterations to the truth that were coming so easily to me.

She giggled. It was soft and quiet, but it was a laugh. "Hey, look. Maybe I'm just rationalizing since I'm not lucky enough to live in Florida."

"Well, you're here now, so soak it all up," I said with finality, laying the subject to rest.

I relaxed in my chair, taking in our surroundings. It was late afternoon, heading into early evening, and the sun was sinking in the west. We could still feel the heat of the day, but a light ocean breeze had picked up, ushering in the evening. Seated together at a café with the sun's glow on Bess's brown hair, slight curls forming around her face from the moist air, her face fresh and dewy—we probably looked like a young couple in love.

"Listen, before we order, I really want to thank you," she said. "I don't want you to think that I'm not appreciative. This is the chance of a lifetime for me. I don't get to travel much, and I can't believe that I'm here, but it's super exciting to be in this gorgeous paradise."

She gestured to the view, pulling me from my heated thoughts, and I looked straight into her eyes as she went on.

"I just want to make it clear that I've never done this before. This is so absurd when I really think about it, and I hope there are no huge expectations for, um, you know . . . intimate behavior." Her words were broken by small gulps and tiny glances at me, but she finished with her gaze cast downward as a slight pink blush overtook her neck.

I grabbed her hand and pulled it into mine, running my thumb over hers. "That's not why I brought you here, Bess. I mean, I would be straight-out lying if I didn't say I felt the heat when we kissed over Christmas, and I want more of that. But that's not why you're in Florida. I want to get to know you, and mostly, I want you to have fun."

A second light sweat broke out over my body. Of course, I meant all of what I said, but I also wanted to sink into Bess. If I could, I would bury my cock and possibly my soul deep within the folds of her body and mind. So deep, I might never pull either one out, which was why this was about her having a fun time in Florida and not my overly anxious dick . . . or heart.

It was also supposed to be about me coming clean with her, yet I didn't.

"Okay," she said, and squeezed my hand back. "To fun."

Before I could tell any more half truths, a peppy little server in a bikini top and sparkly boy shorts popped over to our table.

"Hey, guys, my name is Andi. What can I get you to drink?" she asked while bouncing back and forth on her feet.

I looked at Bess and asked, "You want to get a pitcher of

margaritas?"

She looked down again. "No, thanks. I'll just have a Diet Coke with lemons, please," she said while casting a hesitant glance at the server.

And like a fucking grenade flying through the sky, it hit me.

Bess didn't drink.

The water with lemons—it wasn't a cute healthy thing. I felt like smacking myself in the head, but couldn't.

Fuck, I'm stupid.

I mean, I knew she had a problem with drugs years ago and clearly was cleaned up, but I didn't give much thought to what that all meant now. It meant she was dry.

Andi was still jumping around, more than likely hopped up on coke herself. And not the soda variety.

"Um, I think I'll just have a beer on tap," I said, then immediately regretted it. Should I drink? I did the last time we had dinner. I didn't want to be obvious, but I had no clue what to do. What was right and what was wrong?

Fuck. What had I gotten myself into?

"Sure thing, babe," Andi said, and was off and running to grab the drinks.

In an effort to redirect, I picked up the menu and asked, "So, what kind of Mexican do you like?"

Bess looked up and her eyes were glistening.

Shit.

She licked her lips, then said, "Look, I know we just finished up one heavy discussion started by me, but there's something else."

"No problem. You aren't gonna tell me you like girls?" I teased, trying to lighten the mood.

"No! That's not it at all."

At least she cracked a wide smile.

"Whew," I said and feigned relief.

"I'm in recovery. Well, not actively in it, but I guess you kind of always are. I used to have a problem with drinking . . . and other stuff. And now, I don't do any of it. I've been clean for almost five years, but I constantly work at staying that way. I'm sorry if you don't think that's cool or fun, but it's me. And part of the program is we don't lie about it or make excuses."

This was my opening. My chance to not lie or make excuses, but I couldn't. This was becoming a pattern for me. I'd hated myself for doing it for years, and now I wanted to gouge my eyes out for doing it with Bess. Yet I couldn't make the declaration of truth come out of my mouth.

Instead I said, "I think it's just fine. You, Bess, are cool and fun just as you are."

She wiped at her eye with her finger, swiping a tear out of the way, and an avalanche of guilt fell on my heart. But still, I couldn't start the conversation that needed to be had.

Before I could speak again, chirpy little Andi was back slinging our drinks onto the table.

I took Bess's hand once again, and asked, "How about some chips and salsa?"

She nodded, and Andi chimed in, "Great! I'll go grab that for you!"

As she walked away, I asked the inevitable, "Is this okay?" while eyeing my glass of beer.

"I think so," she said slowly, then looked me in the eye. "Truthfully, I haven't really been around drinkers for a long time. Other than when we last had dinner or I do dinner service at the hotel, I pretty much spend my time around other people who are dry. So, yeah, I think it's all right. I'm really sorry to make you feel uncomfortable. I didn't tell you about me with that in mind."

A thought hit me of at least one thing I could make right. "You know what? I think you're pretty amazing to tell me, and you know what else? A Diet Coke sounds awesome right about now."

I lifted my hand in the air and waved our peppy server over. "I'm sorry, but I changed my mind. I'll have a Diet Coke like the lady. Just take this and pour it out." I handed over the beer and noticed Andi looked confused with a crinkle in her brow.

"You can still charge me for it. I just don't want it now."

"Oh, cool! Thanks," the waitress said and left us again.

After all that, dinner went smoothly as we washed down the saltiness of the chips with sweet soda and small talk about her job and mine. Totally mesmerized with the young woman in front of me, I couldn't stop watching her. With brown hair and eyes nearly the same shade, she was naturally beautiful with nothing enhanced or enlarged. Just subtle, simple beauty. And I couldn't take my eyes off of her.

We plowed our way through some enchiladas before deciding to walk along the beach to work them off. When we took off our shoes and stepped onto the sand, Bess's hair blew wild in the wind, her sweater billowing out from her small frame. I wrapped my arm around her back and pulled her in close. She smelled like fajitas and citrus, and inhaling deeply, I took my fill.

"This is so incredible!" she said, tucked under my arm as we walked along the shoreline. "Wow! God, if I lived here, I would never leave. You're right, who needs four seasons?"

If you were here all the time . . .

My thoughts were going haywire. I took a deep breath, trying to fill my lungs, playing it off as taking in the ocean air.

"It is pretty damn incredible," I admitted. "But you know, living here, we don't do this stuff all the time. We work mostly and play a little. At least, that's what I do."

Kicking up little bits of sand with her feet, she teased, "Yeah, yeah. Make a girl feel good. You probably have a different 'hotel employee' down here every week to soak up the sun and fun."

She had to pull her arm away from me to make the air quotes around hotel employee, and I felt her absence immediately. This woman did something to me, something no one else had ever been able to do—she'd melted a tiny layer of the permanent ice around my heart. A thick layer that even the Southern sun and humidity hadn't been able to defrost.

And yet she thought she was one of many "hotel employees" to catch my attention.

"No way!" I stopped dead in my tracks and turned Bess to face me. When she stared down at our bare feet, I tipped her face to look at me. "Listen to me. I have never done this before. Never. Do you hear me?"

She nodded but said nothing.

"I've never invited anyone here, never got myself involved with a hotel employee—beyond a one-night thing, which I know isn't what you want to hear, but it's the truth. I can't stay away from you, Bess. Like a lost puppy, I keep finding myself crawling back to you, and I can promise you . . . I've *never* felt that way about anyone."

She stared straight into my eyes for a moment, and then asked, "Again, why me?"

I grabbed her hands and swung them behind her, pulling her in tight, trapping her in my embrace, then brought my mouth down hard on hers.

I couldn't tell her why, but I could definitely show her.

Consuming her mouth with my own, pushing my way inside, my tongue seeking refuge with hers, twisting like I wanted to be doing with her body in the sheets. But she wasn't ready for that yet, and neither was I. Because truth be told, I knew it would be addictive. I'd been obsessing over Bess in one way or another for several years, and right now with her tongue exploring my mouth and her body pressed against my erection, I recognized the disaster my life would become with and without her. She was my salve—the balm able to ease the pain of the past—and currently the flame lighting my body on fire.

My lies had gone on too long. My chance to make anything right was long gone, but the ache I felt for this woman was so intense that it raged war with my conscience and won.

Standing in the moonlight, the stars twinkling above us in a dark velvet sky, I wanted to lay Bess down in the sand, rip off her clothes, and plunge deep into her depths without a life jacket.

And in that moment, I wasn't worried about drowning.

CHAPTER TWENTY

bess

I'D known from his e-mail that Lane had reserved a room for me at a nearby hotel that was a client of his. So I wasn't nervous about my sleeping arrangements before I left Pennsylvania.

But as he made love to my mouth on the beach under the starry sky, I'd never wanted to go home with someone so badly. I wanted to ditch any reservations—mental or physical—and hurry back to wherever Lane lived and do whatever I'd never done before.

Which, looking back, was probably not much.

Except, I wanted to do it all. And remember it. Savor it. Catalog it. Brand it to my brain.

He'd pulled me close, captured me with my own hands and driven me hard against his frame. Then he released my hands, allowing them to wander freely. I was like a blind person feeling my way home, touching each and every plane and surface I encountered, finding my way to comfort. And paradise.

Finally, I grabbed Lane's back as his tongue sought refuge in my mouth. Gripping his T-shirt with fear that I would sink into the sand

and disappear from the moment, I pried my eyes open to make sure this was actually happening.

I captured his gaze, like two searing blue planets. Set against the dark sky, the color of his eyes was even more pronounced. His dark hair blending into the night, Lane watched me.

I was kissing a man I'd admitted the awful truth of my past to, and he plowed through it as though it was no big deal. A man who wanted me enough to bring me to Florida and wait for me at the airport. Amazingly enough, he wasn't running in the opposite direction, but pulling me closer.

For the briefest of moments, a faint scent of pine crossed my senses, and I was reminded of AJ. Another man who recently devoured me, and at the time I thought I'd *learn* to like it. I was wrong.

AJ might have brought me awake sexually, revived my appetite for the touch of another human, but his heavy-handed approach to get my attention left a bitter taste in my mouth, much like sugar-free candy. He might have *looked* like the real thing, but he was nowhere near it. Not even close.

I knew how AJ's mind worked—better than he thought—and knew he was chasing another type of high. It wasn't necessarily about me. That's how addictive personalities work.

Lane was chasing me, and I didn't know why. But instead of playing hard to get, I was toppling right on top of him.

Literally.

The kiss had deepened to a point of no return and with Lane holding me tight, we drifted toward the sand. He fell backward and I tumbled right on top of him, our lips never losing their connection.

I brought my hands up to run through his untamed hair, dragging my fingers along his scalp, and my touch elicited a moan from somewhere deep inside his chest. I felt it reverberate against mine and answered with a hum of desire I didn't even know I could make. With the water lapping the shoreline the only noise in the background, our symphony of moans filled the air around us. Even fully clothed, as our bodies drew together, Lane's desire made itself known. I pressed into it, looking for friction, anything that might relieve the need that consumed me.

He brought his hands up from where they were locked tight around my back and drew them over my shoulders, bringing my cardigan down with his fingers. My skin tingled and burned as his rough fingers made their way down my bare arms, the breeze doing little to cool the heat radiating off of me.

We were like two teenagers, my hands tightly woven in his hair as he ran his up and down my arms, then brushed his fingers along my side cleavage. Grinding into each other, we pushed and pulled, desperately looking for release in the middle of a public beach in Miami. And I couldn't have cared less.

I never wanted to leave this moment. I wanted to stay there for the next twenty or forty years.

"Bess," Lane whispered, breaking the moment. His one hand remained steady on my arm as the other reached around to hold my neck when I lifted my head up.

"Bess," he softly repeated as he lifted his forehead to meet mine. "We have to stop."

I nodded, feeling my eyes start to fill with tears. What was I thinking? Was I that desperate to push this man to screw me in a public place?

Thankfully, my emotions were masked by the night.

"I don't want to," he said, rubbing his palm back and forth over the nape of my neck. "But we have to because I want more, so much more. I want all of you. And I need to respect what you said at dinner. You didn't come here for a roll in the hay—or the sand—and that was certainly not my expectation. But in about three seconds, I'm not going to be able to stop."

"Okay," I breathed out.

He lifted his hip and ground into me one more time, allowing me time to digest his desire. "Believe me when I say I don't want to. I want to carry you up to the road and check into the first hotel we see. I want to dive inside you, and I mean deep, any way I can. But I can't tonight. I meant it when I told you we need to have fun while you're down here, and if I get inside you right now, I may never leave for the next forty-eight hours. You won't see daylight."

"Oh," I said, but thought, *Why not*? I don't need the daylight.

But he was right. I needed to cool my raging hormones and take stock of what we were doing, which was pretty crazy for someone who was stone-cold sober.

Before I could say anything more, Lane kissed me tenderly. It was a gentle caress, so different from the raging kisses of just moments before, but it stoked my inner fire just the same. Despite the cool night air, I was roasting.

So, when Lane helped me to stand, I allowed my cardigan to fall while brushing the sand off my body. As I bent over to catch my sweater, the moonlight caught my tattoo, and Lane reached out to touch it.

"Wow," was all he said. His finger traced around the outline, then moved to the teardrops, circling them while his brow furrowed.

I brought my hand up to cover it. I'd forgotten it was there for the first time in . . . ever. It struck me how long it had been since I'd bared my body or my true self to anyone. Sadly, I couldn't remember the last time I did. I was probably drunk or stoned or high or all three. Yeah, I'd been naked with AJ, but he didn't count. The lines were so blurred with him; he'd been my friend first, a shoulder to lean on during the worst of times, and then he took advantage of that.

"I don't normally uncover it, which is one advantage to not living in Florida where it's hot all the time," I said.

"What is it? What does it mean?" he asked while continuing to trace the outline of the eye with his fingertip. I could see his brain churning, his eyes scanning the design over and over like the cars circling South Beach earlier. With a quick glance up at me, he asked, "Why is she crying?"

Standing there on the beach, I looked anywhere but straight at him. "She's crying because she's me," I said as I watched my pretty pink-tipped toes sift between granules of sand. "I guess you could say I've always been a lonely soul. At least, since I was a little girl and my mom walked out on me. I couldn't shed real tears myself, so I had this put on my arm as a permanent reminder of the ones I held in when I stood in the doorway watching her walk away from me."

Lane grasped my hands and twined his large fingers around my smaller ones, bringing us face-to-face.

I whispered, "Now it's just a reminder of how stupid I was to put it there."

"You know what?" he whispered in my ear.

I shook my head.

Leaning closer again, he spoke into my ear, making sure it was just for me and me alone to hear. "I think it's a reminder for anyone who cares for you to make it extra good for you. All the time, extra good. In bed, out to dinner or lunch, or just sitting and watching TV, everything in your life should be a little bit better than for everyone else because of what you went through."

I couldn't speak. I'd never heard such sweet words, let alone ones meant just for me, and they sent a tiny shiver over my body. I chalked it up to being cold, but it really had nothing to do with that.

When we turned away from the beach, holding hands as we walked slowly back toward the street, I asked, "So, what are your deep, dark secrets? I'm certainly spilling all of mine tonight."

CHAPTER
TWENTY-ONE

lane

PULLING up to the five-star Hotel Dylan, I tossed my keys at the valet and yelled, "Leave it up front." As if they wouldn't. They kept all the hottest cars out in front, and my shiny midnight-blue German-engineered convertible was nothing less than the best.

But that wasn't why I needed my ride in the circle. I was going to require a fast getaway after checking Bess into her suite. The heat circling the two of us was thicker than the air in Miami in August. The heavy clouds of passion that were cloaking us in their dark fury were about to burst. And while I wanted nothing more than precisely that, I needed to escape.

Fucking Bess right now would screw everything up. I wasn't even sure what *everything* meant, but right now I felt as though the fate of my heart and mind were tangled up in a waitress from Pennsylvania, and I needed to dissect that wide open—but in the privacy of my home.

"Good evening, Mr. Wrigley." James, the dapper, way-too-chipper guy at the front desk, greeted me. "Welcome back to the Dylan. What can I help you with this evening? Will you be dining late with us? Should I call the restaurant?" he said with a wink.

As usual, he was eating me up with his eyes, and I could only imagine what must be running through his mind. With the relaxed casual clothes I was wearing and my hair more mussed than usual, I looked nothing like I normally did.

His cheeks pinked before he turned his gaze on the woman beside me. Bess was flushed from our time on the beach, her hair tousled and wind-whipped, long tresses partially obscuring her face and running down her back. Her gaze roamed the lobby while she wrapped her arms tightly around herself in her pink cardigan.

"Hello, James. No, I've already eaten, but I'd like to check in my guest from out of town."

He leaned back, further inspecting Bess as his tongue took a lap around his lips. He smoothed a hand down the skinny European suit hugging his frame, which set off his hair that was perfectly combed like a pop star's. "I see. And who may she be?"

"James, meet Bess Williams, a friend of mine from Pennsylvania."

Who knew my little gay blade, my hook-up for quick reservations at one of South Beach's hotspots, would put me through such scrutiny?

"I didn't know you had any friends . . . from Pennsylvania," James said drolly.

I narrowed my eyes and said, "Well, now you do. Can we get Ms. Williams checked in for the evening? She's had a long travel day."

"Yes, of course. Right away. Nice to meet you, Ms. Williams," James said as he started banging away on the computer in front of him, his movements exaggerated.

"Thank you," Bess finally said.

I wasn't sure who she was addressing, him or me, but James answered. "Oh, that's what I'm here for, doll."

When I eased my hand to Bess's lower back, James eyed the action pointedly before he focused his laser beams on Bess, laying it on thick. "Have you been to our establishment before, Ms. Williams?"

What was he insinuating? She wasn't an available-by-the-hour type, and he knew it.

"Um, no."

"How about South Beach, doll?" He winked and batted his eyelashes.

She shook her head.

"Well," he said to her with one eyebrow raised, "it looks like you found the right VIP bachelor to show you off around town."

All at once, the scent of coconut coming from the candles in the lobby overwhelmed me. "Thanks for the vote of confidence, James. Do you have a room ready for Bess?"

I wasn't having a dick-swinging contest with a lightweight whose feathers were ruffled over my attention, or lack thereof. James knew I was about as hetero as they came, and he also knew I didn't do relationships. But there was no fucking way he was swooping in and pretending to be best-fucking-friends with my date. If he was trying to get to me, it was damn well working.

James stiffened slightly, then collected himself. "Of course. A suite just like you requested, Mr. Wrigley."

"Good, now give her the key. I'll help her upstairs."

"Certainly."

Once she had her room number and instructions for finding the elevators, Bess tried to grab her bag, but I got it first. I was annoyed enough with James, and I certainly didn't want a valet either.

As we walked down the wide hallway with white curtains billowing on either side, tiny votive candles lit along the stone walkway marking our path, lust filled the air all around us. I had no idea how I was going to leave her at the door.

We stepped inside the elevator and I pulled her in close—her back to my front—after the elevator doors shut behind us, then I kissed the nape of her neck.

"I'm going to be a good boy and say good-bye at your door," I whispered, "but it's going to be fast because I don't think I can trust myself for much longer."

With her eyes averted, staring at the elevator floor like it was the most fascinating tile ever, Bess replied, "That's good, because I'm not sure I trust myself to hold true to my word either."

She ducked her head, shyly trying to hide her face, but I caught the faint hint of her blush. And if that didn't ratchet me up further, I was a goddamn liar.

I was running my tongue up the side of her neck, taking deep inhales of her scent now mixed with the salty ocean air that clung to her skin, when the doors opened. Bess glanced at her key and said, "Twelve nineteen." I pulled her hand into mine and walked toward the placard with directions to the room numbers and pointed left toward room 1219.

We traveled slowly down the hallway, our footsteps muffled on the expensive carpeting. I felt like a lion going against his instinctive nature, resisting temptation by locking his prey up for the night. Bess was like an innocent kitten, welcoming my closeness, throwing caution to the wind with her hand tucked inside mine, and both her ass and long hair swaying sensually from side to side.

I'd never wanted to put my dick inside a woman so badly. Anywhere and everywhere she would let me.

The situation sent red flags waving inside my mind. I knew I should leave Bess alone, but at the same time I wanted to claw my heart out of where it had been buried for most of my life and hand it over to a woman I barely knew, yet understood better than she thought.

Safely locked inside the four walls of my house an hour later, I lay down on my king-sized bed, sinking into the thousand-thread-count sheets and duvet my decorator selected for me. Slipping my hand inside my boxer briefs I'd quickly stripped down to, I replayed our kiss at the door to her suite.

I'd trapped Bess against the heavy mahogany door, bracing my palms on either side of her head before leaning in and capturing her mouth in a brutal kiss. I didn't wait for the green light; I'd pushed my way in and fucked her mouth.

My dick was hard just remembering it. I grabbed hold of myself and squeezed before running my hand up and down my length. More than just a little pre-cum dripped out of the top and I rubbed it along my shaft, easing the way for my hand to work faster.

With Bess trapped in my arms, I'd bitten down on her lower lip as I pressed my hard body into her soft, lush one. My erection, begging to be freed from my pants, rubbed along the bottom of her sweater, and I'd pushed it against her abdomen, making sure she felt what she did to me.

We'd been moaning so loudly, my hipbone grinding into hers, I'd been ready to roar when sanity crept back in along the edges of my brain. I'd released Bess's lips reluctantly and took a long, deep breath.

"We're going to wake the whole floor and get arrested for public indecency if I don't sprint for the elevator now," I'd said quietly.

"Okay," she'd said softly, and a slight pout had appeared before she smoothed out her features. "Good night."

"Good night, Bess." I'd dipped my forehead to touch hers. "I'll call you in the morning and we'll make a plan to do something fun, okay?"

She'd nodded, then I'd kissed her one more time, brushing my lips along her cheek.

Now I was pumping my dick at full speed, my release barreling its way through me, hardly taking the edge off my desire.

When she'd called after me, I had the urge to run to her, to bust through the door and fuck her right on the floor of the suite.

But instead I'd turned to hear her say, "Lane? Thank you," before I nodded and raced to the elevator bank.

My sheets and my hand were now a sticky mess, but my cock hadn't received the signal. It came back to life, standing at attention as it berated me for not taking it into consideration.

As I headed to the shower, my heart pounded and my brain whirled with bad ideas. It was going to be a long night.

CHAPTER TWENTY-TWO

bess

SATURDAY and part of Sunday flew by in a whirlwind of taking runs with Lane along the beach, eating leisurely brunches together at the local diner, sharing a candlelit dinner in a tiny tucked-away Italian joint, and walking along the shoreline, stealing kisses any chance we had. There was something about Lane that both put me at ease and also unsettled me.

I think it was his eyes. They were confusing, often saying something different than the rest of him. His gorgeous baby blues were mostly open and honest, but every so often they would darken with something secret. A small shade of hesitation, a concern or worry would transform his eyes, and I would stare deep into them, trying to understand what it was or where it came from.

Like the first day I spotted him all buttoned up in his suit in the WildFlower restaurant waiting for a table, it was as if he was in some kind of weird trance where he was wrestling with inner demons. Which was strange, because to the casual onlooker, it didn't appear that he had any problems, any demons.

Of course, I was the last person to think everything was always rosy. Looks could be deceiving. If you went to an AA meeting, you wouldn't believe the normal-looking people there who struggled with addiction.

So it bothered me, this knowledge that there was something not quite right with him; I just didn't know what.

It was usually during those odd moments when Lane would change the subject or come up with something I had to see. The steps where Versace was murdered, the gym on the beach with all the muscle heads, the funky pedal taxis with advertising hanging from the sides, and my favorite distraction—the hammock swing in the courtyard of the Dylan where we both climbed in and swung gently from side to side while holding hands.

With my head nestled in the crook of his neck, Lane asked, "Wouldn't it be great to do this year round?" while kissing the top of my head, making his way around to nibble on my ear.

I couldn't see his eyes, so I had no idea if their blue was burning bright like the sky or if they were clouded with some dark emotion.

"I think so," I said, "but this isn't real. At least, not for me. I have a routine, which is how I survive. I go to work, walk my dog, spend time on my quiet piece of the mountain, and go to meetings. I don't think that translates into life here."

It was Sunday afternoon, and the shadows were drawing long. My room beckoned to me, the satiny sheets calling my name. But not just my name. Lane's too. We had had another earth-shattering make-out session at my door the night before, and I felt the frustration when Lane made his way back down the hall, leaving my panties soaked and my heart racing.

But now we were in the hammock, swaying in the breeze, and I wanted to make love to Lane more than I ever wanted to catch any buzz. The only thing stopping me was that I was leaving soon, and the reality of me coming back, let alone staying for good, was nonexistent.

"I know," he said, and pulled me closer. "But this is fun, more than fun. I like having you here, and I never spend time like this with anyone."

He kept making reference to this over the weekend. *He never spent whole days with anyone. He never invited anyone to Florida for a weekend. He worked all the time, only making time for the occasional dinner or social event with a woman.*

"It is fun," I said softly, "but you have to know. I came with a piece of paper tucked in my pocket with an AA meeting time and location scribbled on it."

"I don't care about that," he whispered, then dropped a foot outside the hammock and swung it, picking up a little speed in our swaying.

I closed my eyes, somewhere between being lulled to sleep and feeling myself spiral out of control. "You've been so kind. Not drinking at dinner and all. It's not necessary. I'm not falling off the wagon anytime soon, but this life wouldn't be for me. The high energy that envelops this place is not for me. Not long term, I'm afraid. That's my reality."

Then out of nowhere, Lane asked, "What if I am? What if I'm for you long term?"

I tried to twist out of the hammock, but he held on tight.

"I can't think like that, Lane. When I left rehab, I thought I would never get involved. That it would be my dog and me forever, and then when you first invited me to dinner, I questioned that, which led to something so stupid—"

"What?" he interrupted.

"Well, I got involved with my sponsor. It was foolish, and he caught me in a weak moment. Maybe my weakest since sobering up. Could have even been the time when I reached for an illegal pick-me-up. The feeling of being alone, the isolation, it was choking me, and my sponsor made me feel that I didn't have to be alone. And then you kissed me in the staff hallway on Christmas, and I was destroyed."

He pulled my face back toward his, twisting my neck, but I didn't care. "I could kill this fucker," he joked when he released my lips.

"It's fine, Lane. It's fine." I said it twice, once for him and another time for myself. "I got my head on straight and found a new support person, but the reality is that I live in the middle of the woods for a reason, and you live here for another. I don't think I can change for anyone."

"Well, who said anything about you changing?"

I didn't have a chance to answer.

Lane flipped us out of the hammock and onto the ground, going first and taking the brunt of the fall, pulling me in for more kisses.

We were a sight rolling around on the grass of the Dylan, lips and bodies locked, holding on for dear life, not caring one bit about the ridiculous public display of affection we were putting on for the whole world to see.

And then Lane whispered for my ears only, "Can we go to your room, Bess?" He leaned back and observed my reaction, his eyes bright with anticipation.

"Yes," I said, and he lifted me in his arms and ran to the elevator.

We fell onto the bed in a mad scramble of hormones, grabbing at each other like teenagers, kissing and licking every available inch of skin until Lane froze for a moment and closed his eyes, then murmured, "Let's slow this down."

Disappointment made me frown. I didn't want to slow anything, and I certainly didn't like the direction he was heading.

He rolled off of the bed and walked over to the mini bar, which was no ordinary mini bar, considering he'd set me up in a two-bedroom suite swanky enough for celebrities. I think Madonna stayed in this room at one point.

After changing into pajamas the first night, I had padded through the room, enjoying the feel of my feet sinking into the lush rugs, when there was a knock on my door from room service. The waiter pushed in a room service cart, then removed anything alcoholic from the bar and replaced it with sparkling cider and artsy, designer bottled water, along with specially chosen snacks. There were bright lemons and limes in small bowls, and dark roasted almonds and chocolate-covered cherries in jars. I'd smiled to myself at the thoughtfulness that went into the gesture.

As Lane returned to the bed carrying two glasses of the bubbly cider, I watched his approach. My blood simmered, my body boiling over with passion like a pot of pasta left on high. Happy we weren't slowing anything too much, I pretended to be content.

He set his knee on the bed next to where I was sitting and handed me a glass, saying "Cheers" as he lightly clinked his against mine. Lane drained his glass while I was in the middle of my first sip, then dropped his delicate flute to the carpet and grabbed mine, leaning over and rolling it on the floor where it collided gently with his.

So much for slowing things . . . thank God.

At Lane's gentle nudge, I slid up the bed until my head rested on one of the oversized down pillows. He crawled up right after me, landing softly on top of me, using his leg to spread mine open. My shorts were riding up my legs and my panties were getting twisted, but I couldn't have cared less. I wanted friction. And more of it. Squirming underneath Lane, I found a spot where we were aligned perfectly, his hardness rubbing my hot spot.

He closed his eyes for a moment with a groan before saying, "Bess, you are incredible. I can't believe I've kept my hands off of you for this long."

He lifted the hem of my tank and kissed along my stomach, driving straight through my cleavage before circling each of my breasts with his tongue. He covered one nipple with his mouth as he tugged at the other with his hand.

A shiver ran through me and I threw back my head, calling out his name, my voice hoarse with need. I might as well have been tapping a vein and shooting up, because even as I begged for more with my body, my mind knew this was an addiction I wouldn't survive.

Desperate for him, I reached down and slid my hands over his ass, a very well-defined ass. We ground against each other until it was no longer enough, and I fumbled with Lane's pants zipper as he tugged at the waist of my shorts. It became a race to the finish line as piece by piece, our clothing joined the empty glasses on the floor.

When our clothes were gone he inched down, heading south until his hot breath fanned over my belly button, but he didn't stop there. He slid a finger and then two inside me, and seconds later, his tongue came to put pressure where I needed it most.

This time, I was the one who moaned. Like a dam released, wetness seeped out of me. I was so hot and turned on in ways I'd never experienced naturally, I couldn't even be worried about making a damp mess on the fancy bed.

My orgasm tore through me like a five-alarm fire, and I floated off to somewhere I didn't recognize. It was an island of bliss, a place where I'd never been on Molly or coke, a destination that a steady diet of alcohol and pot would never transport me to.

Exhilarated, I never wanted to leave. In that moment, I wanted nothing more than to pack my bags and permanently move to this unknown zip code.

Lane's gentle stroking brought me back to Florida, to the hotel and the present. His fingers glided in and out of me, coaxing out every tremor and wave of sensation that rocked my body. I looked down to find him watching me intently, his hooded eyes intensely blue from his own desire.

"Gorgeous," he said in a low voice. "So fucking stunning that I did that to you, Bess, and I watched the whole thing like it was in slow motion."

Then he shifted and pulled his fingers out, and my body immediately felt hollow, aching for something more. When he licked his fingers, his eyes darkening with excitement, my belly and other parts clenched at the sight. I was so turned on—I'd never felt this range of emotions without the help of something pharmaceutical.

And then his mouth was on mine and he tasted like me, but better because it was mixed with him. I reached down and wrapped my hand around him, drawing in a sharp breath. He was big. And wide. And so hard.

His length twitched in my hand, reaching for my center, and I guided him there without a second thought. He pushed inside and started to slowly glide in and out of me. Once again my head rolled back, and his tongue lapped my exposed neck.

I was back to my island, reveling in the sensations as Lane took long, slow strokes in and out of me, when he suddenly pulled out completely.

"Shit," he said.

Startled, I lifted my head and squeaked out, "What?"

"I didn't put on any protection."

"Oh. Well, do you have some?"

He inhaled deeply, then said, "Yeah, I'm just freaked. I've never done that before."

"Sorry, I forgot to ask. We both had our eyes on the prize." I wriggled a little beneath him, stroking my hand down his back to the dimples above his ass, and felt a tremble run through him. Knowing I could have that effect on him made me feel like I was soaring, which was another unrecognizable high.

A cool draft swept over me and I shivered as Lane reached down to his pants and grabbed a condom, ripping it open and putting it on as fast as humanly possible.

With him deep inside me again, I was no longer chilled. The heat began to build once again, and Lane picked up speed. I wrapped my legs around his back and held him tight as he rocked in and out of me, his balls tickling my ass.

When his finger came down to put pressure right where I needed it, I came apart and he followed right behind me. Blown to bits, I took time to visit my new favorite island destination known as orgasm by Lane, before he pulled out, threw the condom away, and pulled me in tight.

CHAPTER TWENTY-THREE

lane

I DIDN'T want to move. With Bess snuggled into me, our bodies slick from sex, my fingers still smelling like her, I wanted to stay at the Dylan forever. But it wasn't fair to Bess. She didn't come to Florida just to fuck, although I knew that wasn't what this was. I'd never made love before, but I was pretty certain that was what we just did. Christ, I'd been balls deep without any protection, and nothing had ever felt better.

But I wanted to make her last night special. Have dinner, and convince her to come back to my house for the night. Maybe we could take a swim together, if she wanted.

I moved her hair to the side. Trying to find her cheek in that mass of brown waves was almost impossible. I leaned over and planted a gentle kiss there when it was uncovered.

"Bess."

"Hmm?"

"That was incredible."

"Um-hmm."

"It's nearly dinnertime. We should go eat. Do something fun for your last night."

"This is fun."

I laughed out loud. A big, loud laugh. "I know, but we need to eat."

"Room service?" she murmured.

"How about Chinese takeout? At my place."

"Really?" When she turned her face toward me, her eyes were twinkling with surprise.

"Yeah. Why?"

"Well, I don't know. We haven't been there at all since I arrived, and I just thought you wanted to keep it private."

With that, I smacked her ass and said, "Silly girl. No way. I just didn't want to pressure you."

She gave me the biggest smile I had seen her make yet, and I didn't need to see any more.

"Come on, pack your bags. We're spending our last night together at my house."

I stood in the airport on the same spot that I had a few days ago, except this time, Bess wasn't riding down the escalator toward me. Her small but oh-so-perfect ass was riding up and away. More than anything, I wanted to yell for her to come back, or to chase her down caveman-style, but I did neither.

Instead I stood there like a class-A idiot, replaying our last night together in my head.

Bess had looked so perfect in my space with the sunset shining through the windows, giving her face a soft golden glow. We'd had Chinese as promised, had eaten it right out of the takeout containers with chopsticks, feeding each other bites before we'd fallen into bed.

After quickly stripping her out of her tiny jeans shorts, long-sleeved T-shirt, and sexy as all fuck black bra and lace thong, my hand had found its way inside her with no directions needed and she rode my fingers.

As she bucked on my hand, I licked and sucked on her nipples until she was screaming my name. Her voice echoed hoarsely through my house as she asked for more, over and over again. At the sound of those words, I became completely undone and flipped her over, then yanked her ass back until she was on all fours. This time, just barely remembering to put a condom on, I hurried to take care of it, then dove in.

I drove my dick into her hard, each stroke causing my body to slap against her ass, and she gasped, her cheek buried in the mattress as she clenched herself around my dick and begged for more. Leaning forward, I brushed her long hair out of the way and pressed my mouth to the soft part of her neck and between her shoulder blades.

Goose bumps formed in my wake as I kissed my way along her smooth skin. They were faint, almost not visible to the naked eye, but I saw them and became even more aroused at the knowledge that I put them there.

By the time we both finished, night had fallen around us, darkness falling completely around the house. We were both hesitant to fall asleep, not wanting the weekend to come to an end, so I suggested a swim.

"Let me grab my suit," she said.

"That won't be necessary."

With a playful growl, I swept her into my arms and carried her downstairs to my back patio. We were both buck naked, but privacy wasn't a problem; my grounds were protected by huge palm trees and shrubbery. Still, when I set her on her feet, she crossed her arm over her tits and held a hand over her tiny landing strip.

"Babe, no one can see you but me, and I like what's underneath your arms, so let go," I told her. Without a second's hesitation, she did as she was told. Our eyes met and I winked.

"Oh yes, I love the view," I said before grabbing her hand and leading her to the pool.

When I got to the edge, I jumped in and she stood on the edge, somewhat timid.

"What?" I asked.

Bess looked warily at the water, then at me. "Is it cold?"

"No fucking way. You think I'd take you into a cold pool? Ninety-two degrees. This baby is heated up and ready for you," I teased, wiggling my hips under the water.

Apparently convinced, she let out a little scream as she jumped in after me, and I moved quickly to grab her in my arms. She wrapped her legs around my waist and as though it hadn't just been there, my cock was at attention, poking and reaching for the promised land between her legs.

We kissed as I moved toward the steps where I laid Bess out in front of me.

Her elbows went to rest behind her on the top step as her ass bobbed in the water. Practically on my knees in the shallow end, I let my hands wander under her glorious ass and lifted it above the water line before dipping my head to meet her even more glorious pussy. It glistened from the water and her arousal, and I ran my tongue up and down its soft valley, finally settling where I knew she liked.

Sadly, it didn't take long enough for Bess to explode, her flavor mixing with the chlorine. I wanted more. It was the sweetest honey I'd ever tasted.

But I couldn't dwell on that for too long because she took me by surprise and turned the tables on me, sliding my body to the steps where I was forced to lean back on the top step as she'd done.

Her mouth was on me before I could blink, her tongue running up and down my length, stopping to pay attention to both the tip and my balls. Lifting my head, I leaned over to catch a glimpse of her bending over me, taking such intimate care of my cock that I nearly blew my load right there.

"Oh fucking God, Bess, please don't stop," I murmured, rolling my head back and closing my eyes.

And she didn't. She slid me in all the way, taking every last inch in her hot mouth. She sucked me hard and long all the way to the end, where she refused to move and held on for dear life as I let go of my release down her throat.

By the time we'd left the pool, showered, and crawled back into bed, naked and warm in each other's arms, we'd been exhausted. With only a few hours of sleep, daylight had come too soon, and I'd kissed the fuck out of her that morning over coffee in my kitchen.

After years of screwing Jake's leftovers before becoming quite the lover myself, last night was the single most erotic and sensual night of my life. Now she was gone and I had to go home to a bed that smelled like Bess and a house that was empty without her.

But she didn't want to live in Florida. Couldn't live here.

And I couldn't go back north. The place was a mental trap for me. An endless black hole of memories and secrets.

CHAPTER
TWENTY-FOUR

bess

THE sound of gravel crunching alerted me to a car coming down my driveway, and I ran to the door, flinging it open.

"May! Brooks!" I ran out onto my porch without a coat, not caring that it was only twenty degrees outside.

May got out of the car, and before she could walk around to the passenger side, my Lab came barreling out the driver's side door.

"Hey, sweetie!" May called to me as she shoved her car door closed.

"Hi, May. How was my big guy?"

Brooks had run up to the porch and shoved his snout into my leg, demanding a pet before he ran back down the hill and lifted his leg.

"He was just fine. He's so lazy," she said with a big smile.

"Good boy," I said to my dog when he came back up the stairs. "He's not lazy," I said to May.

"Well, we're glad to have him, lazy or not," she said as she came up the steps. As soon as she'd crossed the threshold, she gave me a knowing look, then plopped down onto the sofa without an invitation. "Okay, spill."

So I curled up on the other end of the couch with my legs tucked under me, still dehydrated from stale airplane air and feeling sore between my legs, and told her all about Florida.

Except for the naughty details.

When I was done, she gave me an approving look. "See? You came clean and let it all hang out, and survived to tell about it. Proud of you, girlie."

Then she said her good-byes and headed for home, leaving me all alone with my thoughts and memories.

The next morning, I got up early. I was due back to work, but had somewhere I needed to go first. Pulling up to the church, I spotted Shirley in her Buick. Bundled in my parka with a hat tight on my head, I braved the cold to walk over to the only car with the engine idling.

She cut the engine as I approached and stepped out of the car. "Bess, honey. You okay? How was it?"

Before I could answer, Shirley pulled me in for a hug, squeezing me tight as she squished my face into her big boobs. I relaxed in the warmth of her scent, a homey mix of grease from the diner and an overly flowery perfume. I wasn't sure why it felt familiar, but even with no mother or grandmother to speak of, the combined scents of cooking and heavy perfume brought me comfort. If I'd had female role models in my life, I was sure that was what they would smell like.

"It was unreal," I said in a low voice, trying to keep my lip from quivering. "So unreal, but now I'm back."

Shirley grabbed my hand and tugged me toward the building. Even though I convinced my lip to remain still, my glassy eyes probably gave me away.

Squeezing my hand, she said, "Oh, honey. It's okay to be happy and have an unreal time. And even more okay to be sad to leave it."

I nodded and then said, "But now that I've had a taste of what could never be, I'm not sure I'll ever be the same. And I'm already unsure of who the heck I am."

She just squeezed my hand a little harder and said, "Come on, you'll feel better after this."

The morning meeting was mostly people who were happy to have survived the night without drinking or indulging in whatever their poison was, grateful to have made it through another twenty-four hours. In my mind, they were the most distraught meeting-goers, the ones teetering the closest to falling again.

As Shirley blew through the doorway with me in her wake, it occurred to me that was probably why she went to the morning meetings. She was a mother hen, always wanting to help other people, to save them, and we were all her chicks.

I knew most of the people there, but there were two or three newcomers, probably recently released from the full-time rehab program where I went. People in that situation usually decided to stay on in the day program until they were truly able to go back to their lives or what was left of them.

Together we huddled in the cold basement as cheap coffee percolated in the background, next to a carton of doughnuts left open on the table. As we waited for the meeting to begin, each of us looked around the room and saw pieces of ourselves in each and everyone there. And hoped we weren't as bad off as the next person.

Shirley got up to speak today, and I sat up a little straighter in my chair. I'd never heard her share her story before, had only heard bits and pieces, so I kept my eyes and ears focused on my new friend.

"Hi, my name's Shirley—everyone calls me Shirl—and I'm an alcoholic. I'm pretty sure I've always been one. Since I was a teen or something like that and I watched my dad railing on my mom. I tried to make a new life for myself when I left home. Back then, I was going to school in the Midwest to be a nurse. But it was taking forever to put myself through school, and I never finished. That was when my drinking and using got real bad. When I felt like a failure for not making anything of my life."

She paused to look at her feet, and I thought I saw a tear drop to the floor. She sniffed a time or two before continuing.

"Then I started babysitting and sort of cleaned up my act again. I lived in a neighborhood where there were a lot of young families, and some of them asked me if I could help them if they needed a break or to go to work. So I did their laundry and cooking while I watched their kids. I know, I know . . . how could I care for children while I was drunk? I rationalized that I didn't, that I wasn't drunk the next day. I loved those kids so much. I'd sober up on black coffee in the morning after passing out from being drunk every night, but it wasn't right. I know that now."

Shirley cleared her throat and nervously smoothed her hair into her tight bun.

"There was one family; I loved these people like they were my own. They often invited me to stay and eat with them, giving me care packages to take home. If I'd had a different family growing up, I wanted this one. They had the cutest kids I ever laid my eyes on. They used to snuggle up to me and say, 'Read us a story, Miss Shirley,' until I let them down."

Tears gathered in her eyes, and as one slid down her cheek, I felt the telltale pricking in my own eyes.

"One day," she said, "I wasn't quite myself. It was the anniversary of the day I should've graduated nursing school a few years before, and I really tied one on that night." Her voice wobbled and she swallowed, trying to clear her throat.

"The next day, I let those kids down. I had to lay down, take a rest, do something to get rid of the ache in my head and my heart. My head was throbbing and I sat down on the couch with them and said we would watch some TV. But I must've fallen asleep and after a while, they got bored. One little guy got into something real bad. After that it was over. Destroyed . . . everything was ruined . . . because of me . . . and they . . . they moved and I lost them all."

Shirley put her head in her hands, crying in earnest at this point. Her shoulders heaved as she sobbed, but she finished her story with her mascara running and strands of hair coming loose, falling around her face.

"It was after that, such a tremendous loss, that I dried up and moved here and made a quiet, boring life for myself. Now I've got a life with a man who loves me, a steady job, and lots of good friends. It's not perfect, but it's good."

She stared out at us with a tearful half smile. "There are days I wish that I'd faced all my demons. That I didn't move, but faced life where I'd been living it . . . or not living it. But I did the best I could, and I'm here. And I wouldn't have met you all if I didn't come here."

Her story finished, Shirley gave us a bittersweet smile. As the group applauded and called out their support, she came back to her seat next to me. I squeezed her hands in mine and kissed her on the cheek before handing her a tissue, then helped her wipe her freckles free of makeup and dry her pretty green eyes.

With all the emotion bled out of me, work felt like a breeze.

I ended up a little late to work because of the meeting, but served breakfast in between chatting with Ernesto, and stayed on through lunch. The hotel was full and the restaurant was busy. My sections might have been packed all morning and afternoon, but that didn't stop me from taking a quick peek over at the bar and picturing Lane sitting there on Christmas Day, or frequently conjuring up his smiling face.

I tried telling myself that it was okay, giving myself permission to ache for the man and the loss of what might have been if I didn't have so many ghosts in my closet.

CHAPTER
Twenty-Five

lane

One month later

A LONG month had passed since Bess left. A very *dry* thirty days. An epic drought, so to speak.

During those weeks we'd only spoken three times. It was mostly my doing.

She did call me to thank me for the trip and the package I had delivered to her place the day after she returned home. I knew better than to believe she would ever pick up the phone and pursue me. She had done that once, and I didn't expect it again.

And I used that to my deranged advantage, because I was a sick and very twisted person. On paper, I was decent. But inside I was fucking tormented. I had been for years.

The nice brother with skeletons in the closet.

After that I'd only called her twice more, making light conversation and never tackling the elephant on the line.

What were we? Or what could we be?

Because the answer was painfully clear. Nothing.

I was in Spain visiting a property for a large hotel conglomerate that wanted my services. The weather was gorgeous, the women were exotic and beautiful—not to mention ready, willing, and able—and I couldn't get my head out of my ass.

Every afternoon, when the whole fucking nation disappeared to take a siesta, I paced my hotel balcony. With a small tumbler of scotch, I would roam the tiny open space, looking out at the wide countryside in front of me as I thought.

Thinking was very bad because it brought up my past, and that was a part of me I didn't like to think about. I'd moved on, created a fucking dynasty through my own hard work, and the past had no place in that world.

At the moment, I stared hard at the amber-hued liquid in my glass, the oaky aroma mixing with the salty seaside air. All it did was remind me of her brown hair spread out in front of me, salty waves crashing in the background. Of course, Bess's face was in the middle of all that glorious hair, smiling up at me as I enjoyed her body, taking my fill.

Sex had always been my escape mechanism, my secret weapon to burying everything else that tormented me. Now I was on a starvation diet from it, and it wasn't working out for me. The nightmares had returned, and they wouldn't stop. Bedtime had come to include a healthy drink and a long hot shower, where my own stroking did little to relieve my stress.

I had just tossed the rest of my drink back when my phone chimed with a text.

JAKE: Yo, bro! Where you at?

ME: Spain. What gives?

JAKE: I need some help.

ME: Of course. What now?

Jake didn't text back. Instead my phone rang, his contact info coming up on the screen.

"Yo, Jake," I answered, already lacking patience where my fucking twin was concerned.

"Listen, Lane, don't be mad. I need money."

I'd stepped into my hotel room to take the call, but the four walls and the stale damp air were stifling. Walking back onto the balcony, I said, "What the fuck, Jake? Money for what?"

"I had a deal go south. It went really bad."

"What deal? You own a gym, you're not in finance."

"Well, remember Courtney?"

I let out a long breath before answering. "Yes. From Christmas."

"She was a rep for this protein smoothie company, and convinced me to sign off on a PO for a huge recurring shipment. I can't sell the shit. It sucks, and it keeps coming and the company wants to be paid. At least through the next six months, and then they'll let me out of the contract."

"Jesus Christ, Jake! Can't you keep your dick and your business separate?"

"I said don't be mad."

"Well, I am fucking mad. I can't always clean up your messes, bro. Time to come to terms with that." I sat down in the lounge chair and leaned my head back, closing my eyes in hopes of keeping a pounding headache at bay.

"Yeah, I know. Just this time, Lane, and then I'm gonna get my act together. I would have the cash, but I just signed the lease on a second building and put a down payment on equipment. I'm opening a second location. I know the gym business, you know that. And I need to clear my credit to make the second place happen. I'm desperate."

I decided not to get into it anymore. "How much do you need?"

"Twenty-five K."

"You're a little fuck, you know that? Twenty-five K in smoothies? Courtney's pussy better have been worth it."

"Yeah. I know."

"You know what? You're a fuck or Courtney's pussy was worth

it?" I let out a snort. "Just fucking stop with the fucking yeahs and all the agreeing and get your shit together, Jake."

"Okay," he said, his voice muffled.

"Where is this vendor? I want to have a chat and see the contract before I bail you out."

"They're sort of local."

"How local?"

"Youngstown, Ohio."

"Shit. You know how I feel about that place, Jake."

"I know. Please?"

"Fine. I'm scheduled to leave Spain in two days. I'll have my assistant change my flights and head straight to you. Make all the arrangements on your end, Jake. I'm not waiting when I get there. I have a life and a business."

And no one to rush home to.

Not waiting for one of his lame okays or yeahs, I disconnected the call and sent an e-mail to my assistant to change my travel.

Then I sent a text that made my heart pound and my pulse race, a few typed words that I had dared myself not to send.

> ME: Hey! You're probably at work since it's morning where you are. I'm in Spain, but traveling back to PA tomorrow night. Can I come visit in a few days? I miss you and I'd like to see you.

I didn't hear back, but told myself she was busy at work, her phone tucked securely in her locker.

CHAPTER
TWENTY-SIX

aj

S PRING had finally fucking come. With it the ground thawed and my shopping center project started to pick up speed. Which was good because my demons were eating at my gut. I was being consumed alive, and I needed to keep myself busy.

Bess was back. She'd been back for a month, but I knew better than to push her to see me. I'd already made that mistake once or twice.

Throwing my truck in gear, my eighth cigarette of the morning hanging out of my mouth, its smoke coiling around me like my emotions were doing in my belly, I headed to the morning meeting. I couldn't beg, but I had to see her. Just lay my eyeballs on her.

I knew she was going regularly to the early one. Fucking Shirley. God-fucking-dammit. I'd known that lady for a long time. She thought she could save every fucking soul. I'd had enough coffees at her diner counter to know, and now she had her claws in Bess.

I knew because she had told me as much.

It had been late one afternoon and I'd been fucking freezing from standing out on a site. I'd just smashed my cigarette out in the canister in front of the diner and made my way to the bar as I held my last breath of nicotine in, letting it out as I took a seat.

Who the fuck are all these people who say we can't smoke inside buildings? Controlling assholes, that's who.

"Hey, AJ, what can I do for you?" Shirley had asked me.

"Coffee, black," I'd said.

"Please. Thanks, Shirl," she'd said, mocking me.

"Don't get all high-and-mighty with me, Shirley. I know you took my girl, turning her against me. God fucking knows what you're filling her head with."

She'd slammed the coffee mug in front of me and leaned her elbows down on the counter as she gave me that glare that mommas everywhere do so well. "Don't you dare speak to me that way, Andrew Jon. Not now. Not ever. Maybe I used to be a pushover once, but no more," she said as she pointed her finger at my face.

I lowered my head. I had a conscience—whether I let it show or not lately.

"Sorry," I mumbled.

"You better be, boy. You had no business getting involved with that young lady other than helping her as a sponsor. What the hell is wrong with you? I should've stopped your sorry ass."

"I know, but she's my Bess. Anyone who meets her once knows she's fucking special. And I could give her a good life. I get where she's been." I took a slug of my coffee, allowing it to burn its way down my throat, making its way to my acid-filled stomach.

Shirley shook her head, giving me a pitying look. "AJ, honey, she needs to find her own way. You can't solve that for her, no one can. Not me or that man from out of town. This I know, doll."

"What man, Shirl? What the hell are you talking about?"

I grabbed my forehead.

This is why she went to Florida. I had to stop this. Whatever this cat-and-mouse game was.

"You know what, Shirley? Never mind. You should mind your own fucking business when it comes to Bess too."

I threw some money on the counter and hightailed it out of there.

That night I went ballistic when I got home, tossing shit around my house—a lamp, my side table, and a fucking framed picture of my parents—before I sat up the rest of the night smoking out on my porch. I couldn't have given two fucks if it was freezing.

Early the next day, I blew off morning roll call with my crews to catch a glimpse of the little tramp.

Guiding my truck into a spot in the church parking lot, I saw her car and flung myself out of the cab. My heavy boots ate up the asphalt and I was in the church before I could take stock of what I was doing. When I threw open the door, reality came crashing down on me as heads turned and all eyes in the room focused on me.

Shit. I was using a meeting, doing the ultimate sacrilegious act, all to manipulate Bess. I could be hindering her sobriety, and even I knew that wasn't what I intended or wanted.

Without saying a word, I turned around and walked back to my truck.

A cold wind whipped all around me, its mood about as angry as my own. It wasn't quite spring, but winter wasn't totally over. The air was damp and moist, a chill running through it. It hit my face and tears burned at my eyes.

From the wind. Yeah, right.

"AJ! Wait!" she called out from behind me and there she was, running toward me.

I froze in place, my feet glued to the asphalt as my throat clogged with emotion, something I wasn't used to and didn't like one damn bit. I'd tamped down my feelings for years before learning to live without them.

"Bess," I said as she approached.

She didn't hesitate; she came right in for a hug. A friendly bear hug.

"Hi," she said.

"Hi."

I held her close, unable to let her go. Eventually she pulled back, and I noticed she didn't have her jacket on.

"Come on," I said. "Let's go sit in my truck where it's warm." I cocked my head toward it.

When we climbed into the cab, I turned on the engine and cranked up the heat.

Bess wrapped her arms around herself and lifted her shoulders to her ears as she tried to get warm. "Listen, AJ, I'm sorry I've been avoiding you. I'm sorry for everything. I've had a lot on my mind, but what I did was wrong. I love you, but not like that. I *need* you in my life, and I hate to think I ruined that. But I feel like I did." She stared straight out the windshield with her admission.

"Babe, you know I care for you a whole fuck of a lot, but I'm not ready to accept that you're not hiding your true feelings for me. You're scared of how good we can fucking be, and running. Like your mom ran from you."

I shifted in my seat to face her and reached out to smooth back her windblown hair, taking in her innocent eyes and natural beauty. I wouldn't use a meeting, but I would use her past.

She tucked her chin in her chest and stared at her Nikes as she said, "I met someone else. I know it's not gonna work with him, but he made me feel something huge for the first time since I was little. Since before my mom left and everything got messed up."

Hearing these words roll off her tongue was like a punch to the gut in a bad bar fight.

"I'm sorry that I wasn't honest," she said softly. "It just felt so strange and unique and everything in between, I wanted to keep it to myself." She shot me a sideways glance, a small line appearing between her brows as she added, "Plus you and I had crossed so many boundaries, and I was so ashamed of the way I acted. You didn't deserve to be taken advantage of like that. You're right, I did run, but for good reason. From you. From him. From everyone."

My mind whirled as I listened, struggling to find an argument that would make her stay.

"Listen to me," I said, trying to keep the desperation I was feeling out of my voice. "You didn't deserve for me to start any of this, but some things happen for a reason. Like us. I pushed my way in because I had to. There was something driving us to be together, but I should have seen you weren't ready. I left myself wide open for whatever you did. My heart was on my sleeve, and now I need to tuck it back in. For a while, anyway. Because I'm waiting for you, Bess."

She wiped her face. A tear had made its way down her cheek, making me want to pull her in and kiss her. But that wasn't where we were. She wanted to be friends. Friends who'd fucked a few times.

She reached for the handle and popped the door open. "I'm sorry. I have to go," she blurted before she ran back to her meeting.

And I fell off the wagon. All because of some sweet piece of cunt.

CHAPTER
TWENTY-SEVEN

lane

HEADING to Pittsburgh turned into a major cluster fuck. Instead of renting a car, I had Jake pick me up at the airport. Good thing he was driving when he dropped the bad news; otherwise, I would have strangled him.

"We're not meeting with the smoothie company until Monday," he said offhandedly. "That's the best they could do."

"Fuck," I roared before slamming my hand into the dashboard. My carefully constructed facade was beginning to crack, little fissures slowly making their way into my polished finish.

I'd finally heard back from Bess and made a plan. She'd texted that she would "love" to see me, and I figured I'd be able to head up Friday night or Saturday morning at the very latest before going home first thing Monday morning.

"I have a life, Jake," I said after composing myself.

"I know. I did the best I could, but we could have fun over the weekend. Hang out?"

"No thanks, I don't do pity invites. Besides, I'm going to see someone up in the country, and now I'll have to come back here on Sunday night so we can hit that hellhole known as Youngstown on Monday."

"Oh, who?"

"You don't know her."

He glanced over at me, finally taking the hint. "Well, at least we could chill tonight."

"Sure," I said through clenched teeth. The only thing worse than my brother sleeping with five women at the same time was Jake sleeping with no one.

We ended up in a dark sports bar with TVs everywhere and Iron City on tap. It was a shithole, but a good one. Seated in a booth in the back, we ordered a plate of wings, and I pulled out my phone. After e-mailing my assistant—again—instructing her on my latest change of plans, I texted Bess.

> ME: I'm here. Back in the USA. Just got to Pittsburgh and turns out I'm free all day tomorrow. What's your work schedule?

My beer arrived as my phone dinged.

> BESS: I'm off tomorrow and Saturday. I have to work on Sunday, though.

> ME: OK. Can I come out in the morning?

> BESS: Sure. About what time? I've been going to a morning meeting.

> ME: Let's say 10?

> BESS: Great. I'll text you my address for your GPS. I'll give you the main road. It works better when you put that in.

ME: See you then.

I might have seemed calm in my texts, but I was anything but relaxed. I was especially unnerved now that I needed to extend my trip at least until Tuesday, delaying my time to get in and out of Youngstown.

That place was my worst nightmare.

Downshifting my rental Jeep into third, I slowed my speed on the curvy road leading to Bess's place despite wanting to floor it. I'd been up half the night. My old nightmares had returned, and after tossing and turning for hours, I finally called a cab at the crack of dawn to take me to rent a car.

I left without saying good-bye to Jake, but I did grab some of his casual clothes. He could at least let me have those after all I'd done for him over the years, and was about to do next week.

The farther I drove from him and what Monday would bring, the calmer I felt. But every time I thought about the weekend coming to an end and what lay ahead, I started to panic again. It was a vicious cycle of up-down-up-down throughout the whole ninety-minute drive to rural Pennsylvania.

Fields rolled out for miles from the road. Cows grazed in the grass and horses roamed, making me feel small in my pursuits. I was a man pursuing a woman. The wrong woman for me, for so many reasons. Yet I couldn't stop myself.

Her long silence following my initial text showed me she felt the same hesitation, but when she used the word "loved" in reference to seeing me, there wasn't much that could stop me.

Finally I made it to the address on the main road, where Bess instructed I should make the first left immediately beyond it. As I turned onto her small road, a winding country path lined with trees, her small house came into view. Tucked back against the woods, small branches framing it, the house beckoned with its gray wraparound porch.

I parked the Jeep behind another small SUV, which I assumed belonged to Bess, and bolted to the stairs. The door flung open and a huge dog came running out, barking, tail wagging, tongue hanging out.

"Hey," Bess said from the doorway.

"Hey. Some guard dog you have here," I replied, unable to move because her dog was jumping at my feet, panting and begging for my attention.

"Brooks Bailey, leave it!" she shouted, and he didn't hesitate. The dog turned away and bounded down the hill, heeding everything Bess said like every other hot-blooded male.

Alone now, we met halfway on the steps to her porch. She blinked and said, "I can't believe you're here."

"Me either." I pulled her in for a hug and an inhale. She still smelled familiar, but instead of salty ocean air cloaking her this time, it was pine and evergreen.

She pulled back and said, "Welcome to spring in a place that has four seasons. Enjoy the damp and muddy conditions we have to face before we get glorious sunshine."

I didn't have a chance to answer because Brooks was back on the porch, now circling both of us with a ball in his mouth.

"Should I throw it?" I asked.

"Only if you plan to spend the rest of your weekend doing that," Bess said with a laugh. "Come on in."

We headed through the door into a combined sitting area and kitchen. Loyal and lucky to belong to the brown-haired beauty, Brooks followed right behind Bess, never leaving her side now that I was in their domain. The crackle of the fireplace and the smell of something baking greeted us as we walked inside.

"So, this is my place. Not quite as big as yours and no swimming pool, but we do have zucchini bread baked with chocolate chips."

"It smells amazing," I said with an appreciative sniff.

Bess walked toward the oven and waved her hand around while saying, "Make yourself at home."

I couldn't move. My feet were like two boulders in the ground when she grabbed oven mitts and bent over to take the bread out. Her ass was just as perfect as a few years ago when I first saw her in the downward dog position. I was transported to that day, and a tidal wave of guilt flooded my stomach at what I was doing.

Lying or deceiving or whatever this was, it was wrong. It had become an evil pattern, one that dug its claws deep within me, and I couldn't wrestle my way out. Instead, I kept pushing forward, trudging through life with guilt's stranglehold in place over my heart.

As the bread cooled on the counter, Bess made her way over to me. Studying my expression, she said, "You okay?"

"Absolutely. I just didn't sleep well last night." I wrapped my arm around her waist and pulled her closer.

"Oh," she said into my chest.

I kissed the top of her head and wanted so much more.

She looked up at me, her eyes uncertain. "I was gonna suggest a little hike, but if you just want to chill, that's cool."

Placing my index finger under her chin, I tilted her face up toward mine, then I bent and placed my mouth over hers. There was no way to describe what I did next other than I devoured her lips and tongue. I couldn't bring myself to stop.

Finally, I broke away and said, "A hike sounds perfect."

CHAPTER
TWENTY-EIGHT

bess

LANE was in my house. Rather than his usual expensive suit, he was wearing worn-in jeans and a dark blue thermal shirt, standing in the middle of the sitting area with his mouth covering mine.

In Pennsylvania. In my little house.

I was freaking out—baking and suggesting a hike—when all I really wanted to do was lead him back to my bedroom. Although I had vowed that one weekend with Lane was enough when I returned home, then he texted me. And I'd relented, because once would never be enough when it came to him.

My life was still complicated. AJ and I were not in a better place, but our swords had been drawn. He knew where I stood and wouldn't accept that, but I was holding to it.

I was lonely other than my occasional time with Shirley. Being alone and cold with no one other than Brooks to warm my feet was getting old. And I liked Lane more than a little. Maybe even a lot. I just couldn't figure out how he fit into my carefully crafted life. But now he was in my house, kissing me silly.

So when Lane interrupted my thoughts with, "A hike sounds perfect," I quickly took him up on it. It seemed the smart thing to do at the time.

We hiked through the woods, taking a path from my house. Brooks followed along off leash, but Lane noticed he wore the collar he'd sent in his second package. He also noticed the giant container I was using for Brooks's treats that he'd sent in his most recent package.

I thought that would be my last package and cherished the tiny mementos of our weekend he included. The miniature snow globe with a swimming pool inside sat on my window sill, and the votive full of sand and shells held a permanent spot on the mantel. He probably noticed those too, but I didn't point them out.

As we made our way along the narrow paths wearing almost matching puffy vests, we held hands and had conversations we shouldn't have been having.

"So, you got this dog pretty much under your little finger?" Lane asked as we rounded a bend and Brooks came as soon as I called him.

"I don't know about that, but we came into each other's lives when neither of us had anyone else. I think he knew how much I needed him."

I stopped and caught myself from going on and on about a time of my life that would certainly bore anyone.

"Hey, go on," Lane insisted, grabbing my hand and keeping us moving through the trees.

"Really? It must sound so silly and touchy-feely."

"Let me be the judge of that," he said, and pumped my hand.

"Well, it was right after I left rehab and was on my own for the first time in ninety days. The worst was behind me, I hoped, but I still felt really alone. My dad wanted to come and be with me, but we were never close like that, and I grew up without a mother."

Bess paused for a moment in her story, reaching out her free hand to stroke Brooks's head as he trotted beside her. "So I got a dog. One Saturday I went over to the pound, and they had a litter of puppies that had been abandoned in a barn. I felt so bad for those little guys, I wanted to take all of them. But I could barely take care of myself, let alone eight puppies." She tugged affectionately at Brooks's ear. "And then this one tumbled over to me. He was tripping over his own big paws and kept trying to jump in my arms. I picked him up and didn't put him down until it was time to get in my car to go home."

This time, Lane came to a halt and grabbed my cheeks, bringing me in for a kiss before he said, "Bess Williams, you *are* magnificent."

Brooks sat down right at our feet in between us and stared up at us like we were the two weirdest creatures he'd ever laid eyes on.

"Would it be wrong if I said I want to turn around and go back to your house and strip you naked?" Lane said, interrupting my thoughts.

"No," I choked out, already breathless and barely able to speak.

Practically racing back up the hill, we made it to my door in record time. I unlocked it, let Brooks in, and by the time he was finished shaking the moisture off his fur, we were ripping our coats and shoes off, leaving a trail of clothes behind us as I led Lane to my bedroom.

We fell onto the bed in a tangle of limbs. Lane helped me scoot over, smoothing the hair around my face as my head fell into the pillow, lightly tracing down my neck and collarbone with his tongue. A hot trail formed where his warm breath laid tracks barely cooled by the mountain air swirling around my room.

My hands and hips reached for him of their own volition, betraying any rules I had put into place where it came to my heart or unwanted disruptions in my very organized simple life. Apparently my body didn't mind complications as long as it meant Lane was inside me.

He slowly licked a path up my inner thigh, taking so long that I was squirming when I begged, "Lane, now!"

"Be patient," he breathed out, and went back to teasing me.

My heart pounded in my chest, my own breathing coming in pants, and when he finally landed where I wished he would, my body yelled, *Yes!*

His strokes were both tender and rough, patient and urgent—a living, breathing contradiction, much like our lives and paths crossing.

With a final sweep of his tongue, I came. My orgasm was hard and furious, my body angry that I'd waited so long since I last saw Lane, sending chills spiraling through me that were almost punishing.

With my tremors still running their course, Lane slipped on a condom and was inside me. He pulled me up to meet his chest, my nipples rubbing against his very hard body, the friction causing peaks to form as he shifted me back toward the headboard, and I caught a glimpse of his six-pack working hard.

With one hand on the headboard, the other holding me tight, his tip hitting the spot that drove me wild, I was pretty sure I was going to come again when I felt Lane pick up speed, hunting down his own release. As soon as he started jerking and I felt him losing it inside me, I followed suit.

Toppling down on me, yet careful to hold some of his weight back, he slid the condom off and tossed it on the nightstand. While I lightly scratched his back, he held me until all the sensation passed.

We spent most of the afternoon this way. Lounging and talking with lingering touches.

Tucked in the crook of Lane's neck, our bodies sticking together in the sweaty aftermath of sex, I didn't want to move. I said in a hushed whisper, "Wow, Spain. So that's where you were?"

"Mmm," he said into the top of my head.

"Was it amazing?" I asked, unable to keep a touch of melancholy from my words. Not sure where it was coming from, I couldn't help but feel a longing to travel and explore with Lane. But that would never be possible.

"It was work. Of course, it is a beautiful country, but I was there for work," he answered, before rolling me on top of him and smiling. "But it would have been better if you were there."

"Don't," I pleaded. "Don't make promises you can't keep."

"I'm not. Actually, I've never really traveled much with anyone else. It would be fun with you, and hot."

Our eyes met, and I blinked back the wetness in mine. "Lane, let's not get carried away. I'm a waitress in rural Pennsylvania. You're a mega-successful entrepreneur from South Beach. I'm a recovered addict and you're essentially a playboy. Even I'm smart enough to know this has a short shelf life, whatever this is. What I'm not smart enough to do is to say 'no thanks' to you and your fabulous offers, but I know this will end sometime soon."

And I hope I don't fall apart. I pray I'm strong enough not to crumble.

"Bess," he whispered, steadying my face with both his hands so I couldn't look away. "Don't make this into some awful self-fulfilling prophecy. I don't know what this is either, but like I told you on Christmas, I feel drawn to you in a way I've never felt before. I can't stop the pull and neither can you, so we shouldn't. And for the record, when I'm with you, I don't feel like a playboy. I'm a man chasing a woman, scared I'm not gonna catch her."

He didn't use any more sweet nothings to capture my heart, only actions.

After another round in the sheets, this one slower and less frantic than our first hit, we drifted off to sleep. As dusk deepened outside the house, I was jolted awake with a swift punch to my ribs.

"Ow," I mouthed, unable to make the sound come out with the pain rushing through me.

Lane was thrashing in the sheets, his hands fisted, punching the air. "No! No! What did you do? What?" he yelled, his cries hoarse and raspy with emotion.

"Lane," I whispered while holding my side after shifting to the other side of the bed. "Lane," I said quietly again, afraid of what might happen if I said it louder. I wasn't equipped to care for someone this way. I'd been tasked with doing it for myself all my life, and look how shitty that turned out.

What was he screaming about? Was it the darkness that lingered in his eyes, that indefinable something I'd seen in him before?

Luckily, Brooks had gotten up from the corner of the room where he had been resting, and came straight to the side of the bed where Lane was sleeping. Apparently concerned, Brooks poked his wet nose into Lane, jarring him out of his nightmare.

"Shit," Lane said, coming awake. He ran a trembling hand along his forehead, then pushed it back through his messy hair. He wasn't facing me, but I could feel anger and an unwelcome embarrassment radiating from him. Whether he admitted it or not, he was a playboy, and this wasn't how playboys drifted off to sleep after fucking their girl.

Unsure of what else to do, I placed my hand on his shoulder and asked, "Lane, you okay?"

He slowly turned my way, his eyes no longer the cornflower blue of a bright sky, and they were certainly no longer happy. They were muddled and pained, a sea of roiling emotions that I couldn't dive into. I wasn't a strong enough swimmer.

"Shit, Bess. Fuck!" He sat up in bed and rummaged around for his shirt, whipping it on before grabbing his boxer briefs and throwing those on in a fury. "Fuck, I'm so sorry. I didn't mean to scare you." He stood up and paced beside the bed, his brow furrowed, his mind more than likely racing between fight or flight.

His breathing was heavy, his eyes frantic and wild, and I felt the need to go to him. Gingerly, I brought my feet out of bed, pain jabbing my side from the movement. As I stood, I held my ribs, trying to act like I was stretching. No such luck.

"Jesus Christ, what the hell happened?" Lane asked, marching over to me when I should have been running to him.

"Nothing. You just clipped me in your sleep," I said, trying to be vague.

"Don't do that, Bess. Don't be all naive and pretend what just happened didn't freak you the fuck out. One minute I'm making . . . I mean, we're having sex, and the next I'm punching the shit out of you and waking up in a terror."

"Well, I was worried," I said, trying to keep my voice calm and soothing. "But you're up and we can talk about it now if you want." I ran my hand down his cheek.

Isn't that what I should say? I felt like I needed to call Shirley or May. I was at a loss, clueless about what to do next.

He swatted my hand out of the way and stepped back. "There's nothing to talk about. It's an old bad dream. Haven't had it in years, and now it's back. Probably stress."

I didn't have a chance to respond because before I could open my mouth, he turned away and said, "I gotta roll. I'm really sorry, but I have to cut this visit short. I can't stay and risk hurting you."

Lane was out the door and peeling down the gravel driveway in his Jeep before I could even wrap myself in my robe and get to the door to watch him pull away.

CHAPTER TWENTY-NINE

lane

"JAKE! Pick the hell up!" I yelled into the phone as I barreled down the hill faster than I should have been going.

Of course, my fucking brother wasn't picking up when I needed him to. It had always been a one-way street when it came to us.

Frustrated, I tossed my phone onto the passenger seat.

Screw him.

I drove straight to Pittsburgh's airport, not stopping for gas, food, or anything. I kept my foot heavy on the accelerator, feeling myself gain control with every push. I was in charge of the car, where I was going, and my own destiny. Not Jake. Not Bess. Not my nightmares.

Fuck 'em all.

My phone rang, startling me as the sound blared through the dark car.

With my left hand and knee on the wheel, I reached over to grab it. Swiping my finger across the screen, I didn't need to see who it was. It wasn't Bess. She wasn't strong enough to call me, let alone survive my lies and nightmares without getting hurt. Not only emotionally, but physically too.

"Hello—Jake?"

"Yeah? What the fuck is up?"

"Oh, I don't know. My nightmares are back, you little shit. I had them the whole time I was gone, thought it was the hectic travel schedule I'd been keeping. Then I had one last night, when I got in from Spain. No way this was another one-off, no such fucking luck! Fuck you, Jake. You started all this!" I yelled into the phone.

"Calm down, Lane. You're losing it."

"Me? I'm fucking losing it? No, you're gonna be the one losing it because I'm going home. No way I'm staying until Monday to go to Youngstown. You got that?" I said this as I leaned into a curve, the Jeep just about on two wheels, the dark mountains on one side, a straight drop into a ravine on the other.

"Lane, listen, come back to Pittsburgh. Let me buy you a beer and you'll calm down."

"Nope. No fucking way, Jake. 'Bye."

I disconnected the call without waiting for him to answer. I'd had enough.

It was time to go back to my world. Business and bikinis.

CHAPTER
THIRTY

One month later

"**G**OOD evening, Mr. Wrigley? Checking someone in tonight?" Stuffed like a pig in a blanket into his fitted dress shirt and skinny chinos, James greeted me with his usual sarcasm as I walked into the Dylan.

"No, James, I'm not, but thanks for asking. I'm here for a late dinner. Can you call down to the restaurant and see if they can accommodate me?"

The snarky little shit. He'd seen me come in a few times this month for a drink, never once checking anyone else into the damn fucking hotel.

I had no idea why I continued to go there; it only held memories I would have liked to banish. Yet I kept torturing myself with quick glances at the hammock or toward the suite where she'd stayed.

"For how many, Mr. Wrigley?"

James interrupted my thoughts of Bess spread out on the bed, my head between her legs. Unable to talk yet, I held up two fingers, my fantasy so real I could almost taste her pussy. When he waggled his eyebrows at me, I was tempted to make two fingers into one. The middle one.

James hung up the phone. "If you'll head over to the patio, they have a table ready for you. Should I direct your guest that way?"

"Yes. Randi, I mean, Ms. Pepper should be arriving any minute."

I hadn't sealed the deal in a month. Not since I shoved my boxers back on and ran out of Bess's, fleeing the scene, leaving only bullshit in my wake. My balls felt like they were going to burst, even after rubbing one out—often.

I'd gone on a bit of a bender when I first returned home, spending the remainder of the weekend holed up with a bottle of aged scotch. Then I thought of Bess and her struggles, and scolded myself.

On Monday I jumped back into my life with a renewed vengeance, ignoring twenty-five frantic calls from my brother, and then I remembered Bess and her story of helping the puppies. I called him back, Skyped with the smoothie fuckers, wired them their money, and solved my brother's problems again. Except he wasn't a lost puppy.

After that, back to work I went. I had closed three new accounts in a month. It was a new record for me, traveling eighteen days of the month. I'd even been back to Spain once for forty-eight hours. All I thought about was Bess and how dreamy-eyed she got when thinking about traveling.

Losing myself in my preferred rigorous workaholic lifestyle, I felt my shell snap back into place. But every time I ran or twisted in yoga, it felt like it was going to crack wide open again. I couldn't help but think of Bess holding her side. Christ, I'd hurt her; I'd physically injured a woman. The very one who held all my fantasies, and as of recently, my heart. I almost felt her pain when I bent into the side crow pose, or pounded down the beach.

She was all I thought about. Essentially, I'd traded one nightmare for another. At least I'd been able to somewhat control the awful dreams of my past since returning to my refuge—sunny Florida— where all that mattered was people's appearances, no matter how contrived they were, and nothing was more important than a tanned, firm body.

Like the fake beauty walking my way at the moment. Randi had arrived and was taking the outdoor dining patio by storm, air-kissing a plastic face here and another one there before sitting down across from me.

Tonight was about exorcising my latest living hell, burying myself deep inside some faceless woman so I could forget the girl who had taken up permanent residence in my head.

"Hi, Lane. How are you?" Randi asked as she slinked into her seat. Her tits were popping out of her miniscule black minidress. Thank God someone came and put a napkin on her lap as she sat down, because if she had to bend over, one of those fake C-cups was going to come popping out onto the table.

It didn't even look remotely sexy. My tastes had turned toward skinny jeans and Nikes.

"I'm fine. You?" I asked, not really caring.

Randi flipped her auburn tresses back in a practiced gesture, her long French-manicured nails catching the light. "Oh, great! I just got booked on a shoot in Australia! I can't wait. I wonder if the toilets actually flush the wrong way there . . ."

She never shut up, yapping incessantly about herself, and as she waved her hands in the air to emphasize a point, I couldn't stop thinking about Bess's hands. They were small with short nails that felt so good scratching up and down my back as I rode her hard. Bess was smaller than the average model I dated, but we fit together so perfectly.

Oh fuck! I wasn't going to get her out of my head. Not tonight.

Interrupting Randi, I stood up and said, "I'm sorry, I'm not feeling well. I have to go." And like that, I walked right out of the Dylan, calling my assistant on the way out.

"I have another package to send."

CHAPTER THIRTY-ONE

bess

N oT bothering to look up when the bells above the diner door chimed, I heard, "What the hell are you doing here?" The tone was gruff, and a waft of cigarette smoke and Jim Beam hit my nose.

"Um, working," I said as I looked up into AJ's angry face. "The question is, what are you doing, AJ?" I stepped back, giving myself some fresh air.

"What does it look like I'm doing? I'm getting a coffee," he said with a snarl.

Concerned that he'd been drinking, I tried to bring my palm up to his face to touch the man who had saved me years before, but he slapped it out of the way with his own rough and heavy hand.

"AJ, what are you doing to yourself?"

"I'm getting a coffee, Bess," he answered, my name coming out long and slurred.

Narrowing my eyes at him, I crossed my arms over my chest. "You know what I mean."

"Why don't you get me a large coffee to go. And while you're at it," he sneered, "you can tell me why you're working in this shithole of a diner when you have a cushy job over at the WildFlower. You slumming it again? Like when you gave me a whirl in bed?"

I turned around to the coffeemaker and grabbed a Styrofoam cup, filling it as I willed myself not to cry. I closed my eyes tightly for a moment, pulling air in and out of my nose.

Whipping back around, I handed AJ the coffee and said, "No charge, it's on me," before moving toward the kitchen.

Once behind the swinging doors, I ignored the light film of grease covering the linoleum floor and slid down to sit on the dirty piece of shit, dropping my head between my knees as I gulped for air.

I'd picked up a shift or two per week at the diner over the last month, ever since the day Lane left. The emotional bruises were taking much longer to heal than the physical, and I found even one day off work a week was too much time to be alone with my thoughts.

By chance, I'd hobbled into the diner the morning after Lane ran away, hoping for coffee and a hug from Shirley. She'd been short a waitress, and since I was off work that day, I filled in.

Sadly, I didn't do a good job of hiding my injury, and ended up at Doc Riley's after painfully serving breakfast to locals and tourists who wanted real rural flavor. The gentle gray-haired man assured me that my rib was bruised—not broken—and since I was an addict they preferred not to prescribe pain pills for, I just needed to grin and bear it.

Shirley had run home and retrieved a hot pack, which she wrapped tightly around my middle with a bandage, and tucked me into bed with a steaming mug of tea and Brooks. Then she'd sat on the side of my bed, stroking my hair as she made false promises that everything would get better.

Much like she was doing now on the kitchen floor of the diner.

Shirley slid down next to me. "Come on, girl. He's a big boy. When he wants help, he'll get it. No one knows the program better than AJ, honey. He knows we can't offer him help when he isn't willing to accept it. I've been keeping an eye on him. Me and one of his buddies."

My heart breaking, I sniffed back my tears and asked, "Why didn't you tell me?"

"Aw, Bess," she said and grabbed my hand, squeezing my knuckles. "You've had so much on your plate, I didn't want to trouble you any more than I had to. With Lane gone and your side injured and the way you were pushing yourself at your other job—not taking any sick days even when I told you to—I couldn't let you know about this."

I leaned my head against her shoulder. "But it's my fault. Everything."

"This is not your burden, Bess. AJ should have never messed with you; he knew that. You were his responsibility to be there for in times of need, not sex. If he confused it all, that's on him."

"But I participated, Shirl. Ugh, And Lane. He was helpless, flailing in the bed, all tangled up in the sheets, screaming, and I couldn't even figure out what to do for him. I'm such a failure at anything but this ridiculous life of mine with nothing but work. And it's not even meaningful work."

"There's nothing you could do for Lane, honey. He just needs time."

"How do you know?" I practically wailed. "You've never even met him. It seemed pretty final when he walked out . . . ran out with his boots in his hand, his button fly open."

"You'll just have to trust me on this one," Shirley said as she ran her hand soothingly down my arm. "Go home, sweetie. Get a warm bath, take a rest. I'll call you later."

There was no rest in the cards for me, though, because as I pulled down my gravel drive, I saw a courier waiting for me in front of my house. Slamming my car into park next to his vehicle, I began to wonder how much more I could take today.

"Can I help you?" I yelled as I walked toward the truck.

"Delivery, ma'am," the guy in the uniform said, stepping out of the truck.

"For who?" I asked foolishly. I didn't get deliveries except from
. . . Lane. This must be a mistake.

"Bess Williams, is that you? I was told this was your place
and instructed to wait for you, make sure your hands touched the
package."

"That's me," I said with a sigh.

"Great, sign here," he said, shoving a clipboard at me. Obviously,
he was through waiting for me.

I stood in the driveway, holding the small box with trembling
hands until he was gone. Then I opened my door and let Brooks do
his business before sinking to the floor for the second time in one
day.

Still wearing my jacket and Nikes, I stretched my legs out in front
of me. With my dog's head resting on my shin, I tore the brown paper
wrapping off the box.

It was a blue box. A Tiffany's box. I only knew this from watching
movies; I'd never been to Tiffany's in my life. Had never even dreamed
of going.

My heartbeat picked up its already frenetic pace as I tugged at the
narrow white satin ribbon, allowing it to fall to the floor like I had
done with the airplane ticket months before. And like my heart had
done when Lane walked out.

When I removed the lid, my breath halted.

I set my hand on my dog's head, and he looked up at me with
what looked like compassion. A letter fluttered out of the box and
into my lap. I picked it up, my eyes almost too blurry to read it.

My beautiful Bess—
I'm sorry for my horrible behavior
when I left your place so abruptly last
month. I'm most sorry for hurting
you and not staying to take care of
you.
There are no explanations or excuses.
Just know that it wasn't about you.

There are pieces of me you don't know, and I hope you never do. They are buried deep where they belong, but recently some stressors made them move to the forefront of my mind. The nightmares are not new. I thought they were contained; they had been for some time.

I never meant to hurt you, either physically or emotionally. Your feelings and your body and its safety are of equal importance to me. I've come to cherish both more than I care to admit.

You also need to know that I've maintained my distance over the last month for your sake. Obviously I wasn't in a good place, and I had no intention of drawing you further into any of that. It's age-old business that needs to stay where it was—in the past.

But the more time passes without you in my life, the greater the void I feel. Like an idiot, I thought maybe time would make it easier, but there is nothing more that I want than to see you again.

This is a little gift from me to you, but no expectations are laid on your receipt of it. Whether you agree to see me or not, I want you to have this.

Please call me if you want. I can make arrangements to come see you or for you to see me.

Bess, know this—my heart was on autopilot until I met you, and you made it beat steady and strong again.

~Lane

P.S. The various shapes are for us— you and I are different, but together we work. The yellow is for the bright lemons, their zest only rivaled by your essence.

My eyes stung, my pants leg soaking from where my tears had dripped on it, and my body was hot and cold at the same time. I was sweating, but a fine layer of chilled goose bumps had formed along my arms. Sensing my tension, Brooks whined and stood up, pacing back and forth next to me.

My fingers shook as I took the gift out of the box. It was like nothing I had ever seen before. A heart pendant hung from a white gold chain. I didn't think it was silver. Not from Tiffany's.

It was a big heart, framed in white gold and filled with diamonds. Not just little chips of diamonds but *diamonds*. They were all shapes and sizes, clustered together in a random pattern that only made sense as a whole. Mixed in every few stones was a yellow one. I assumed these were some type of special stone or colored diamond, I didn't know. But their yellow brilliance sparkled and shone brighter than the clear ones.

The piece took my breath away; I was afraid to pull it out of the box. Tentatively I slid my finger into the box and stroked the piece without removing it, massaging it to life like the letter was doing to my heart.

Then I shut the box, set it on the counter, and went to take a bath.

My emotions were whipping back and forth like a yo-yo, something that was never good for me. When I was in high school and my feelings overwhelmed me, I found alcohol. When the boys took advantage of my body, I found pot and other light mood enhancers. When I got to college and didn't know who I was, I demanded the harder stuff.

Right now my emotions were in overdrive. My body was still reeling from the effects of AJ's harsh, cold touch and the warm, gentle stroke of Lane's tongue. At the same time, my mind spun because I had not one single clue what my life should or could be. The cumulative effect of all this upheaval in my life was very, very bad—bad times one million for me—and I needed to calm myself, not run away or slip into old habits like using drugs or alcohol or men to dull my pain.

I didn't know how to do this, how to cope with stress. I only knew day-to-day boring, and that was all I could handle.

CHAPTER
THIRTY-TWO

bess

FOLLOWING Shirley's instructions, I filled my massive claw-footed tub with bubbles and sank in, leaning my head back against the small rolled-up towel on the ledge. Outside the bathroom window, dusk was painting the sky with hints of orange and purple that filtered through the glass, the bubbles picking up the color in their iridescence.

With my eyes tightly closed, snapshots like Polaroid photos flitted through my mind one after the other, highlighting snippets of my life.

There was an image of my mom leaving, her beat-up brown suitcase rolling behind her as her long dark hair blew in the wind, her black boots carrying her far away from our apartment and me. I'd always imagined her with a big smile on her face as she left me and the responsibility that came with being a mom, but now I understood it. In my own way, I'd fled from any responsibility in my life too, first with alcohol and sex, and then drugs. I still did it today, creating a life for myself devoid of any true responsibility other than showing up to serve food to strangers.

When I released that image, another took its place. It was me, a very drunk me, dancing on a table in college as I shook my hair all around me, my jeans riding low, boots up to my knees, and a guy standing below with his face at the level of my crotch. I was reckless, without a care other than feeling good. Later I lay underneath the same guy on a damp and musty futon, his small, almost-limp dick sliding in and out of me, his pelvis slapping against mine with little to no regard for making me feel good. The scene was blurry, but it was there burned in my memory. The alcohol and whatever else—weed, maybe—was enough to dim any responsibility on his part or mine. If I had demanded any sexual pleasure, it would mean I'd have had to care about his, and I had never done *caring*. Not since my mother abandoned me.

Using my foot, I turned on some more warm water. The tub had chilled, and I wasn't done yet with the photos in my mind. They might be awful and painful, but I needed to stop escaping.

As if a video was playing in slow motion, I watched AJ driving away from me time and time again. Not because he was abandoning me, but because I was emotionally unavailable. I might have been sober and standing in front of him, but I was as shut off and unavailable as anyone could be.

Then I saw Lane running away from me, truly escaping with the fear of God instilled somewhere deep, and I saw a lifetime of myself in his own actions.

Running.

I caught a glimpse in my mind of a blown-up picture of my friend Camper and me that I'd pinned to a bulletin board in my old apartment. We were standing in front of a long row of tequila shots, her wearing skinny jeans and a bright red tank top, and me in a navy minidress. We looked a mess, our pupils like pinpoints, our faces shiny from sweat and our makeup smeared all around our eyes.

I was a fucking disaster those days, but didn't know if Camper was; I'd never asked. I might have wondered, but didn't want to care. She'd been with me the night I ended up in the hospital after the disastrous yoga class, and it was the last time I saw her. I had no idea if she'd tried to see me in rehab, and had never wanted to know.

I could still see the nurse on the first day I was in rehab, standing in the doorway to my room as I'd yelled, "I don't want any calls or visitors. Nothing! You hear me? Now leave me the fuck alone." Starting that very day, I'd asked to be alone, planned to be by myself, asked for this life of loneliness.

Me. I'd done it to myself—this was all on me.

At that realization, I opened my eyes and took in the blue dimness of dusk wrapping its way around my bathroom now that the sun had set. The color made me think of Lane's eyes, like a beautiful blue sky, but with a storm lingering in the distance, a furious, angry storm. I'd never asked what was behind those clouds in his eyes. I had gone on and on about my past, my demons, but I'd never asked about his.

An empty glass on the floor came to mind. The sparkling cider. He heard me when I told him about my addictions, and he didn't run. Instead he'd accommodated me. And what the hell did I do?

I now knew Lane was constantly racing, trying to stay ahead of his own dark clouds. I hadn't made the effort to care last month or the month before, but I should have. He hadn't really mentioned his family, which now made me wonder since my problems stemmed from my family, and I'd left it at that. But I should have asked.

For the first time in my life, I felt like I had it in me to care about another person. To take care of someone else. To want to become concerned about their well-being. To be attached. To be their family.

The pictures stopped flashing through my mind, having done their job, so I stepped out of the tub and nearly slipped on the cold tile. I knew now that I couldn't abandon Lane. I would open myself up and learn to be caring. For him.

While I was toweling off, a knocking started on my door. It echoed through my small house, punctuated by Brooks's frantic barking.

My heart raced as the thought hit me that it was Lane. Would he follow behind his generous gift, the gorgeous heart I didn't deserve but wanted to more than anything?

I put on my robe and padded out to the living room, where the knocking grew in intensity, becoming loud bangs.

"Bess! Are you in there? Open the door!"

Shit, it was AJ. Was he drunk? For the first time since moving to the mountain, I felt unsafe. I hesitated, leaning against the door as Brooks came to my side and pressed against my leg, letting out a low warning rumble.

"AJ, what do you want?" I called out. "Are you okay?" I raised my voice, hoping it would travel through the wood door to the other side.

"I'm fine," he said. "Open up."

"Are you sober?" I foolishly asked.

"Yes! I want to talk with you, Bess," he roared.

"Okay," I said weakly before unlocking and opening the door slowly. Darkness had started to settle on the mountain like it had on my heart.

AJ's boots ate up my wooden floor as he stomped in, stopping by the mantel before laying into me. "Bess, you're driving me crazy. I fucking fell in love with you the day I picked you up at rehab. What the fuck? You give me a chance and then change your mind?"

I stayed where I was, my back to the cool door, my dog at my feet on high alert.

"AJ, it's not like that. We had this talk, and I apologized. I confused my feelings for you with something more than they were."

He swung his hands out, his movements exaggerated, large and clumsy. "Damn right you did, and you fucked with me while doing that shit. And I'm a sad fucking sack because of it."

"I don't know what else you want me to say, other than I'm sorry." I reached behind me, gripping the door, looking for purchase as though I might fall.

"Sorry doesn't cut it." He spat out the words, his eyes narrowed. "Quit the diner. I go there. Quit Shirley. She's fucking bad. Didn't you ever hear her story? She's bad fucking news. In fact," he said with a sneer, "why don't you go back to your new man, Mr. High-and-Mighty in Florida, and get the hell out of here altogether. This is my small town."

My head was spinning. Shirley? Why Shirley? I needed her. Although, it now occurred to me that I'd also kept a distance between her and me, only sharing about myself. I needed to change that too. Needed to connect with her story and care for her, not just let her care for me.

The sound of glass shattering dragged me out of my head. I jumped and yelled, "What the hell?" not knowing what just happened. And then I saw it. The jar that I'd kept on the mantel with the sand and shells from Lane was spread out all over the floor, shattered and broken like my heart.

Brooks leaped toward AJ, barking, warning him to keep his distance, but AJ didn't pay any mind. He kept walking right toward me. With my eyes on my only memento of my time with Lane, I whispered *no* to myself. I treasured that votive. It was all I had left of that weekend, and now it was gone.

I didn't have time to dwell on it because AJ leaned into my face. "Is that what you do now? Make pretty little pieces of shit to remind you of that guy?" he yelled, his mouth tight, his hands flexing at his side.

There was no time to answer because my cell phone, plugged in on the kitchen counter, started to buzz. AJ spun me around and said, "Get it! It's probably Shirley. Tell her you're busy!"

With a trembling hand, I picked up the phone. When I saw who was calling, my heart cracked.

"Hello," I said, trying to control the shakiness in my voice. I turned away from AJ, pressing my hip into the counter, leaning all my weight into it until it pinched my side.

Lane's voice swept over me. "Bess, I know I said you should call me only if you wanted, but I couldn't wait. I know I messed up, and I need your forgiveness. Please?"

From the other side of the room, AJ shouted, "What the hell is this expensive piece of shit? You on the job, Bess? I didn't make enough money for you? I said, what the hell is this? Tell me now!"

Frozen, I couldn't make myself turn around; the countertop would have to hold me. I was all limbs and no spine.

"What was that? Who is that? Are you okay? Bess!" I heard coming from the phone, but I couldn't answer.

I jerked as something sharp hit my head and fell to the floor. It was the Tiffany's box. Stunned and disbelieving, I rubbed the spot where it nicked me, unable to move other than lifting my hand to comfort myself.

"Bess, hang up the damn phone and turn around and answer me!" AJ demanded.

I closed my eyes as Brooks went crazy, barking louder than I'd ever heard him as AJ's footsteps pounded toward me. My world spun all around me; the voice on the phone sounded so far away.

I felt it slipping from my hand, and then everything went black.

CHAPTER
THIRTY-THREE

bess

SOMETHING wet was on my forehead, but my arm didn't feel strong enough to reach up and touch it. Maybe it was Brooks licking me? No, it didn't feel like that.

I heard a few hushed voices.

"It doesn't appear as though she hit her head, so it's probably more a reaction to stress. She'll come out of it. Her pulse is steady and her heartbeat sounds good."

"Are you sure?" a deeper voice asked. "Maybe we should be more careful and take her to the hospital in the city."

"No, she'll be fine. Let her rest on the couch and she'll come to."

The voices all sounded garbled, as if they were underwater. Or maybe I was underwater? Was that why my forehead was wet?

I concentrated on lifting my hand and it worked. Bringing it to my forehead, I felt a towel or something soft there. It was cool and wet. I patted it in place, making sure it stayed put, and heard all the sounds in the room go quiet.

"Bess?" the first voice said. It sounded like Doc. I'd just seen him, so I would know.

"Bess?" he said again.

I think I nodded my head, or at least I was trying to. Prying one eye open, I tried to turn my head to the direction the voice was coming from.

I squinted and saw a blurry Doc, May from work, and someone else who looked like Lane, but he had short hair. A buzz cut.

When did he do that? Where am I? How did Lane get here from Florida? What happened?

And then I remembered. The call. AJ. Lane yelling on the other end of the phone.

I shut my eye and attempted to open both together. It took two attempts, but I did it. Taking in my surroundings, I noticed it was still dark out. I wondered if it was the same night or a night or two later.

I swallowed. "Doc?" My voice was broken and raspy.

"Bess, honey. Don't strain."

"What happened to me? How long have I been like this?" I said while patting my hand along my body, making sure I was still all there. "Where's Brooks? Forget me," I added, straining to look around the room.

"He's in your bedroom. He was pacing and nervous while you were unconscious, and he seemed to settle down back there."

"Get him." I managed to say it firmly, and Lane with short hair turned and walked away.

Doc frowned down at me. "As for you, I think you had a panic attack and passed out. You sort of came to shortly after, but fell into a deep sleep right away. Probably stress-induced."

I took a shuddering breath and pressed my hand to my stomach. "How long ago was that?"

"Well, AJ called Shirley about two and a half hours ago as he was peeling down your driveway, and said you were passed out. He was having some kind of fit himself, so Shirley decided to go after AJ and called May to take care of you. May found you about fifteen minutes after AJ called. That's when you woke for a moment." Doc came close and bent down, taking my pulse.

Brooks ran to me after being released and nearly knocked Doc out of the way, sticking his snout right in my face and giving me his own snuffling once-over.

In the soft light coming from the lamp, I reassured my dog as I watched Lane continue to stay back. He was hesitant, so unlike his normal direct self.

"Lane?" It came out all wrong, hoarse, unsteady, questioning.

He stepped closer and shook his head. "No, I'm Jake. His brother, Jake Wrigley."

When I tried to frown, he explained.

"His twin brother. Identical. I can see he doesn't talk about me much . . . I get it. But he called me in an absolute panic when you went silent on the phone. He said there was screaming and fighting in the background, and he was beyond worried. I've never heard him yell like that. He begged me to come here."

"You're his twin?"

"Yes."

"Where do you live?" It was a stupid question, but it came out.

"Pittsburgh."

"Doc, can I sit up?" I asked.

Doc put his arm around my back and propped me up against the back of the couch. Brooks didn't go far, staying put right at my feet on his hind paws, staring down anyone who came close.

"Do you feel light-headed?" Doc asked.

"No," I said, trying to sound firm as I rested my hand on the top of Brooks's head.

"What happened, Bess?" May asked, coming to sit down next to me.

I told them what I remembered about AJ showing up and flipping out, demanding my attention and feelings.

"That was before he saw the necklace," I explained.

Jake frowned at me. "What necklace?"

I pointed toward the counter where it had been. "Lane sent me this necklace today. A heart. It was why he was on the phone, why he called. To see if I received it."

I tried to stand up and my robe gaped open. Oh my God, I was still in my robe. Had anyone seen my body?

"Not right now, missy," Doc said, settling me back into the couch.

"But I have to find the necklace and the note . . . and get dressed."

"There's nothing there, Bess," May said. "I checked all around the room for clues as to what happened when I got here. Nothing was out of place other than the vase and sand by the mantel. I cleaned it up."

"Wait!" I called out. "What did you do with the sand?" Tears started to flow at the thought of losing that memento of my time with Lane.

"It's in the garbage."

"Get it out!" I yelled with as much strength as I could.

"Bess, darling, you've had a rough day. Lots of stress. Let's just try to stay calm now," Doc said in a soothing voice.

Calm?

"There was a letter? Where is it?" I leaned forward. "And a necklace?" I tried to stand again, but May held me back as I freaked out, mumbling to myself.

May was running her hand up and down my back when Jake interrupted, "Hey, Doc, maybe something to calm her nerves? A Xanax?"

"No!" May and Doc shouted at the same time.

"I can't take that," I said quietly, absently rubbing the leather collar around Brooks's neck.

"Okay, suit yourself," Jake said with a shrug. "Listen, my brother is on his way. He'll be here soon, and I'm sure he'll solve all this. He's very good at cleaning up messes."

I nodded and said, "Really? He's coming here?"

"Yeah," Jake said, then edged toward the door. "I gotta go. Take care, Bess."

Watching him leave, I could have sworn I saw something deep and tormented behind his blue eyes—just like in Lane's.

CHAPTER THIRTY-FOUR

lane

L ANDING at the smaller regional airport by charter plane put me at least an hour closer to Bess. I jumped out of my seat, grabbed my bag, and ran to a car my assistant had ordered to be waiting for me and instructed the driver to "Haul ass all the way to the middle of Nowhere, Pennsylvania."

I hated not being in control, let alone stuck in the backseat of a ridiculously posh car, but this was the only way I was going to make it alive to the mountains. It was still black as night out, to say nothing of my ratcheted nerves, pulsing through my entire system.

As soon as I sat down, I called Jake.

"Lane, what the fuck?"

This is how *he* answered the phone for me.

"What the fuck to you?"

"I sped all the way up to Buttfuck, Pennsylvania, to check on your piece of ass in distress, and at first I thought maybe I slept with her years ago. She looked so damn familiar, I couldn't stop staring. That country doc probably thought I was mental."

"Jake, don't go there now," I warned him. I knew where he was heading and I wasn't in the mood.

"Oh, I will," he shot back.

Fuck.

My hair felt damp from sweat. I pulled my leather jacket and sweater off, leaving me in just a plain white T-shirt.

"Lane, do you want to tell me what you're doing messing around with the girl who almost died in my gym years ago? I may not have showed up until you destroyed my chance at pussy for the night and she was being loaded into an ambulance, but her face hasn't changed. Jesus Christ, can't you get laid in Miami?"

"She doesn't remember that night."

"What? You're bullshitting me."

"No." I cracked the window open, still feeling incredibly hot.

"And you haven't told her?"

I began to wonder if I could ever tell her, let her in on the fact I was there to witness that piece of her personal history. Especially now, it felt beyond the statute of limitations. She probably didn't even want to remember that night. I'd tried to forget it so many times myself.

Yet, it still haunted my thoughts. No longer in the limo, my thoughts were back in the gym.

After I'd realized the whole place assumed I was Jake—he'd been copying my longer hairstyle since he finished playing college ball—I'd decided to play the role. I hadn't been happy about it, but I'd done it.

With Bess out cold on my mat, I'd pretended to be busy taking vitals when her eyes opened and looked straight into mine, dazed and confused.

"Bess, come on, we got to get out of here. Get you home," the friend said, trying to lift Bess up.

"All right, everyone, stay focused with Lexie while I take care of this," I said out loud over the DJ, playing the part of Jake, and began to help Bess over to the side of the room. She'd barely come awake, her palms sweaty, face pale, eyes out of focus. The other girl and I semi-carried her out of the yoga room and to a bench, where she slumped over once again, becoming unresponsive.

I grabbed the friend and demanded, "What the hell did she take?" She looked like a deer caught in headlights. "Don't fucking clam up on me now. Your friend needs help," I said, shaking her shoulder a bit.

"I don't know for sure, she parties pretty hard," was all she said, turning her own glassy brown eyes the other way while Jimmy or Timmy or whatever the fuck his name was stood nearby and called 911.

"Why the hell would she come to yoga like this? Unless she's so addicted she can't go anywhere without being like this? And what kind of friend are you to bring her like this?" I crowded the other girl while I berated her, who I'd learned was named Camper.

Pacing the floor, my bare feet sinking into the plastic bullshit material, I waited for Camper to answer me.

Quietly she said, "Well, she's always like this, but I didn't ever think it was a problem." Then she ran out of there, not even bothering to grab her shoes, flying by the paramedics running in.

The EMTs were annoyed. You could tell they thought Bess was another college girl who couldn't handle her alcohol or whatever. They started taking her vitals, placing a neck brace on her small form, and sliding her on to a portable gurney. One was on the phone, calling ahead, "Yeah, gonna need a stomach pump, charcoal. Out cold, slowing pulse, but did come to for a minute or so. Dumb friends moved her from her original place."

I was just trying to do what I thought was right, but I wasn't Jake, and I didn't have the credentials to run a gym.

"Hey, you, do you know her name? Or what she took?" the guy yelled at me.

I shook my head. "Bess. That's all I know. That was her friend hightailing it out of here when you showed up."

We were causing a scene by now, a few patrons coming over to check out who was passed out.

"A lot of help you are," the EMT said to me before going back to his call.

And then they were wheeling her out as fast as they ran in when

Jake showed up. Apparently, the guy who called 911 called him afterward—we couldn't fool that smart dude.

We ran after the paramedics, following them outside, my bare feet pounding the cold concrete.

"Goddamn, Lane. What the fuck?" he scolded me, stopping to watch Bess being lifted into the back of the ambulance.

"Me? What the fuck?"

"Yeah, you!" he yelled back.

We hadn't even noticed the ambulance turn its lights on until the siren alerted us to it leaving.

"Fuck! Fuck you! You just let them go without even riding with that girl," I berated Jake. "She's in there all alone and you're mad at me?" I went on, stomping back to the gym to get my shoes and shit.

As the two of us walked back inside, Lexie peeked her head out of the yoga room and looked like she was seeing double. Because she was. Apparently she didn't know Jake was a twin. An identical one.

And I'd become so consumed with exacting revenge on Jake for a lifetime of fixing shit that I didn't go to the hospital. Instead I'd fucked Lexie.

My trip down memory lane was interrupted by Jake yelling at me.

"Lane! While you're at it, explain to me how she doesn't know you have a twin brother. That's my fucking play, if you recall."

Yeah, I know.

"Well, you also know I'm very good at keeping secrets, bro. Now, can you fucking tell me if she's okay?"

"The girl is fine, and a fine piece of raw meat too, if you ask me. But she's fine. Had some sort of panic attack and was making a big deal about a necklace and a letter you sent being missing."

"What? Missing?"

It's worth a small fortune.

"Gone. Some dude was harassing her and pitched a fit, causing her to black out from stress, and I guess he left with the necklace."

I rubbed my chest. My heart hurt. My head ached.

"Jesus Christ," I said. "Where the fuck are you now?"

"On my way home, brother. I can't stay around all day and clean up your mess while you screw some chick who nearly croaked on drugs during yoga, and you're pledging your undying love or some shit to her by snail mail."

"Jake! You owe me and you know it."

"Well, when you want to come clean to the little lady, let me know."

"Yeah, come clean. Is that what you really want?" I put the window back up, the vibration of the wind making my already pounding head worse.

"Do whatever the fuck you need to do, Lane. 'Bye."

I slammed my phone on the seat next to me and looked out the window. As pastures lined with white fences zipped past, I prayed I could keep all my emotions contained on this trip. I didn't have the time or patience for nightmares right now.

The car turned around and descended the driveway in the darkness, I watched the red brake lights pulling away, steadying myself before I entered Bess's little house. The last time I'd been there hadn't exactly ended spectacularly.

As I turned toward the door, it opened, flooding the porch with light, and I made out the silhouette of a man walking out carrying a medical bag.

He looked at me in the haze of the floodlight and made his way over. "Hi, I'm Doc Riley. You must be Lane. We met your brother, Jake, earlier," he said while extending his hand.

I shook his hand and said, "I am. Thanks for everything. I'm anxious to see Bess, but what do you think happened?"

"Panic attack. Stress. An old friend got her worked up. She can tell you the rest herself. She's laying down inside."

"Thanks," I said and walked to the door, holding my breath.

Slowly peeking in the door, unsure of what was behind it, I whispered, "Bess," in case she was sleeping.

A middle-aged woman greeted me. "Hello, Mr. Wrigley. I'm May. I also work at the WildFlower, so I've seen you there," she said with a soft and sweet smile.

"Hi, May," I said before turning toward the couch. Bess was curled up in the fetal position, Brooks at her feet.

"Hi," I barely croaked out.

"Hey," she said back to me, her voice thin and worn.

I approached with caution, unsure of what to say. Behind me, I heard May doing something in the kitchen.

"You didn't have to come," Bess said when I got close and slid down on the floor by where her head rested on the end of the couch.

"I shouldn't have ever left."

She didn't know the double meaning behind those words, but I felt my regret deep in my bones, a familiar but unwelcome ache.

"I was worried about you," she answered, not moving a muscle.

"Well, I was worried about you."

Both times.

With an unsteady hand, I reached out and rubbed her cheek, smoothing her hair back as I took in her pale skin and dark eyes. Even disheveled in a robe, she looked beautiful.

"I'm okay. I guess I passed out. That's what Doc said."

Not moving my hand from the side of her neck, my thumb caressing her neck where her pulse fluttered. "What happened, Bess?"

She looked toward the floor. "It was nothing."

Using my thumb, I tilted her chin so we were face-to-face. "It wasn't *nothing*. I heard screaming and you passed out. That's something. Now, tell me what happened."

She cradled her face into my hand and spoke in a low voice. "Well, it was AJ. Anthony. The man I told you about in Florida. He's gone a bit crazy for me, except it's all my fault. I was with him. *With* him before you. It never should have happened because he's my sponsor." A tear fell down, splashing my fingers.

"People make mistakes, Bess."

She shook her head. "No, this is one I shouldn't have made. We crossed all these invisible lines and broke the rules, and I ended up taking advantage of his affection for me. It's what gave me a little spark of life back, but it wasn't enough because I had met you."

I kissed her cheek, my lips grazing her soft skin, desperately wanting to move over to her even softer lips. But I didn't. It wasn't that kind of moment.

"Bess, you may not realize this, but you gave me my spark back."

"I don't know. I don't think I'm a good person, Lane. I never even knew you had a twin, an identical one. When I came to and saw him, I believed it was you with short hair." Her brow furrowed as she added, "And I see something deep in your soul that I want to dig out and take away, but I haven't even attempted." Her voice was scratchy and broken, matching my mood.

What does she see?

"Bess, let's not worry about me. Let's take care of you. Okay?"

She didn't answer, just lay there.

"Are you hurt?"

She shook her head. "Tired."

"Why don't you take a rest?"

"I can't. I'm worried about AJ. He ran off. My friend from AA chased after him. No matter what, he's still a person and now he's drinking again. I can't stop thinking about how I could have done something differently." She stopped for a breath before she went on. "And I can't stop thinking about your note and the necklace—it was so breathtaking, both of them were—and now they're gone."

Bess's whole body shook as she dissolved into tears, trying to speak but unable to for her sobbing. Tears slid down her face, dropping to fall on Brooks's fur where he curled up beside her.

"Bess, it's fine. It's insured," I said into her ear, trying to steal this moment for the two of us. May was still busy clinking some glass in the kitchen, picking it out of the garbage. I was too busy to ask what the hell that was about.

"But the letter wasn't insured."

I grabbed her hand and brought it to my heart. "It doesn't matter, it's imprinted right here," I told her.

Brooks stood and circled in place, interrupting the moment.

"I don't know when he was last out," Bess said.

"I'll take care of him if you promise to close your eyes and try to rest. I'm here and I'm not going anywhere."

I stepped out onto the porch, gently closing the door behind me. Dawn was coming and the air was moist.

"Take your time, buddy," I told Brooks as he ran to a tree.

I sure as hell needed a few minutes to figure out what the fuck just happened.

I'm not going anywhere?

Well, I couldn't stay here forever, even if I wanted to.

Imprinted right here . . . in my heart?

It might very well be, but my heart was only half the heart she deserved. There was a black cavern of lies deep within it.

And now my brother was involved with Bess, and he had a habit of killing everything.

Chapter Thirty-Five

Bess

I ended up sleeping through most of the morning. Brooks sat on the floor by my side, and Lane settled at the other end of the couch, my feet in his lap. Occasionally, I woke and saw him, all disheveled and looking nothing like the buttoned-up executive I first met.

I moved my finger to pinch myself, making sure I wasn't imagining him in a wrinkled white T-shirt and jeans, his shoes kicked off, exposing argyle socks in shades of gray.

Around lunchtime, I needed to use the bathroom and desperately wanted to shower and change. May had left, so Lane helped me up and toward the bathroom, where he waited on the other side of the door until I needed help getting undressed.

I didn't really require anything, I was just desperate for his touch, needed to feel his fingers singe my cold skin, not just warming my body but my heart too. It was a stupid ploy, but my only one at this point.

Gently, he unwrapped my robe, letting it sift through his fingers as it slipped down my body. His hands caressed my naked breasts, his thumbs circling my nipples as they hardened into tiny buds. Seconds ticked by, then Lane's breath fanned over my neck as he leaned in and kissed his way up to my ear. He sucked on my ear lobe, eliciting a moan or three from me. I felt like I could be floating away, and I certainly shouldn't have been feeling that way, let alone asking for it.

"Bess, did you like the necklace? I meant what I wrote in the letter, that we're different, but together we work."

His words, breathy in my ear, were exactly what I needed to hear, and all I could do was murmur something unintelligible.

His hands explored further, making their way up toward my tattoo, smoothing over it before heading down to rest on my rib cage, the silent plea for forgiveness in his eyes was not necessary. Finally landing on my butt, his hands pulled me against him so I could feel his reaction to me. And then he stopped.

And I might have whimpered.

Leaning his forehead into mine, he said, "As good as this feels, this isn't the time for it."

With a sigh, he reached over and turned on the shower full blast, letting the steam carry throughout the small bathroom before helping me step in.

"Oh, this hot water feels so good," I said while he stood guard on the other side of the shower curtain.

"I have lots of hot water in Florida. Why don't you come back with me for a few days?"

I was going with him. I couldn't believe I'd agreed so quickly, but with my newfound resolve to be there for others and my recent bout with clinginess, I just said yes.

But first, I was going back to Pittsburgh.

For a girl who had little to no travel experience and hadn't really been back home since college, I was a regular world traveler these days. This trip to Florida would be an entirely new experience for me, though, since Lane chartered a private plane to fly us out of Pittsburgh. Which worked out since Doc refused to give me his blessing to travel commercially, and it meant Brooks could come too.

We took my car to Pittsburgh. We drove toward the sunset, its soft colors fading into the horizon as we made our way out of the country toward the city lights. It was so relaxing, it was hard to believe only twenty-four hours had passed since the incident with AJ.

Lane drove and talked on the phone. One call he made was to his insurance company, who was sending someone to investigate the disappearance of the necklace. Shirley called to say AJ was holed up with a rehab friend, hopefully drying out. We all knew the necklace was probably there too, but Lane thought it was best to let the insurance people do their job. He was happy to leave AJ to the higher powers if it meant we could head out sooner.

On the drive, Lane's overall tone and demeanor was gentle, but his jaw was tight. I didn't know what to make of it. He was wrestling with something more than what I'd seen pass over his eyes in the past. The closer we got to town, the tighter his hands gripped the steering wheel.

Watching him from the corner of my eye, I got the impression he would do anything to get the hell out of Pennsylvania; he seemed to truly hate it. His coming to see me several times was apparently a chore he only survived because of me. But why he was so intent on making me happy, on setting my mind at ease, was a mystery to me. Who was I to him, after all?

Well, I couldn't dwell on it. Instead I accepted whatever part I played in Lane's life like an alcoholic begs for a cheap forty.

One issue I dug my heels on was that I wasn't leaving town until I thanked Jake for his help. When Lane was reluctant, but gave in, I learned he was willing to do anything for me to go with him. He wasn't happy about it, but it was the only way I would agree.

It was our first standoff. I was on the stool in the kitchen, freshly showered and in jeans and a sweater, waiting for Lane to finish making travel arrangements. He'd been on the phone, ordering the plane he took here to be fueled up and ready to roll, when I interrupted him by waving my hand in front of his face.

"Lane," I said in a low voice, "before all this happened, I made a promise to myself to be a better person to others. I owe your brother a thank-you for all he did for me."

"Hold on," he said into the phone before hitting the Mute button, then looked at me. "Bess, it's not necessary. He knows."

"But it is," I said. "After your letter, I realized how much I tossed on your plate, and now there's all this. I need to pay it back and forward."

We glared at each other, neither of us giving in until I whispered, "Please."

Lane didn't say another word to me. He pressed the Mute button before putting the phone back to his ear. "Yeah, we're going to fly late. After dinner." Then he texted his brother and made arrangements to meet him for a quick coffee before we left.

Now we were barreling through the tunnel making our way into the city, the Cathedral of Learning on University of Pittsburgh's campus coming into view.

Lane reached over and took my hand. "You doing okay?" he asked, his jaw only slightly more relaxed as he touched me, seeming to get himself in check.

"Uh-huh. Thanks for doing this for me."

He nodded and brought my hand up to his mouth, placing a chaste kiss on the inside of my wrist.

"Seriously," I said as I squeezed his fingers. "I know you didn't want to. It means a lot to me."

He took his eyes from the road for a second to meet my eyes. "Well, you're right. I don't feel like sharing you any more than I have to, so we're going to meet Jake at a coffee shop by his new gym location. He owns a fitness club, by the way, and he's interviewing some marketing girl there. And then we're hightailing it back to my place."

This time he gave me a genuine smile. His unruly hair fell over his eyes, begging me to brush it back, which I did. Then I dropped my hand to his shoulder, stroking the muscles there, unable to resist running my palm lower over his firm chest, looking so broad and delicious in his cashmere sweater. The whole look was doing something for me, and it quickly took my mind off the word "gym." The last time I'd been in a gym hadn't ended well for me, and I tried not to think about it.

"Okay, sounds like a plan," I said, still distracted.

Bridges and tall elm trees whizzed by as I lost myself in memories. Childhood reminiscences of growing up in Carnegie—a nearby tiny hole-in-the-wall town full of factories—came flooding back, as well as recollections from my college days in the big city.

We pulled into a parking lot in a suburb south of Pittsburgh, a wealthy one close to where I grew up. The residents all used to bring their cars to my dad for repair.

My dad. I hadn't thought about him until this moment. I felt a little twinge of guilt at what an afterthought he'd become to me, but for close to two decades, that was what I was to him. I should have called him to let him know what happened to me. Or made a plan to see him now that I was so close.

Next time.

"Will Brooks be okay in the car?" Lane asked as we got out. "With the windows down?"

"Sure. Let me give him a chance to pee first, though," I said while opening the back hatch and letting Brooks out.

"You have to leash him here," Lane reminded me.

After glancing around at the perfectly manicured streetscape with expensive cars and bistros lining both sides of the sidewalk, I nodded and grabbed the red leather leash from the back of the car.

I walked slowly down the block, taking in my surroundings as my dog stretched his legs and sniffed at everything in sight. This neighborhood was different from what I was used to, neither the country quiet like where I lived now, nor the sheer madness of South Beach where Lane resided. It was a place where people laid down roots, where they built lives and families. It occurred to me that in a way, both Lane and I had set ourselves up in places that weren't really conducive to family life.

Lane waited for me by the car, a small smile on his face as Brooks and I made our way back to him. After Brooks was settled in the backseat again, Lane handed me my keys and then took my hand. "Ready?"

I shoved my keys in my pocket and said cheerfully, "Yep!"

As we left the parking lot and turned onto the sidewalk, he frowned. "I just want to warn you," he said in a tight voice, "my brother can be a bit wild. He and I haven't always seen eye to eye because of it." He glanced away as he added, "That's why I don't mention him much."

After absorbing Lane's words for a moment, I said carefully, "Well, he did come to see me as soon as you called, so he can't be that bad."

"He owed me a favor. Actually, he owes me a lifetime of them."

We walked the other direction toward a small coffee shop. It was both quaint and upscale, its facade framed in mahogany, and the smell of fresh roasted beans wafted all the way outside.

As we entered the store, small brass bells chimed above the door. "What about your folks?" I asked. "Do they live here?"

"They're not around anymore." Lane waved to his brother, who was seated facing us in the back, finishing his interview.

I mentally scolded myself for only asking about their parents. A girl who knew more about families would know to ask. And by Lane's response, I could tell there was more to their family's story than what he was telling me.

And I was distracted by why he never mentioned it when he said, "Let's set our stuff down and then I'll grab us some drinks, okay?"

"Sure."

As we headed toward Jake's table, my thoughts were still consumed with Lane's parents. Were they blue collar or business people? Loving and doting or emotionally distant? I wanted to know all about them, curious about what I missed growing up and what he must have had.

Then everything started to spin for the second time in two days.

Jake stood to say hello and I opened my mouth to thank him for meeting with us, but I froze in place, adjusting to the sight of the twins next to each other. They were so alike and so opposite, a mass of contractions, that it took my breath away. Lane and his calm personality and wild hair, and Jake the opposite, his hair short and neat, but his personality chaotic. At least, according to Lane.

Then the young woman stood and said, "Holy shit!" Lustrous curls framed her full face, setting off her brown eyes, now wide and staring with surprise at me.

"Bess? Bess? It's you!" she said, grabbing me and pulling me into a bear hug.

Jake shook his head and rolled his eyes while Lane grabbed his forehead, appearing to be in pain.

"Camper?" I said, stiffening in the girl's arms before pulling away. Concerned about Lane, I turned to him and asked, "Are you okay?"

How many times am I going to say that today?

But he didn't look right. He was pale, his eyes were a stormy dark gray, and his brow was pinched in distress.

"Bess! I can't believe it!" Camper exclaimed. She was like a broken record, repeating my name, so excited to see me that she was oblivious to my discomfort.

"Wait!" she said, waving her hand between Lane and me. "Have you stayed in touch all this time?"

"Huh?" I asked.

Out of the corner of my eye, I caught Lane shaking his head, his eyes wide as he stared at Camper.

"What do you mean?" I asked. "Do you know each other?" My attention pinged back and forth between the three of them like I was watching a game of doubles tennis and I was the fourth. But I'd never played tennis before.

"Well, yeah, Bess. This guy," she said, pointing at Lane, "was the person who helped when you collapsed in yoga years ago. Don't you remember him helping you out to the bench? God, you fell right on top of him."

My mouth dropped open as I tried to make sense of it all, while

Camper went on like she always did.

"When I showed up here for the interview," she said, "I thought it was Lane sitting there, and then he introduced himself as Jake. Now that I think about it, you got an odd look on your face when I asked if you had any brothers who went to Pitt." Her voice trailed off as she glanced at Jake.

Lane was now white as a ghost, his dark hair falling down his forehead from him pulling on it. His normally vibrant eyes looked flat as he stared at the black-and-white checkerboard floor.

"I didn't want to mention that night," Camper went on, still looking at Jake, "in case you had no idea what happened, or didn't have a brother, or I was just totally wrong. I'd hate to not get this job."

While Lane glared at Jake, and Jake smirked back at him, Camper grabbed me in another bear hug.

"What happened to you, B? I missed you. You went to rehab, they wouldn't let me visit, and then you disappeared. No Facebook or Instagram, nothing. I've been hoping to find you for years."

Stunned and confused, I hadn't said a single word since asking Lane if he was okay. I wasn't even sure if I was still breathing.

All eyes turned to me, waiting for my answer.

"You were there?" I choked out as I stared at Lane, my voice so tight it was unrecognizable. "You knew?"

He nodded.

A little light-headed, I placed my palms on the table, hanging my head for a moment as the chill traveled all the way through my spine while I tried to collect myself. My heart was already ice cold.

Nobody moved as I took a few deep breaths, then stood up and turned to Jake. "And you knew when you showed up at my place yesterday?"

He nodded, giving me a little smile as he said, "Not right away, but I figured it out while waiting for you to come to. It's okay, I didn't judge you back then."

"No, it's not okay," I said through clenched teeth as my emotions spun out of control. "I left that whole life behind me. The coked-out college girl with the party boots is my past, a past I wanted to forget.

I work hard every day to move forward, to leave it behind, and I don't share it with anyone." Turning to Lane, I shrieked, "And you knew? You knew when I told you I was in recovery? You knew when I didn't order a drink? You knew!" Turning on my heel, I stormed out of the coffee shop and ran down the sidewalk, headed to my car.

"Bess! Wait!" Camper yelled after me. "Hold up!"

She caught up with me and bundled me tightly in her arms, where I cried for what felt like hours, not caring who saw me. She rocked me gently from side to side, her voice low as she said, "I'm sorry, Bess. I never really understood how bad you were. I let you down as a friend. You're so beautiful and perfect, you didn't deserve that." Pressing her cheek against my hair, she sighed as she rubbed one hand in soothing circles on my back, trying to calm me down.

"I need to get out of here," I said, and my heart sank as I realized that Lane didn't come after me. Hiccupping, I pointed at the parking lot across the street. "That's my car."

"Let me come with you," Camper said as we crossed the street, her tone brooking no argument.

"I live ninety minutes away near Ligonier, that's crazy," I said, but by that time Camper was already standing at my car door, ignoring Brooks's excited barking as she held her hand out for the keys.

CHAPTER
THIRTY-SIX

lane

"How could you just stand there like that?" I yelled at Jake. "You're an even bigger asshole than I thought!" Furious, I hit him in the chest, but since he was as fit as I was, he absorbed it with barely a flinch.

I was no longer the well-dressed, well-educated, well-mannered brother. Unraveling by the second, my emotions were a ball of yarn undone, a bunch of string sitting in a big, twisted, mixed-up heap on the floor.

Fuck that; I was a bull pawing at the dirt, about to charge. Standing there in the middle of a civilized coffee shop, I was losing it like a little girl with a foul mouth.

"Jake! Fucking look at me," I shouted as my hair flopped into my eyes. "You! You've got the nerve to say you *didn't judge her*? I've never once asked you to do anything for me when it comes to women. You had to know this one—the one I sent you to check on in the middle of the wilderness—meant something to me. And you can't say something that would help *me*? No, you fucking made it worse!"

"Lane, get a hold of yourself," my brother said, putting his hands on my shoulders, trying to calm me.

I pushed his meaty hands out of the way with my own. Mine might have been smooth, unlike his rough ones, but they were the same size. A reminder that we were from the same DNA, so how could we be so very different?

"I will not get a hold of myself," I hissed. "I've had a hold of myself for too damn long! Did you know that chick too? Did you know she knew Bess? Was this a fucking setup?"

"No! She looked at me kind of strange and asked if I had a brother, and I thought maybe you or I slept with her, but never this. Never." He tried to get me to sit, trying to push me toward a seat.

Fuck him.

"Listen, Lane," he said in a low voice. "You're sounding crazy. And you're letting her get away." He pointed toward the front door.

"Don't you fucking tell me I'm crazy. You and I both know what you owe me. *Everything, Jake.* Everything! So, give me a break and don't tell me what to do or who is walking away. We were never meant to be, Bess and me. Let it fucking go!"

I didn't have a chance to hear what my pain-in-the-ass brother said next because the manager came over and politely told us to take our disagreement elsewhere.

Since I was in a dense fog, Jake guided me out the back door to the alley that led to his gym. Unable to think straight, my brain was clouded with images of Bess—coming down the escalator in Florida, wading nude in my pool, and resting on her couch with her feet in my lap.

When my brain fog cleared a moment later, it occurred to me that I didn't have a car, had no way to escape. I had nothing, not even my self-respect.

"Fuck!" I roared to no one, my voice bouncing off the brick walls, swallowing me up. I was pathetic, nothing but a shell of a man, broken beyond repair.

When they wheeled Bess out of Jake's gym years ago, it was my chance for redemption, to do something selfless and good for someone who was truly in need, but I didn't. I could have stayed and made sure she was okay, climbed on board the ambulance and sat next to her while they took her to the hospital, but I didn't.

I added another fucking lie to a box full of them that were buried in my black heart. My body was a graveyard for dead lies, ones that couldn't be resurrected and fixed. Like a fool, I'd thought I could slip my way into Bess's life, leaving the transgressions of my past decaying in my soul, and act like we could have a fresh start at something spectacular. But we couldn't because my life was shit.

I'd never been a violent person, but years of guilt and holding things in had built up inside me and were pushing on my pores to get out. It was an impossible situation—either let the demons out, or keep them captive inside my own living hell.

I wasn't even sure which side was going to win.

"Fuck!" I yelled again in the alley as Jake kept a respectful amount of space between him and me. We hadn't fought or wrestled since high school—and he might work out for a living—but he knew I packed a punch. I'd never fought anyone else in my life, leaving that to him. Jake had taken people out on the baseball diamond and at various fraternities scattered around campus, but not me. I was always the one with a perfect GPA and my emotions in check.

Well, not any-fucking-more, and I knew exactly where I was going to start. I might have lost any chance at redeeming myself from my sins of the past two decades, but in the last few hours, I'd changed into a darker version of myself. A deeply sordid Lane. The demons were rising, and I couldn't stop them. Not anymore.

I had succumbed to the evil I'd tried so hard to keep at bay. Finally free, it rushed through my body, spilling onto the concrete wherever I stepped. It both preceded and followed me, my new fucking calling card.

"Get your car, Jake. Now."

I think he nodded. While I waited, I paced the alley, stalking its length as I made my plans.

And then he pulled up in his black-on-black Hummer. Which was perfect, because I was prepared to steamroll an asshole or two.

"Hurry the fuck up!" I yelled at Jake. He was speeding up the curves of the mountain in the pitch black, but it wasn't fast enough.

"Faster," I shouted.

My fingers were working overtime on my phone, beating the thing to a pulp. With twenty percent battery left, I screamed, "Yes! Got you, motherfucker!" And then I punched an address into the GPS.

I might not be getting my girl back, but that didn't mean anyone else could have her. Or my precious fucking diamonds.

Yes, I was a possessive prick. How the hell did I get to be so goddamn rich? I'd toppled over everyone else to get the accounts I deserved. I'd never been that way in my personal life, believing I didn't deserve the riches of love and happiness. But I was going to make an exception, because neither did AJ Streets.

Doc had given that asshole's name to my insurance company as a person of interest in the necklace's disappearance. Earlier today, I had decided to stay out of it, only concerned with Bess and her health. But now, as nighttime fell dark and heavy, things were different.

With Bess gone, I was no longer chasing forgiveness. I wanted retribution.

I made a quick call to Doc, pretending to ask a question related to Bess, and a little chitchat was all it took for him to reveal Anthony Jon Streets's full name to me. All I had to do was ask, "Hey, Doc, refresh my memory, who was it you told the insurance company was at Bess's house today?" And he ran right down the list. I already knew everyone involved except for *him*.

The fucker who'd been inside Bess.

The man who wanted to lay claim to the woman I had fallen for.

The piece of shit who I was going to set straight.

The glow of the GPS and the annoying woman's voice did little to calm my nerves as Jake drove without a word. His silence bought him freedom from my wrath. We were fucking identical twins, so he knew how to deal with me. We'd been through it all together—birth, the death of our parents, wet dreams and puberty, college—we knew all of each other's hot buttons. And since Jake knew when to shut the hell up, he didn't disappoint as he drove me to my destruction.

As we barreled up a gravel road to nowhere, a huge house came into sight. So the motherfucker apparently had money, which let him buy a new life. But that wasn't going to help him now.

Jumping out of the passenger side while Jake rolled to a stop in front of a three-car garage, I didn't wait for him to shift into park. I ran up the set of stairs to the impressive wraparound deck and threw open the screen door, then pounded my fist against the front door.

"Open up," I yelled.

The door flung open, banging backward into the wall with a thud.

"Who the fuck are you?" he growled.

I was fit, but AJ Streets was big. The guy screamed blue-collar tough in flannel with his oversized muscles flexing through the thick fabric.

Oh, fuck it. I can hold my own. And I had Jake.

"That doesn't matter," I bit out with my hands balled into fists at my sides. "I'm here for the necklace we all know you took from Bess. And while I'm here, I'll warn you—stay the fuck away from her. You don't deserve to be in the same goddamn country as her."

We were in a standoff. I was on one side of the threshold, him on the other. Neither of us gave an inch, both of us with our chests puffed out, staking a silent claim.

He let out a snort. "Oh, I should've known you were that guy. The rich fucking prick, the asshole who thought he'd swoop in with his money and expensive sweaters and take my girl," he said, a little spittle running out of his mouth. The dude reeked of nicotine and booze.

He grabbed a handful of his own shirt and slurred, "This is what real men wear. Flannel. Not cashmere, you fucking pussy."

I grabbed his neck and pushed him back into the wall behind him, entering the hallway of his house. It was fucking freezing in there; all the windows were open, the cross breeze running the length of the house, howling.

Leaning into his face, I spit out, "I don't need to know what to wear, buddy. I don't need any lessons from you unless you want to tell me how to break a young girl's soul, you lying sack of shit."

I only broke hearts.

He pushed me off him and I went flying into a table. From the corner of my eye, I saw Jake step into the foyer, ready to jump in at any moment. I righted myself and motioned for my brother to hold back. I didn't need him to wade in and rescue me; this son of a bitch was all mine.

Rolling my shoulders, I stalked forward. "Well, I know who the fuck you are—Bess's so-called sponsor who seduced her while you pretended you were being her goddamn support. Fuck you, you lousy drunk bastard."

I had a good hold of his flannel shirt this time and I whipped him into the wall. A trickle of sweat slid down the center of my back as adrenaline surged through me. "So you go over there and fucking torment her some more until she passes out, then you fucking run away . . . you coward!"

Lifting my knee, I caught him off guard in the belly. The balls would have been too obvious, although I wanted to cut those fuckers off.

AJ bent over to catch his breath and gagged. Smelling the contents of his stomach as they came back up, I quickly sidestepped out of the way before he emptied a gallon of cheap liquor on his floor.

"Asshole," I muttered as I kicked him all the way down to the floor.

And then the sorry excuse for a man started crying like a baby. "Shit, I'm a mess, man. Don't you see that? Been clean for coming on a decade, but your girl messed with my head. I thought she wanted me, cared for me. Maybe she did, but then you stepped in with all your fancy-ass shit, and now I'm all alone with a bottle of Jim Beam." He rolled over to his side, allowing me to stare at his back.

Running a hand through my sweat-soaked hair, I caught my breath. God, I'd never been a violent person, yet I wanted to kill this guy. If he hadn't gotten sick, I probably would have kept going.

As Jake finally came forward to intervene, it occurred to me that this was my retribution for a lifetime of bottling up secrets. Pure, unadulterated rage, and I was willing to wield it on anyone who crossed my path. Even a sad excuse for a man who couldn't resist the bottle, who needed help—not to be slapped down.

But I wasn't the nice guy anymore. Putting my foot on his shoulder, my designer boots probing him to move, I gave one last order. "Where's my necklace?"

"Man, she doesn't even like that kind of shit," he whined. "I could afford to buy her that, but she would have rejected it, but from you— it's all special. Fucking whore."

That got him another swift kick, this time to the thigh. He rolled into the fetal position, and Jake crouched down by his ear.

"Listen, asswipe, I've had to haul ass twice today to this desolate excuse of a place because of you. I would suggest that you tell me where the jewelry is, then you can text someone to come and help you dry out."

"Or," I added, "I can hang you over the deck and let you do it the easy way. Cold turkey."

Then Jake took the guy's arm and pushed on some pressure point until AJ was screaming bloody murder.

"In the freezer! You fucks," he yelled.

Jake dropped his arm and kicked him in the leg again before trailing behind me to get my shit.

"Her cunt wanted me first! Sweet little thing practically begged for it, clamping down on my cock—you hear that, you sorry sack of rich shit?" he shouted, slurring his words and moaning as he rolled on the floor in pain.

We didn't bother to shut the door on the sorry excuse for a man when we left. I hoped he fucking froze to death.

Jake revved the engine before he spoke, staring at the necklace clutched in my hand. "Holy shit, that Bess must mean a whole lot to you. Look at that sucker—it's worth more than my gym."

I slammed my door shut, then snarled at him as I slapped my

other palm against the dash. "It doesn't matter anymore, let's go."

As we barreled down the driveway, an old piece-of-shit Buick passed us coming up the hill. The driver—a middle-aged woman—slowed a little, and I swore I knew that face.

Fuck, I needed some sleep.

CHAPTER THIRTY-SEVEN

bess

Two weeks later

IT had been two weeks. Fourteen days. Three hundred thirty-six hours since I last saw Lane. Over twenty thousand minutes since any notion of ever having true love was shattered into dust. Like the hail now falling on the porch, that was the way my tears fell for the first three days after I fled from Pittsburgh.

Camper had driven me back, and I'd wanted her to leave. I'd been in no shape for any kind of reunion with my only friend from college. Not her, the one I had to shut out when I went to rehab at Rambling Brook. She was the one I was with when I used to pop Molly and smoke Mary and down Jack—all my oldest, closest friends. In the old days, we'd giggle and gossip and party some more, and that bad influence was the last thing I'd needed as I dried out in rehab.

Which made me think she was once again the last thing I needed as I fought my demons along with my pain. But Camper had stayed in the mountains with me for three days, lying in bed with me, wiping my tears, and making me tea. She'd been a huge help, and I wished she was still with me now as I sat on my couch over a week later, not knowing what to do with myself.

My hands shook, chills running up and down my spine as the memory of Lane standing in the coffee shop played on a continuous loop in my mind. I'd had the same conversation with Camper over and over those three days she was here. The words still reverberated in my head.

She and I had been cuddled on my bed. My head was tucked in her arm and she was stroking my back just like we did sometimes while watching a movie back in college. At twenty years old, I had no idea how much my body and heart craved that kind of touchy-feely attention. Now I knew why I'd loved Camper back then. Not because we partied together, but because she was the only person who'd ever given me any affection.

This most recent bout had been all her giving and me taking. Actually, it had always been that way. I'd always been a taker.

Anyway, we'd been snuggling and I'd repeat the same word I'd spoken for two days straight. "*Why* didn't he just tell me? Why the secret? Why? I told him I was an addict, and he could have said it then. I told him I went to Pitt, and he could have mentioned it then. Why didn't he? Why?"

My throat was raw from the word that seemed to be stuck on repeat, falling from my lips over and over again.

"I don't know the answer to that, Bess," she said as she stroked my hair. "He didn't. I'm not an innocent bystander either. I ran off that night, leaving him to deal with you when he started asking questions. I was afraid I'd get busted too."

Waving my hand in front of my face, I said, "Forget that. We were stupid, young, naive, and dumb, especially me. I'm glad you didn't get busted for anything. You seem to be fine, and in a good place now. Me, I was an addict through and through. I needed a clean break."

More tears came, flowing freely down my face as I returned to the subject of Lane. "But why didn't he tell me? I mean, I don't know what I would've done. I've been so dead set on leaving that time in my past, but he didn't know that. There's something else, some other reason why." I paused for a moment, thinking back to all the times he became different, moody somehow in a way I didn't understand. "The cloudiness in his eyes, the hard clamp I've seen him hold on his jaw, other little things I've noticed. That's why, Camper."

"I don't know, sweetie," she said with more back rubbing.

"I guess I didn't matter enough for him to tell me. Maybe that's why," I'd said, settling on it as an answer before falling asleep in my old friend's arms.

Now I sat alone on my couch, except for my dog who had jumped up and plopped his big head in my lap. Staring out the window, I still thought, *Why?*

But I knew I would never get an answer.

These days, I was back to night meetings. AJ was in rehab. I'd learned this from Shirley, who insisted he was sorry and also kept telling me that I should give Lane a chance. I was sick of listening to it, so I took advantage of AJ being gone and went to my old meetings.

Working my regular shift plus overtime, I still found myself with too many idle hours that I despised. I would watch the clock during those minutes, counting off the seconds like a kid waiting for her mom to get home from work. At least, that was what I imagined it felt like as I didn't have the first clue.

Dwelling on the past, present, and lack of a future became my only pastime.

Even Brooks was sick of sitting. He'd jumped off the couch and was circling the door, when I decided to take him for a walk. Slipping on a lightweight sweatshirt and heading out the door, I was surprised when an enormous black Hummer came up my driveway.

"Brooks, stay," I told my dog. He dutifully sat down next to my feet, waiting for further instructions.

I stood still, awaiting what latest drama had found my doorstep when Jake stepped out of the enormous vehicle. When he walked toward the porch, I didn't move.

"Bess," he said simply.

"Jake."

He breathed out my name again as he came close, and I could smell his cologne. It was so different from his brother's smell. Lane was drenched in cool confidence and sand and sun. Jake was cloaked in sheer masculinity and sweat mixed with Calvin Klein.

Lane was a refined Jake.

Jake was a raw Lane.

My head hurt from the comparisons, but I realized that Lane's scent was only a cover-up for his real stench, much like the department store cologne was masking Jake's latest workout.

But what was Lane's regular scent? Was he normally cloaked in a mixture of expensive perfume from Miami babes or the cheap Walmart eau de toilette of hotel staff? Or was it that of a liar, a man who took pleasure in duping young women? Preying on their weaknesses? He certainly knew mine beforehand.

"Are you heading out?" Jake asked, interrupting my psychoanalysis of his brother.

"I was taking my dog for a walk."

I started down the porch steps and yelled, "Let's go, Brooks." Of course, I had the stupid red leather leash in my hand.

"Can I join you?" Jake asked from behind my back.

"Sure," I said without stopping.

Heading down the hill, my boots sticking to the spring mud, I glanced at Jake's feet.

Brand new athletic shoes. Serves him right for bothering me.

"So, why are you here, Jake?" I said, cursing myself for saying the word *why*.

"Lane's not doing well."

Not looking his way, I shrugged. "I don't know what you think I can do about that, even if I wanted to do something."

"Bess, he's a mess, but I'm the only one who knows it. He's got his suit on, all perfectly tailored, and he's wheeling and dealing, playing the role of big, accomplished CEO. He's got this Florida bimbo and that Southern babe on his arm, but I know Lane better than anyone. This is haunting him." He was by my side now, easily walking down the hill, his wide shoulders taking up almost the whole path.

Southern babe ... Florida bimbo. That stung.

"Sounds to me like he's fine."

"He's never been fine." Jake grabbed my shoulder and stopped me in my tracks, turning me to face him. "Lane hasn't been fine since our parents died."

I gasped as a shiver ran through me from head to toe.

Jake frowned at me. "What? He didn't tell you?"

"No."

Jake grabbed his forehead, looking so much like Lane on that day in the coffee shop, it pinched my heart. "Geez, I would have assumed."

"No," I said slowly, my mind churning as I processed what he'd said. "But I didn't really ask. It's something about me I realized that day after Lane sent the necklace. Apparently I'm pretty self-absorbed, but I'm working on it. I need to learn how to be there for others in a way that no one was ever there for me." I felt a lone tear drip down my cheek, at first thinking it was a raindrop, but knowing better.

Jake grabbed hold of both my shoulders and shook me. "So, why are you shutting him out now? I know he was wrong, and it's not my business to even guess what the whole lying to you thing was all about. But he needs you now. All this coming back north, it's never been good for him, yet he did it for you."

A thundershower was pouring down my face now. "Why?" I asked, my throat tightening on the one syllable.

"You need to go to him, Bess. That's for him to say. He won't accept my help, but he needs someone."

"What's his problem with the north?" There I went questioning again.

"Let him explain that," was all Jake said before turning and climbing back up the hill to his ridiculous car.

Four days later, before leaving work, I changed clothes and took the elevator to the eighth floor, looking for my only ally who could be impartial and objective.

Camper, Shirley, and Jake were all pro Lane. "Help Lane," they'd say. "Hear Lane's side, Lane needs you." Or the kicker, "You don't know what he's been through." I heard their words in my sleep and when I was awake, and they drove me crazy.

Ducking my head inside room 802, I called out, "May?"

May, who had been wishing for me to meet Mr. Right longer than anyone, seemed to be the only person I knew who could take a neutral stance, not pushing or pointing me in any one direction.

Well, her and AJ. I'd seen him in rehab the day before. His green eyes were cold and lifeless, his posture aloof as he slumped on the window seat, barely tolerating my visit.

"May?" I called again, this time a little louder, pulling myself out of my negative thoughts.

"Hey, Bess." She peeked out of the bathroom, her hands and lower arms lined in yellow rubber gloves.

"You have a sec?" I asked.

"Of course," she said, waving me in before peeling off the gloves.

I sat on the edge of the couch in the room, keeping my eyes down as I smoothed my hand over the paisley fabric. "I need your opinion."

She sat next to me without a word, covering my hand with hers.

"I mean, your opinion without any of that Prince Charming bullshit. I'm a waitress, you're a maid, and we work in a hotel in the middle of nowhere. Nobody is going to come and swoop me up."

Squeezing my hand, she said, "Bess—"

"No, it's all right," I said, interrupting her. "It's all right because at least that realization lets me understand why I fell for AJ when I shouldn't have. I believed I didn't have a chance with anyone else, so when he kissed me, I just let it happen. But then I felt what things could be like with Lane, and now I know what *real* feels like. All of a sudden, I understand commitment and unconditional love, those things I always thought were myths. But now they're gone."

I sighed deeply, then looked May in the eye. "And I think in order to move on and have anything close to that with someone else, I need to make amends with Lane. His brother came to see me and told me Lane's hurting. Maybe I owe it to him to check on him, to put his mind at ease and let him know that I forgive him."

"Honey, he's hurting because he lost you," May said, weaving her fingers through mine.

Laying my head on her shoulder, I said, "No. He just needs to be absolved of his guilt, and I should give that to him. After he gave me my heart back, it's the least I can do."

May dropped a kiss on the top of my head. "Bess, love, that man did more than give you your heart back. He pumped oxygen into it and watched it dance. If you're asking me if you should go to him, I say *yes*. But not to absolve him. To love him."

Her answer made my heart smile. Looking up into my friend's face, I leaned in to place a kiss on her cheek and asked, "Can you watch Brooks again?"

CHAPTER
THIRTY-EIGHT

lane

"LISTEN, Alan, I don't care what you budgeted for software upgrades next year. This is my cost. Either take it or leave it, because this price isn't going to be on the table for much longer. I have a long waiting list." I barked into the phone, tapping an expensive pen rapidly against the arm of the chair I sat in, sick of this guy's runaround.

But inside, I was just plain sick. And tired. Inside, I felt like the young boy I once was, afraid to risk feeling again.

I was in my office in downtown Miami, unable to appreciate the stunning sight of the bay glittering in the window behind me. My Italian leather shoes propped on the desk, I'd been making phone calls, taking out my aggressions on anyone who crossed me as my perfectly pressed jacket hung on the back of my office door.

To look at me, you would never suspect there was a brutal war raging inside me. My brain's foot soldiers were standing guard at my heart, not allowing anyone entrance. I had fully retreated to my safe space, the four walls within which I controlled everything. For there were no loose ends when it came to my business; there I was the master of my fate, the controller of my destiny.

My office was on the fiftieth floor of the tallest office building in southern Florida, and that was where I'd spent the last few weeks. Outside my domain, my control wasn't guaranteed. After all, I couldn't mastermind the world. And I knew all too well what happened when there was no one in charge.

I hadn't been home since returning from Pennsylvania. Home was where chaos only bled into the nightmares, where the sheets still reminded me of her scent, even though they'd been washed countless times. *No, thank you.*

"Okay, Lane," I heard from the other end of the landline. "You drive a hard bargain, but we desperately need what you're selling, especially since our competitor has your software. You have a deal, sir."

You bet I do. In business, I know what the fuck I'm doing.

I was in the middle of saying, "I'm going to put you through to my assistant, so she can set up when I can come back to your property," when my cell phone started vibrating on my desk.

Setting the landline back in the receiver, I swiped the smartphone. It was an unknown caller.

"Wrigley here," I grumbled into my headset.

"Um, Mr. Wrigley?" a man said with a Mexican accent.

"Yeah, who is this?"

What now?

"Sorry to disturb you, sir, it's Chaz. Um, I take care of your pool."

"Chaz, if there's something you need or a bill is outstanding, please call my main office number and ask for Shelly. This is my private cell." I dropped my feet from my desk, thinking about heading down to the hotel for some lunch.

"Uh, sir. It's not that. I'm here now at your place, taking care of some things, and there's a girl here. A young woman who's sitting by the front gate, with her bag by her feet."

"What?" I stopped dead in my tracks, bracing myself against the floor-to-ceiling window facing the water, my hand chilled against the warm glass.

"A girl, sir, all wrapped up in a sweater even though it's seventy-five degrees out. I asked her if she needed help, but she said she'd just wait for you to get home." He paused for a moment and said in a strained voice, "I'm not prying, sir, but I noticed you haven't been around."

I was putting on my jacket, wrinkling it all to hell as I tried to shove my arms in the sleeves while still on the phone. "I'm coming," was all I said as I ended the call, willing my private elevator to get me to the garage faster.

Grinding the shit out of the clutch, I shifted like a lunatic all the way home. As its tires shrieked a protest, I slammed my car into park in front of where Bess waited at the gated entrance to my home, and jumped out.

Bess got to her feet, the sun blazing down on her dark hair, casting a glow on her face as she turned it expectantly toward me.

"Bess." "Lane."

We spoke at the same time, cautiously closing the distance between us on the scorching Florida pavement.

"What are you doing here?" I asked, my voice sounding gruffer than I wanted.

God, I'm so tired.

Her brow crinkled, and she took a step back instead of continuing to move forward.

I held out a hand, embarrassed that I was already screwing this up. "No, I didn't mean it like that. I'm not mad, just disappointed . . . in myself. How did you get here on your own? Why are you just sitting out here by the driveway? You didn't call?" I tried to steady my tone, tamping down my own inadequacies and anxiety.

She stood her ground, her arms wrapped tightly around her own narrow waist. "I wanted to say I was sorry, sorry for dragging you into everything with AJ and me. And, well, I wanted to thank you for when you saved my life years ago."

Before I could say anything, she continued. "That day was both a beginning and an end for me, you know. An end to who I'd been for a long time, and the start of who I am now. I can't ever be that Bess again, and I'm not sure this new one is much better," she said as she looked down at her Nikes. "My selfishness replaced drugs as a survival mechanism—both of them let me off the hook when it came to really getting close to anyone. So, I'm sorry for that, both now and then."

I couldn't move. *She was sorry?* Standing there in her athletic shoes, wrapped up tight in a sweater that hid her tattoo, she looked like a young college girl, but her attitude was fierce and grown-up.

I need to get my shit together.

She bought herself a plane ticket with her hard-earned tips to tell me she was sorry?

I'm a dick.

I was so stubborn that I ran from this woman, never considering how that would make her feel, and she turned around and did something like this for me. Something I doubted she could afford— either financially or emotionally.

"Bess, you have nothing to be sorry for. This is all on me," I said. The heat of the car's engine reflected off of me, causing sweat to drip down my back, coating me in a glaze of my own shame.

She shook her head. "No. I need to be selfless and apologize, Lane."

I walked to her and gathered her in my arms. "No, you don't." Because I was the caring one, the enabler in relationships. *At least, I used to be.*

"I need to apologize," I told her. "There were so many times I wanted to tell you, but I couldn't. I knew it would ruin everything, and it did exactly that. It ruined it all."

When I rested my lips on the top of her head, she wriggled out of my arms, and I immediately felt the loss.

"Well, I want to know why," she said as she stared at me. "Why didn't you tell me right away?" Her eyes narrowed, she challenged me on the edge of the street.

"Let's go inside. It's hot. Let's get you a cool drink, okay?"

After settling her in my car, I opened the gate and we drove to the house, not bothering to pull into the garage. I waved to Chaz where he was working by the pool, and we went inside. The house was cool and silent, a welcome and soothing greeting to my pounding heart and overheated soul.

"Wow, it's so clean and quiet here," Bess said, looking around with wide eyes.

"I haven't been home much." I took my jacket off and tossed it over the banister. "Actually, I haven't been here at all," I confessed.

"What?"

She moved a little closer, and the warmth of her body defrosted my lonely heart.

"I've been staying at the hotel that sits under my offices. I've been working nonstop, and I haven't wanted to be home."

Bess took my hand. When her small fingers intertwined with my large ones, a strange combination of lust, possessiveness, and fear took hold of me, making me suddenly want a drink. Would she grant me that one wish? I needed one—my nerves were jumping at her mention of the word *why*—but could she handle it?

"Come in," I said, leading her to the great room. "Would you like some water? Soda?"

"I'll take a glass of water."

I set Bess on the sofa, treating her as if she were some delicate piece of glass even though I knew she'd hate that comparison, but I couldn't help it. Now that her past was spread out in front of us, my involvement intricately woven through it for anyone to see, I couldn't help but to look at Bess and see the messed-up college-age version of her. The young girl crying for help that I ignored, convinced I had to stop fixing others for my own sanity.

I'd forced my way back into her life, and had left nothing but destruction in my wake. I should have never asked for that first dinner.

And I never should have covered for Jake.

This couldn't be fixed, no matter how much I wanted it to be. *This* being my fucking shit life.

Grabbing the water, I came back with one glass.

"What about you?" she asked as she reached for it.

"Do you mind if I have something stronger?" I said as I closed in on the bar, clearly unable to wait for her response.

"No, go ahead. Please don't treat me with kid gloves, Lane. I can see you're doing that, and you need to stop."

After pouring a small tumbler full of scotch, I tossed back half in one gulp.

Silence sucked all the air out of the room. I stared into my drink, unable to find the words that might make this situation right.

"Maybe I shouldn't have come," Bess said in a low voice, "but I don't care. I'm here for you, Lane."

"I'm a living, breathing mess," I said as I barked out a demented laugh. "You can't fix me, Bess. I'm the one who fixes others. I don't have a fixer."

Quickly unraveling, I tossed back the rest of my drink, mindlessly grabbing the whole bottle and settling into the chair across from the recovering alcoholic proposing she'd make it all better for me.

"Well, I could try," she said, staring at me intently. "I've never really been the *fixer*, but I'm up for it. Even with you sitting across from me guzzling down a bottle of high-priced liquor."

Glancing down, I noticed the almost half-empty bottle in my tanned hands. I stared down at the bottle, mesmerized with the liquid sloshing around inside it when she moved in for the kill.

"Why don't we start with you telling me about your parents?" She leaned forward and grasped my hand, her thumb rubbing small circles on mine.

Looking at a point over her shoulder, I said, "There's nothing to tell."

"Jake told me they died."

That was when it was clear that I was nowhere near getting my shit together. I erupted like a volcano, jumping to my feet and yelling, "Jake did what? When did you see Jake?"

Red. All I saw was blood red.

"Jake came to me," she said, her eyes wide as she gazed up at me. "Told me you weren't doing great. He just knew somehow, and he gave me the courage to come. And he said your parents died."

"Well, of course he did. After years of handing his sloppy seconds to me, he wanted to take a run at mine."

Bess gasped. Leaning back into the couch, she looked like she'd been slapped. Essentially, she had, yet she didn't move.

Furious with myself, I hung my head. "I'm sorry, that was rude." *Jake, what a fucking traitor. After all I've done for him.*

Dragging my poison in a bottle, I moved to the couch and sat down next to her, trying to pull her to me, but she wouldn't allow it. "Bess, God, I fucked up. Let's start over. You have my emotions doing backflips in my head."

"No," she said firmly, then stood up and moved toward the door. "Maybe this was a mistake. Here I am facing my own demons," she said pointedly, giving my scotch the evil eye, "and all I want to do is help you stare down yours. And you won't even talk to me. I'm such a fool."

I rushed after her, grabbing her before her hand hit the doorknob. "Bess, don't. It wasn't. I'm tired. I haven't slept since I left Ligonier. I'm so fucking tired, and now I'm sloppy drunk." I whispered the last part as I sank to the floor in front of her, on my knees.

I needed absolution. *For everything.*

My head rested against her knees as she stood above me, and I repeated, "I'm so tired."

A moment passed that seemed like years until she dropped to the floor next to me and wrapped her arms around me, soothing me like a little boy in my mother's lap.

With my head buried in her stomach, her legs crossed Indian-style in front of me, I murmured, "The nightmares, they're chasing me. Finding me down here, and they won't stop."

And then I fell asleep on the cool tile floor in the cocoon of Bess's warmth. I hadn't been so embarrassed since I prematurely ejaculated with Cindi Swanson in the attic at my grandparents' house when I was a teen.

Needy was not becoming on me. I was a man, resolute and firm in my convictions.

Yet there I was nodding off in the lap of a woman I had wronged, allowing her to care for me.

CHAPTER THIRTY-NINE

bess

Lane was asleep like a baby, his head in my lap. I didn't know what to do, so I rubbed his back like Camper had done just a couple of weeks ago for me. I watched his even breaths puff out of his mouth, his back rising and falling. Taking in the death grip he had on my thigh, I felt something I'd never felt in my whole life.

Worry. This foreign emotion burned in my gut for *someone else*, another living and breathing human being, and it simultaneously terrified me and empowered me.

For the first time, I pushed all my ridiculous *poor me* fantasies down, forcing them to remain dormant in the bottom of my heart. The man in my lap, whose behavior mimicked a small child, was pained—tortured, really—and it was over more than just ditching me in Fizzle Fitness all those years ago. More than anything, I wanted to take all the pain and suffering from him, ball it up, stick it in my backpack, and carry it away.

He shifted a little in my lap, and I looked down to see Lane staring at me.

"Hey," I said, running my hand through his damp hair.

"Hey," he croaked out. "I'm sorry I drank myself silly, and crashed like that. Crap, I'm such a fucker." He grabbed his forehead, nearly pulling the hair out of his head.

"Lane, what's going on?" I asked, but didn't expect an answer.

Whatever this was, it was so deeply buried in his mind, it wasn't going to be easy to extract. I'd seen this in rehab and AA meetings, people with such deep-seated secrets. It took time, patience, and often a military-grade deconditioning to get that shit out.

He shook his head, not meeting my eyes. "Not now."

"Lane, we all have pain, misunderstandings we're harboring. I was there during one of your nightmares, remember? You've got to let it go. I can absorb it." As I spoke, my hands smoothed figure eights on his back. I had no idea where this compassion was coming from, but I was going with it.

"No. It's nothing," he said into my lap.

"Maybe you'll change your mind if you say it out loud. It definitely is *something* if it has you so twisted up. Like me, the minute the drugs were out of my system, the shakes were gone and I was left alone in my sterile hospital bed. I cried like a baby for my past losses, for seeing my mom leave and mentally begging her to stay. I'd carried that with me for years, and when it was out, I was relieved. I felt okay with moving forward."

Lane looked up at me, the blue of his eyes swirling with affection and fear.

I brushed his hair away from his forehead. "Look, I didn't make the best choices after that. I insulated myself in a lonely life where I could never be left again. And I led AJ on because I believed he was the best chance I'd ever have. But you changed all that. You, Lane. You made me want to forgive and forget what's been long done and gone, and when I did that, I could see a future for myself. Something different, something better."

He sat up and pulled me in close, his arms trapping my chest to his. We sat on the cool floor with only heat traveling between the two of us, unknown feelings burning my body up, and then Lane kissed me.

I knew this response was an escape for him, but I couldn't deny him. For him it was another defense mechanism, something he used instead of talking. I'd done that for years—pushed emotions back for sex, substances, waitressing.

His tongue sought entrance and I was a goner. I didn't care. If Lane needed someone to seek refuge in, it would be me. When he was ready, he would find redemption inside me. *Me.*

On the way to Florida this time, somewhere while flying over the Carolinas, I realized I was ready to care. The path my life was heading down was self-destructive in its loneliness, barren of all emotion. And I didn't want that.

When I felt him bite down on my lower lip, hunger and desire raged through my veins. Lane wrapped an arm around my back and started to lay me down on the Persian rug in the hallway.

We were falling. Together. Running first and jumping into the deep end.

Our legs twined, Lane used his knee to push my legs wide open. Settling between them, he rubbed himself against my core, his hard length finding the right spot immediately. I moaned, almost begged, despite knowing there was nothing romantic or sweet about this encounter.

As our mouths refused to come apart, our hands explored, pulling and tugging sweaters and dress shirts off. And then, with my chest and my heart exposed in the middle of Lane's palatial foyer, we fucked. This time I was the drug, and Lane had so many open veins, he was filling them all with me.

The hollow look in his eyes, the urgency to get me naked, and the rush that came over him when he finally sank deep inside me were pretty much dead giveaways. Even to someone like me who was new at this relationship stuff.

CHAPTER FORTY

bess

W<small>E</small> spent two days like this, hidden away in Lane's house, the only serious conversation being over the money I spent to get to Florida.

"Tell me how much it was for the ticket, Bess," Lane demanded over coffee.

"Nope." I shook my head with a smile.

"Bess," he growled.

We were half-naked, lounging on the couch with big mugs and pretend smiles. The housekeepers had been shooed out, the gardeners sent home, and the pool unattended. Lane was hiding and I was aiding and abetting.

I texted May to make sure my shifts were covered at the hotel. Her no-nonsense attitude was a welcome mental break from all the charades here in Florida.

My supervisor, Maddie, thought I took some personal time to see my dad. I learned from May that Robbie was filling in for me in the mornings. Brooks was fine. And of course, May couldn't resist asking about the man of the hour.

MAY: How's Lane?

ME: Fine.

MAY: Toast is fine.

ME: Well, he's toast.

And that he was—toast. Lane was burned. Third-degree burns covered his entire heart.

When we first met—or the first time I actually remembered meeting Lane—his wounds were wrapped in gauze, but the dressing had unraveled somehow. And now he was trying desperately to find new bandages. Sex, midnight swims, showers, and shouting on the phone for work were all doing little to cover up his singed heart.

For forty-eight hours, we did everything but talk. Every time I tried to have a serious conversation, he shook his head. "Not now," he would say. I would chatter on about the hotel and he would listen. I even mentioned AJ getting help, and Lane just nodded.

On the second night, standing beneath the seven—yes, seven—showerheads in Lane's master shower, his hand drifted down my side. I was pushed into the tile wall, Lane leaning into me, his dick seeking entrance. His fingers brushed over my center, tickling and teasing before finally entering me. One, then two.

"Bess," he whispered in my ear, his voice barely audible over the roar of the water. "You feel so good. You take it all away, make it all worth it."

"Lane, you need to tell me what it is, what I make go away."

He was full-on fucking me with his fingers now, flicking that spot, and I was on the precipice.

"Just feel this. Lose yourself in me, Bess." He moved his hand a little faster, and the most sensational orgasm shot through me.

It had worked again. He tapped yet another vein and shot up

with my orgasm, and I was a willing bystander. An enabler. I had to stop the madness.

Dried and satiated, before we collapsed in bed, Lane said, "I have something for you." He pulled the necklace out of his drawer. The heart, with our different shapes and sizes and personalities masquerading as diamonds filling it.

"How did you get it?" I asked, reaching out to run my index finger over its decadence.

"All by myself. That fucker thought he could take you and my necklace from me."

"What?" Shocked, I stepped back.

"I paid a visit to AJ and got what was mine. Did him a service, actually, because he called some older chick in a Buick to help him dry out."

Shirl?

"I don't know who or what happened after that," he added. "I didn't stay for the show."

Frowning, I said, "Lane, he may have been awful, but I hope you didn't hurt him."

A cold chill ran through my body. Why did everyone treat me with kid gloves? Was I that fragile? How did I not know about this?

"Bess, he's fine. You told me yourself, he's in rehab. That's a good thing, right?"

I nodded.

"Now, come here," he said and pulled me into bed, tucking me in next to him. Shifting our bodies, he molded me to his form, barely giving me room to breathe.

I woke to shouting, kicking, screaming.

"No! Jake! Look what you did . . . Jake!"

Lane grabbed my wrists and shook me, hard. My head was banging against the mattress, my neck feeling like it was going to snap.

"Lane!" I yelled. When that didn't bring him to his senses, I slammed my knee up into his abdomen. It was my only defense.

"Oh, you're fighting back, Jake? This is all your fault! Take it."

"Lane! It's me! Bess," I shouted, my voice hoarse from trying to be heard over his.

Another knee to his gut, more yelling of his name, and finally his eyes popped open and focused on me.

"Bess?"

Realization of what happened flooded him, his face growing pale in the faint moonlight streaming through the window. "Oh shit! No!" he said as he slumped back and moved all the way to the edge of the bed.

"It's okay," I said.

But I wasn't. My wrists burned from his fingers, my heart ached from the stress, and I had a headache—either from the banging or the screaming.

Lane threw his arm over his face and said, "You have to go."

"What?" When I turned to him, he rolled the other way, giving me his back.

"You have to go," he said. "*Now.*" Then he felt along his nightstand until the glow of his phone filled the room.

He was on the phone, apparently with an assistant, and the details of the one-sided conversation washed over me.

I was leaving.

Now.

There was a car coming.

A flight was arranged.

So I packed my bags silently, determined not to argue with him. But when we made it down to the driveway, I wasn't able to keep quiet anymore.

Standing in the muggy, bug-infested Florida night, I turned and faced the man I'd traveled to help. "You know what, Lane? I'll leave. I'll run like you want me to, so you can blame me or whoever else you want to blame. But you and I both know *you* need help."

Throwing my hands out, I said tersely, "Get it! Not for me, but for your own peace of mind. You're eating yourself alive, and that's something I know all about. The end is never pretty, and I would hate to see you go out like that, but it's happening. You're going to end up empty and soulless."

Lane didn't say a word. He just stood there, expressionless, staring at me with his arms crossed over his chest, removed from any responsibility.

When the car pulled up, he said, "There's no other way. You're right. I'm not going down a pretty path, Bess. So just go. You don't deserve this. Run, and do it fast."

I saw a lone teardrop slide down his cheek before I got in the back of the car, and I couldn't take my eyes off the headlights shining on his brooding figure as we pulled away. Alone in the back of the town car, I cried. For him, not for me.

Lane had two choices now. Find a better, stronger drug than me to wipe away the pain. Or face the truth.

I hoped he picked the second.

CHAPTER
FORTY-ONE

lane
Six months later

I'D gone for a run in my neighborhood rather than driving down to the beach. I was learning to be at home without panic and nightmares, and sticking around my house was part of my therapy.

The house in Florida had never been a hot button for me until everything went to hell. Before Bess came into my life, my past remained in the Northeast. Now it was a frequent flyer, following me wherever I went.

It was fall, but the Florida heat didn't get the memo. Although it was the end of the day, the air clung to the warmth from the sun earlier in the day, and I was sweating quicker than I'd expected.

Rounding the bend, I wondered if the leaves were changing back home. By home, I wondered if it was cold where Bess was—in Pennsylvania.

Of course it was.

A chill wormed its way through me despite the pace I was pushing in eighty-plus degrees. The street was clear and bright in Miami, but in Pennsylvania—and Ohio—they were slick and littered with leaves.

An accident waiting to happen. Like my parents.

Except with them, it wasn't the leaves.

I arrived at the end of my driveway at the same time a cab pulled up to the gate, not allowing me to dwell on that awful day so many years ago. Coming to a quick stop, I brought my hand to my face, wiping the sweat out of my eyes, curious about who was going to step out. My beard bristled under my hand. Another change I'd made—I wore a beard and jeans now instead of my suit of armor.

Was it her? No, she wouldn't come back here.

Then dispelling any hope that it was Bess, a large form similar to mine opened the back door of the cab.

"Jake, what the hell are you doing here?"

"Well, I decided two months of my brother being MIA was enough," he said, wrapping his big arm around my sweaty body.

I shrugged his arm off. "I'm fine, and you know it. I told you I was getting better but needed space, and yet here the fuck you are."

Jake shot me a quizzical look. "Aren't you going to ask me in?"

I didn't want to. The last time I invited someone in from the bottom of the driveway, it went catastrophically bad.

"Come on," I said, punching the code in the gate.

After opening the front door, I showed Jake the kitchen and excused myself for a shower, more so I could gather myself than get clean.

Standing under the spray in the guest bath—I didn't use my master one anymore—I closed my eyes and fought back the emotions of my past. Calling forward my newfound strength, I took deep breaths, allowing the water to wash the sweat away.

Rubbing shampoo through my new beard and the hair I'd kept long, I thought about that night like I did every time I showered.

I'd watched the town car with Bess tucked in the backseat pull away like I'd watched the ambulance drive away so many years ago. Except this time, I'd been the one who needed help, screaming inside for someone to rescue me. And Bess had been trying to be strong enough, sticking around, letting me use her, giving and not taking.

Unlike me, who had run away or literally pushed her out of my life. It made me hate myself even more for my past transgressions.

I'd stared into the night until the taillights became tiny pinpricks, hating myself more with each passing second. When they were gone, I didn't go back inside. I'd laid down on the concrete driveway and looked at the sky, enamored with the universe, its largeness. It was all consuming and I was nothing but a small chess piece in its game of life.

Even if life hadn't been manipulated or altered in the way I knew it was all those years ago, maybe the outcome would have been the same.

What ruled our existence, I thought. Fate? Or our own decisions?

This line of thinking was too existential for me. My world was one of cause and effect. Clients paid me, then I installed my systems at their hotel and they made better money. That was all I knew, like Bess knew waitressing and collecting tips on the morning shift, going to meetings, and walking her dog. It was how we survived, lugging around the burdens of our youth, and we each had our own ways of dealing with it.

But Bess was growing out of it. I didn't know how or when, but she was. She was strong and I was weak.

When I'd stood up with the intention of going back into my big, empty house as dawn broke, I'd decided I wanted to be strong. Not just a facade of strength, but complete. Whole.

And I'd called a number I hadn't used in a few years.

The shower water began to cool, shifting my attention back to the present.

I wanted to touch myself, but I didn't dare. Aside from the fact that Jake was downstairs, I couldn't find relief the only way I'd grown to know. I'd spent years losing myself in women and climaxing—using my brother's leftovers, my own conquests, Bess, and my own hand.

Now I knew I needed to surrender to the pain and relieve myself of the responsibility, rather than masking the pain with substitutes. That was the only way I could move on.

And that was what I'd been doing until Jake showed up.

"So, what do you want, Jake? Money? Help with your latest piece of tail? What is it this time?" I asked as I walked back into the kitchen.

"Nothing."

"Bullshit," I said as I opened the fridge. Grabbing a bottle of water, I guzzled it and tossed it into the trash.

"Well, what is it? Why you so quiet all of a sudden?" I asked Jake.

"Listen, Lane. Honestly, I'm just worried about you. Have been for some time."

"Yeah, I know," I said, unable to keep the anger from my tone. "That's how Bess ended up on my doorstep before I tossed her out like the trash. That was your fucking fault. I wanted to be alone."

I sat on the stool across from him, both of us with our elbows on the island, mirror images of each other except for the hair . . . and beard. I was doing everything in my power to separate myself from that fuck.

"Bess is doing okay, by the way."

I stood, slamming my hands onto the counter. "What the fuck? How are you still seeing her?" Agitated, I spun around and started pacing. "Never mind, I don't want to know."

He completely disregarded what I said and answered anyway. "She's been spending time with Camper, who got the job with me. We've all hung out a little. She worries about you constantly. Even when she's not asking, I see it in her face."

Jealousy raged inside me, whipping and licking at my skin, fighting to come out and play.

"Shut the fuck up, Jake. You don't deserve to hang out with her. You don't deserve to be here, either. Because if it weren't for you, I wouldn't be in this god-awful place. My soul is black because of you. Our whole lives were ruined by your mistake, and I'm supposed to take that shit to the grave?"

My brother stood up, matching my height inch for inch. "That's another reason why I'm here. I need to say I'm sorry for that."

"Sorry?" I yelled, sweeping my hand across the island, sending napkins and little knickknacks my housekeeper always left out flying across the room. "For what, Jake? Say it," I said, taunting him, knowing the words would never make it over his lips.

"You know."

"See! I fucking knew you couldn't say it. Say it, Jake! Say what you're sorry for!"

We were in each other's faces, our eyes the same, our noses exactly alike, but our hearts were not. His was lifeless, like always. Dead. I wondered if he even had a pulse. While mine was shattered and glued back together just enough for me to function in day-to-day living.

"Why do I have to say it?" he yelled back.

"Because you have to own it, Jake. I'm sick of walking around with it in my back pocket." I was so furious I was practically foaming at the mouth. I could feel spit flying around my beard, my hands were shaking, and my knees were weak.

Suddenly done with it all, I said, "Oh, fuck it, what the hell does it mean now. Great, you're sorry." I stepped back, dismissing Jake. "Go back home."

He walked forward, gripping my shoulders with his hands, caging me in with his arms. "I'm sorry, Lane." And then through gritted teeth, he said, "For doing what I did. I shouldn't have done that. I was just playing, and I didn't know any better. And well, you know . . . Shirley fell asleep and you didn't want to play with me."

"Say it, Jake."

I was losing patience; I'd never loved and hated another person more in my life. We shared blood and some innate bond as twins, so I couldn't cut off my caring for him. But compassion was hard to find when it came to Jake.

He broke free from me, taking a step backward and then another. "It was my fault. All of it. The accident. It was all me. I played with the car, pretended to be fixing stuff that I had no business messing with, all because I wanted to be like Dad. Oh shit. Dad . . . he's gone because of me." Then he bent over like a runner trying to catch his breath after a race, and said between raspy breaths, "Okay, you happy? I'm sorry."

"No, I'm not okay," I spit out. "I've carried that shit around with me for years. When I was little, I worried they would take you away from me. When I was older, I was worried others would judge me like I'd judged myself all these years. I'm so ashamed. We killed our own parents." Doing my damnedest to hold my shit together, I sat down and cradled my forehead in my hands.

Jake stepped next to me and rested a hand on my back. "You were an innocent bystander. A kid, Lane. We were the same age. I did what I did, and you had no power over me to stop me. You were the well-behaved brother, the one who went in our room and played Legos while I single-handedly ruined our lives while Shirley slept. Speaking of her—"

Not allowing him to finish, I interrupted. "That's what my therapist has said since I moved here, that I was an innocent bystander. But I needed to hear it from you."

"You don't think I don't walk around with this in my soul, burning my gut all the fucking time? It was me!" Jake said softly, almost a whisper in my ear as he bent over and leaned on the island.

"I see it. It's why I'm always cleaning up your messes, excusing your lousy behavior. I can't imagine . . ."

My eyes stung, and I felt tears fill my eyes. It had been a long time since I'd felt that. Looking up at my twin, I saw that Jake's eyes were wet too.

Right there in the middle of my kitchen, my brother and I finally had a reckoning that was twenty years in the making. We fell apart, dissolving into bits and pieces of emotion that scattered around the room.

As I lifted my hand to swipe away my tears, I wondered if we would be able to put ourselves back together.

CHAPTER
FORTY-TWO

aj

IT felt really good to hit the open road. Rock music blaring through my truck, a cigarette hanging from my mouth as I shifted lanes—I couldn't give up all my vices—and the fall breeze wafting through my open window. I was free.

From her.

From booze.

From everything.

I'd been out of rehab for a few months. I'd gone home for a while, done the meetings, made my apologies, got along on my own just fine. Then I needed to get out.

I couldn't see Bess every day just yet, even if we had made our peace, hugged, and declared ourselves *friends.* The knowledge that she was alone now didn't make me feel as good as I thought it would.

Bess was a good soul. The best. She forgave me for it all—the attack, the stealing, the stalking. She deserved happiness, and I wanted her to have it, even if it ended up being with that prick, Lane.

I stuck my hand out the window, signaling I was stopping for gas to the head of my crew who was following me down to North Carolina. I'd met a guy in rehab who wanted me to do a job for him. I thought it would be good for me, a change of scenery and all that shit.

Jax, my right-hand man, was coming with me, and we'd pick up a crew down there after speccing the job. It would be a long one, and I was looking forward to lying low for a while.

Yeah, I'd go to meetings. I had the details for local ones in my phone. Jax wouldn't care; he knew the drill. Dude had been with me a long time.

Made me wonder how Bess was doing it. Her world had crashed down on her so many times since cleaning up, and she seemed to just get stronger. I envied her that, but was happy for her just the same.

Throwing the truck in park, I got out to pump gas at the same time as Jax. "Dude, you ready?" I asked him.

He twisted the gas cap off of his truck and joked, "The question is, are Southern babes ready for me?"

I just gave him a half smile, but said nothing as I ran my credit card at the pump.

Seeing my reaction, Jax shook his head. "Sorry, man. I know it's a bad subject. Listen, a few weeks of new pussy and you'll feel on top of the world."

I let out a loud laugh. That was exactly what I didn't need right now, but I didn't want to burst Jax's bubble.

Twisting the cap back on the tank, I hopped in the cab and pulled out with Jax on my tail, a small smile spread across my face. Checking my reflection in the rearview, I knew I needed to let go of Bess, both for her sake and for mine.

I still loved her, but she was gone to me.

Maybe some new pussy *was* just the ticket.

CHAPTER FORTY-THREE

bess

"SEE you, May," I said, dodging around a scarecrow.

It was October, and the entire hotel, including the staff corridor, was decorated for Halloween coming up in a few weeks.

"You coming to the staff party tomorrow?" she yelled back to me after I rounded the corner toward the lockers.

"I think so. I've never been before, but I'm changing things up, so I guess. What do you think?" I called back, grabbing my purse from my locker.

"I think you should go, because you deserve to have a good time. But don't wear those shoes," May said, her voice clear and too close. She'd sneaked up on me and was standing on the other side of the locker door when I slammed it shut, looking at my Nikes.

Shit.

"Brooks and I are going to eat pizza and watch horror movies tonight. I don't know of a better time, but I'm seriously considering going to the party tomorrow." I hustled to head out to my car, not giving her a chance to nag me about it any further.

I was back to my old life. I worked hard, serving both breakfast and lunch at the hotel, went to meetings, and spent time with my dog. My greatest pleasure came from eating scones with Ernesto.

Okay, I was doing a little more socializing. I'd been to May's house for tea, Ernesto's for a big Sunday-night dinner, and was trying to make peace with it being more than normal to see movies and grab dinner with a friend or two.

I'd even taken a trip. Camper had suggested that we take a few days and get to know each other again. She'd apparently won a trip through her job—with Jake—to a posh hotel in New York City, and took me as her guest. Even though the whole trip stank of Lane's doing, I couldn't help but have a blast.

We'd taken a regional jet out of the small local airstrip, landing in the Big Apple just in time for rush hour. Even that had been awesome to see. Cars honking, taxis blaring by, people everywhere, bicycles whipping by our cab's window—it was a living, breathing zoo of humans. We arrived at our hotel right on Central Park South, and as soon as we'd entered our elegant suite and I saw the million-dollar view, I'd known.

When I turned and glared at Camper, she made puppy-dog eyes at me and said, "Don't say it, don't ruin it. Let's just have fun. You deserve it, okay?"

I swallowed the lump in my throat and said, "Okay," and I'd meant it. I'd never really been anywhere, other than Florida, and I was going to enjoy this getaway. Especially spending time with my old friend.

We spent the first whole day checking out the Statue of Liberty from Battery Park before taking the subway up to the Village, where we had amazing Italian food and even better conversation.

Sipping on sparkling water with huge lemon slices floating among the ice cubes, Camper asked, "So, do you ever look back and regret meeting me or doing what we did back then?"

"No, of course not. I was long gone, checked out emotionally before I even met you. I would've found my way to all of that even if I didn't meet you."

She leaned in and wrapped her hand over mine on the table. "I'm sorry I didn't take better notice or help."

I gripped her fingers and said, "And I'm sorry for dragging you down and then locking you out."

Then at the same time, we both said, "Enough!"

"Right, we're here to have fun!" I insisted.

We'd spent the rest of the time taking in more sights and a Broadway show. On the last night in New York, we'd stayed in the room, giggling in our pajamas with mud masks on our faces, courtesy of the hotel spa.

Over our room service dinner, Camper had gotten serious again and said, "I wish we'd known back then we could have this much fun without all that shit."

"Yeah, I know. But we still have now."

That was it for the heavy stuff. We went back home the day after, feeling connected and positive.

Now as I made my way to my car after work, I reminded myself of that feeling. I needed to keep it going. Often it took a daily or hourly reminder, but I was trying.

Of course there were meetings, and they helped. I was back at the church for the nighttime gatherings, pouring strength into others and dipping into theirs when I needed it.

My biggest problem was, I still preferred the isolation. There was solace in the time I was left alone with my memories of the first trip I took to Florida, or the words imprinted in my mind from the letter Lane had sent with the necklace, or the shorter ones that followed.

I hadn't talked to Lane directly since the night he watched me pull away in the town car, but there were packages. A small box arrived every month by courier. Each one included something small for Brooks like a doggy bowtie covered in oranges, a lemon for me, and either a bag of sand or seashells. One even contained a sealed bottle of ocean water.

There was always the same simple apology note.

Dear Bess,

Sending you and Brooks some Florida sunshine. I never should have turned my back on you, but you deserve the sun and the moon and the stars. Not just Florida's.
I'm so sorry.

~ Lane

Jake had stayed in touch, also refusing to let me wallow in my preferred solitude. I saw him on my own a few times, and sometimes with Camper.

As for the two of them—Camper and Jake—something was up, but I wasn't savvy enough to figure it out. At the thought, I laughed as I clicked my key fob to unlock my car door. I couldn't even figure out my own love life, let alone someone else's.

I drove past the new strip mall, distracted for a moment with the view of reddish and burnt-orange leaves, and my thoughts turned to AJ. He headed out last week to new experiences, thinking it would give him a fresh start. I hoped so. I forgave him; it wasn't in me to hold a grudge against him. We'd shared some intimate moments—not just sex, but meetings and friendship and borderline stalking. It didn't matter now. He was better without me. My heart belonged to someone else, a man whose own heart wasn't available.

Pulling up to my house, I couldn't hold back the sadness. It had been a year since Lane Wrigley came into my life. Originally, I'd thought it was a death sentence being called to a dinner for my employers' sake.

But as it turned out, Lane breathed life back into me. He was the first one to show me how to live again, during our precious time in Florida as we walked in the woods or made love, and even during that very first awkward dinner in the tavern.

The last few months had been good for me. I had been getting back to experiencing the world, opening myself up to really feeling and seeing it with people I cared about and who cared for me. The problem was that I wanted to do it with Lane, but he couldn't do that with me. Or maybe he *wouldn't*, I didn't know. His life was tethered to something or someone else. I didn't know what the nightmares were about, but I knew they kept him stuck in the past—and apart from me.

After unlocking my door, I was immediately greeted by a wagging tail and gigantic paws stepping on my feet.

"Hey, Brooks, how're you doing?" I said to my dog, half expecting him to answer.

It was hard to believe that I woke up on a chilly morning last fall and Brooks was the only man in my life. But that was *before*, and this was *now*. As if the last year didn't happen, Brooks was still the only guy in my world.

I let him out to relieve himself, leaving the door slightly open so he could come back in while I busied myself with turning on the oven, filling the kettle with water, and scooping a cup of dog food.

"Hurry up, Brooks, we've got a hot date," I called behind me to the half-open door.

"You do? Sucks for me," I heard behind my back. Stopping what I was doing, I squeezed my eyes shut, bracing my hands on the counter in front of me.

I'm hearing voices?

I couldn't turn around—refused to—because I didn't want the fantasy to end. I wanted to hear the voice again. Squeezing my eyes tighter, I wished with all my might for him to say something else.

Inhaling deeply, I took in the essence of a ghost. His scent was clean, tiny hints of sand and surf lingering with soap, the manly spearmint kind. Then I felt his presence—his hand was at my lower back—and if I squeezed my eyes tighter, I could almost feel his fingers caressing me.

I must be hallucinating.

His warm breath tickled my cheek as he whispered my name in my ear. I leaned all my weight into the counter in front of me, pressing my pelvis flush with the hard stone to steady my thoughts and brace myself, since I was obviously sleeping while standing up and I didn't want to fall.

Brooks barked, interrupting my dream. "Shh, be quiet," I said out loud.

I heard the voice again. "Bess?"

"Hmm?" I answered, holding a conversation with a figment of my imagination.

"Bess, it's me. I'm here. Right behind you."

Something pressed against my back a little harder. His full hand. It moved, making circles that were soothing and comforting. I shook my head, trying to separate reality from fantasy, before opening my eyes and turning around.

And there he was. My eyes widened as I took in the beard. *That's new.*

"Lane?" I said so quietly, I could barely hear myself.

"Bess." He leaned in and touched his forehead to mine.

"You're here? How? Why?" I murmured. I didn't move for fear he would disintegrate.

"I'm here." He brushed his thumb along my cheek, pulling back and looking directly in my eyes. "I needed to say I was sorry in person, to explain, to make amends. I never meant to hurt you, but I don't want to interrupt your date. I didn't think," he said, waving toward the now closed door.

"What date?"

"You said you had a hot date. Your door was open, you were yelling to Brooks."

"No, no date. Just Brooks and me. Pizza and a movie."

"Oh, that's good . . . very good," he said after letting out a long breath.

Horses were galloping across my chest. I brought my hand up to my heart, kneading and massaging it back to a regular rhythm.

Lane lifted his hand and placed it over mine. "I'm sorry I startled you. I probably should've called or texted, but I didn't stop to think, I just acted. Came straight here," he said, not letting go of my fingers.

The horses picked up their pace and I couldn't breathe. "I have to sit," I said, my voice raspy and throaty.

Lane guided me to the couch, and I sat. Brooks followed to curl up at my feet.

"I thought you were a dream," I said, looking at the Lane I remembered, but with a beard.

He shook his head. "I'm here." He paced back and forth for a moment before asking, "Can I sit?"

I nodded.

He took up the space next to me, and used his fingers to turn my face toward him.

"Bess, I'm here, here because I was wrong. Wrong to lie to you about being there with you at the gym, even though it was a long time ago. And even more wrong to have just abandoned you that night. And wrong to have sent you off without an explanation when you came to Florida to save me. I've spent the last six months working with someone . . . a therapist," he said, grabbing his temple, pinching his eyes shut.

He stood abruptly and my heart dropped, free-falling to the pit of my stomach.

Was he leaving?

"Christ, it makes me seem like such a pansy. A therapist," he said, roaming the small space of my sitting area. He looked like a caged animal, waiting for someone to set him free.

Was that what this was about? Setting himself free . . . from me?

"Don't say that," I whispered. He shouldn't beat himself up, even if he was saying good-bye.

Didn't we already do that?

"No, it is. I am. But I went for you. For us. Even though I didn't really go about anything the right way, and I don't even know if there will be an us. I had to try," he said, kneeling on the floor at my feet, bracing his hands on my shaking knees.

My heart moved up to my throat, lodging itself in my vocal cords, making it impossible for me to speak.

"Bess," he said, bowing his head, staring at the floor. "You don't deserve anything I'm about to tell you." He took a deep breath as if gathering himself, then looked into my eyes. "My brother, Jake, was responsible for our parents' deaths."

I felt a shudder run straight through his body into mine.

"He's . . . he's not a murderer. It was an accident. He'd been playing with the car, pretending to change the tire like we'd seen our dad do. My dad used to tinker with that car all the time. Our parents carpooled to work and usually took my mom's van, but the day after Jake played car mechanic, for some reason, they took my dad's old one. He loved that car . . . it was a '79 Chevy Nova he bought when he was a student." Lane barked out a laugh, his eyes pained. "It was so beat up, and when he drove it, he looked like such a hippie behind the wheel, with his wild hair blowing in the breeze as he jammed to the Beatles."

He took a breath, still staring at the carpet. I brought my hand to his wild hair and realized it must be some type of tribute to his dad. Even with his fancy pressed suits and his perfectly tailored designer jeans, his hair was an ever-present memorial to his hippie father.

With my hand sifting through his locks, he went on.

"They never came home that day. The tire hit some leaves and rolled off when they braked . . . at least, that's what the Youngstown police believed. But I always knew the truth. Jake had loosened the bolts and hadn't been strong enough to tighten them back up enough the day before. Our sitter wasn't paying attention and I was busy playing Legos, but I was watching Jake in the driveway through the window. I was jealous of him, of his free spirit, of how he did whatever he wanted to do."

His eyes met mine, the anguish in them painful to see. "You see, it's my fault too because I watched and didn't do anything. I saw our nanny go out in the driveway and grab Jake from under the car and bring him back to the house to clean up, but she never checked to see what he'd done. And I didn't say anything."

He took a deep shuddering breath before adding, "By the next afternoon, it was too late."

I watched Lane's back heave with slow, ragged breaths and remained quiet, suspecting he wasn't done. My heart burned with searing pain for the broken man in front of me.

"At nine years old, after we were sent to our grandparents in Pittsburgh, Jake and I made a secret pact in the dark hours of the night . . . after what our sitter told us right before we left. She said they could lock Jake up for murder. That was the night the nightmares began, and they lasted until I moved to Florida. Everyone thought they were just because my parents died, so it was easy to go with that excuse. Those dreams tortured me with guilt and obsession over Jake. I was so mad at him for what he did, but also scared to fucking death that I would lose him. I'd made a deal with the devil to never let anyone take him from me, so for years I covered up for all his stupid shit and went along with all of his dumb games."

"Lane, look at me," I said and waited.

He raised his eyes to meet mine, anguish turning them into two deep-water pools.

"Lane, you were a kid," I said gently. "You weren't responsible, and neither was Jake. He was a kid too. You didn't deserve to let this haunt you as long as it has—"

He didn't let me finish. "It's why I was at yoga that night, the night you collapsed. I was covering for Jake. He was sleeping with the instructor and wanted me to pretend I was him. And like always, I never said no to him. Fuck, it was such a nightmare. You had fallen right on top of me . . . and your friend, she freaked out and ran off. I guess she was lit up on something too. At first, I was confused why no one was coming to help, and then I remembered I was supposed to be Jake. So I pretended to whip into action."

I stopped him, running my hand along his jaw, his beard bristling along my fingers. "My falling, nearly OD'ing, that wasn't your fault either, Lane."

He shook his head. "Well, it was my fault you were all alone in the ambulance. I was so mad at Jake for putting me in a bad place again that when he showed up, I decided it was more important to reveal his little ruse. I wanted to check on you or visit you, something, but I never did."

Glancing up at me, he said, "Actually, that was when the offer to move to Florida came and I took it. It was a new start for me. No more Jake, no more fall weather with winter on its heels, no more emotional triggers. I'd seen a therapist a little when I first moved south and then declared myself fine. I was in the warmth, away from the cold weather that only reminded me of the worst time of my life. Then I met you and the triggers started again, not just old ones, but a new one. *Love*."

He took another long, deep breath and said, "I couldn't give love if I didn't feel worthy of love."

Was that what this was about? He wasn't saying good-bye?

Taking my hand in his, he threaded his fingers through mine before he snared my gaze. "I love you, Bess."

His eyes were so blue in that moment, clear skies for miles, and I wanted to fly away in them. Stunned at his admission, I could only stare at him, wondering once again if I were hallucinating. This couldn't be happening, not to me. How could I deserve this?

"To be honest," he said, "I've thought about you every day since that yoga class. You seemed so beautiful on the outside, but I could tell you were broken on the inside, and there was such a push-pull going on inside me about whether to help you or not. I thought you were beyond repair, but that turned out to be me. You turned out to be the strong one. The one who made me want to fix myself after always fixing everything for Jake."

I frowned at him, frustrated at how hard he was being on himself. "Lane, you were not broken beyond repair. You need to forgive yourself. That's the hardest step for anyone. Believe me, I know."

"Can you forgive me?" he asked, laying his head in my lap.

"There was never anything to forgive." I smoothed my hand over his head, comforting him like I did in his foyer—like a heartbroken little boy.

"But I sent you away," he mumbled. "I used our connection to forget all of this shit, our intimacy, when you showed up in Florida."

He stared up at me in pain, his eyes searching for forgiveness.

With a sigh, I said, "I know. I knew you had something much deeper going on than the secret about knowing me and about the drugs, and as much as that hurt me, you deceiving me, I knew there had to be more. And I wanted to be there for you. *Because I love you.* I have since you kissed me in the hallway on Christmas. You stole my heart that night. And even though I saw you were all mixed up, I couldn't make myself leave you alone."

Relief flooded me. The look I'd seen before deep in his eyes, the hazy fog of indecision and regret, it wasn't just about deserting me—it was something much worse. A horrific event, a burden that no child should have, but Lane had carried it since he was nine years old. To make it worse, Lane had taken on his brother's guilt too, although I suspected Jake felt the weight of his own participation in different ways. That haunted look was evident in his blue eyes too.

"Well," he said, "I took care of that for us. I sent you away, as if I could forget you. That night after you left, I decided to hunt down absolution . . . for you."

Brushing a few stray hairs away from his forehead, I confessed, "I knew you were wrestling something bigger."

Wrapping his arms around my knees, he squeezed. "I couldn't forget you. The need to remember you was stronger than my need to keep this bottled up inside any longer."

I lifted his chin with my fingers, forcing him to look up at me again. "I knew you would slay your inner dragons. I didn't know how, but I knew you would. I just didn't know if you would come back to me. I'm not whole myself, Lane. My life, it's boring and mundane . . . and simple. I'm not a party girl anymore. I can't ever be. Watching movies with my dog is a big night on the town for me."

He kissed the inside of my wrist. "I love that—all of that—about you, Bess."

I half smiled as I teased, "But your playboy image will be tarnished."

I had to joke about something—this conversation was getting too intense. And Lane's pain over his parents still swirling in the air was making me weak with need. I wanted to stick my hand deep down inside the man and pull out his suffering, then stuff it inside my own soul.

He straightened, remaining on his knees, but bent forward and kissed me. It was a gentle kiss, full of promise. It was a promise I wasn't sure he should make, one I didn't know I could fulfill.

"I'm not a playboy, Bess. That was my disguise. Women, partying, pretending to be naughty . . . those were my drugs. But with you, I can be me. Plain, boring, business executive me. And now I can be whole because you know the truth. Can you live with what I allowed Jake to do? What I've covered up all these years?"

"Lane, you were a kid. You have to accept that. I don't have to accept anything."

"I am. I'm trying."

"Can you accept me?" I asked, my voice trembling. "For my past wild behavior? And my not-so-wild life now?"

"I love you, Bess. You have to know that, boring or not."

I leaned forward and kissed Lane, winding my hands through his hair.

And then I stopped suddenly, pulled away and asked, "How's Jake?"

I hadn't seen him in a few weeks. I loved the man in front of me, but I'd come to care for his brother. And now I realized how much they both kept bottled up inside.

Lane gave me a wry look. "I hear you two are friends now. In fact, the little fuck used it against me, pushed all my hot buttons, made me jealous enough to get on a plane and come back here."

I laughed. "He's sleeping with Camper, I think."

He shook his head. "Well, I hope she doesn't get too attached, because Jake doesn't do commitment."

"But how is he?"

"He's okay. How's he been when you've seen him?"

"It's been a while, but he's always his same cavalier self."

His tone impatient, he said, "Well, I think he's going to be shedding some of that. He's going to work with a therapist that my doctor connected him with."

Apparently Lane was done talking. He pushed me back onto the couch and slid on top of me, taking my mouth.

When he whispered, "Bess, I love you," against me, my whole body shuddered.

It was cold and wet outside, but I was warm underneath Lane, his long body covering mine. His hands were everywhere, touching, bringing life to my skin and meaning to the blood pulsing through my veins.

Taking my hand, he lifted it and slipped it inside his pocket without ever breaking the kiss. My fingers caught something sharp inside his jeans, and Lane broke free only to say, "Take it out."

With shaky hands, I pulled out the necklace. It shimmered and sparkled in the evening light, catching stray colors streaming in from the window.

"I think this belongs on you," Lane said, moving to attach it around my neck.

It was the first time I'd worn it; I'd never gotten the chance to put it on before it had disappeared. The pendant was cold against my skin, and I reached up to stroke it as my eyes pricked with tears.

"Don't cry," Lane said, and wiped a tear from my cheek that had dared spill over my lashes.

Then with a twinkle in his eye, he took my hand again and brought it over to his other pocket. Something else awaited me in there.

Pulling it out, I found a bracelet. It had two strands of plain white gold rope that came together into a knot, like you would see on a gift bag. Dangling from the two loose strands were jewel-encrusted charms: a yellow-stoned B and an onyx-lined L.

"Lane, it's too much."

He shook his head and moved back to kissing me.

Brooks interrupted with a bark. Jealous, he nudged his head under Lane's hand, begging for attention.

"I'll do you one better, Brooks," Lane said, grabbing his small piece of luggage he'd dropped by the door and pulled out a huge dog bone. It was shaped like a skeleton for Halloween, and had an enormous black and orange bow tied around it.

Unwrapping it, Lane tossed it in the corner for my dog, and then scooped me up and carried me back to my bedroom. After laying me down on the bed with my hair spread out around my face, Lane kicked off his boots.

"Those are kind of silly," I said.

He gave me a mock pout. "Hey, I was rushing to see my girl in the country, and ran to get a pair of shit kickers."

I giggled. "They're Prada, Lane. They're the furthest thing ever from shit kickers."

"It doesn't matter, they're off now and I don't plan on going back outside."

Once again done talking, he climbed up my body and slipped his hands under my shirt, lifting it up and over my head before flicking off my bra. He unfastened my jeans with his other hand, then began tugging them off as I lifted my hips to help.

Traveling the full length of my body with kisses, Lane snagged my thong and pulled it off with one finger before settling his face between my legs. His warm breath teased me before his tongue swiped up my center, landing where I silently prayed he would. Then he slipped a finger inside me, his mouth sending vibrations straight through my clit, his beard tickling the inside of my thighs in all the right places.

I was burning up, ready to become a fiery inferno of orgasm, when he slid a second finger inside me. And then it burst through me. Flames were licking all around my body, and the only way to douse them was for Lane to dip inside me. But I didn't want to put them out yet. I liked the sensation I was feeling and wanted it to last.

Lane moved back up beside me. He had trapped my arms above my head with one hand and was smoothing his palm up my side when I whispered, "Lane, I need something."

"What, darling Bess? What do you need?"

"I need my hands," I said, sucking in a breath.

Immediately releasing my hands, he said, "Did I hurt you?" with a pained expression.

"No, nothing like that." Using his sweet confusion against him, I tipped his six-foot-two-inch frame over on the bed and worked my way down to his button fly.

One button, two, three, four, and I was shimmying his pants over his hips. He lifted his ass so I could tug his jeans and boxer briefs at one time, springing to life what I wanted. I felt Lane kicking his pants off his ankles and then they fell to the floor, leaving a very gorgeous and naked man in front of me.

I didn't hesitate, just dipped my head and put my mouth where I wanted. Licking his full length, sucking on the tip, tasting Lane's pre-cum, the fire continued to spread all the way through me. I was lit up from the very bottom of my toes to the top of my head. When I felt his hand on my head, not commanding, but suggesting a little more speed and pressure, I gave it willingly. Taking him deep in my mouth and sucking my way back up, I heard a raw moan come from the back of Lane's throat.

"Bess, I'm gonna come, and I don't want to yet," he gritted out, now sounding a bit more demanding.

When I stopped for a moment and looked up, this time he took advantage of my confusion—flipping me off him and on my back so he could dive into my body. He was bare again. This time he didn't notice, just started making slow, luxurious love to me. With long and calculated thrusts, Lane drew the burn out of me, leaving warmth in its path.

"Lane, you're not wearing anything," I said softly.

He paused and pulled halfway out. "Shit. Again," he said, holding himself over me, hovering.

"I'm on the pill, and I haven't been with anyone since us."

He didn't answer. His lips landed ferociously on mine, devouring me with a kiss. I wanted him to move again, but he didn't.

Needing more, I lifted my hips, urging him on.

"Bess, wait. I'm kissing the fuck out of you right now."

"I can tell," I mumbled between the press of our lips.

He let go and stared me down while he was still hard and seated inside me, and I was going insane with wanting to feel him move. "You waited for me?"

"Yeah," I answered.

"Me too, Bess. There's been no one else. I tried to, but couldn't."

That didn't even sting—well, maybe a little—but I knew all too well what it felt like to try to convince myself that someone else was *the* someone for me. And I did more than try a year ago with AJ.

"I love you, Lane," I said, the moment feeling right to return the sentiment.

And with that, he started moving—slowly at first, tenderly kissing me before the urgency rose once again. Then he picked up his pace, his tip hitting me in just the right spot. His hands slid back up, taking mine with his and pinning them above my head. I was like that—completely submissive to the man on top of me, baring my whole soul after he'd poured his out earlier—when my second orgasm ripped through me. It did nothing to extinguish the flames inside me . . . it only stoked the fire.

We ended up kissing and making love and sometimes screwing for what felt like days.

At least, until dawn when Brooks finally whimpered to go outside.

CHAPTER FORTY-FOUR

lane

For the second time in a year, Bess had to call in for coverage at work because of me. I could tell she didn't like doing it, but she also didn't love the idea of leaving me either. Which I liked—a whole lot.

I got up the morning after my apology and our sleepless night of reconnecting, tugged on my Prada boots—I know, ridiculous—and let Brooks out. Taking in the country air didn't provoke the same panic it once had. I was breathing easier now that the truth was out, at least with Bess and Jake.

Having it out with Jake had been my first step, coming clean over how gutted I'd been and hearing him take responsibility was the beginning. Admitting what happened in the past to Bess was another step, one that had me in knots the whole flight and car ride to her. But now that it was over, I didn't feel the usual anxiety I had in the past over traveling back to the brisk fall weather.

Whistling for Brooks, a new panic set in. I had to leave. I was pretty sure that Bess might have passed my business as a priority, but that didn't mean I could let everything go to shit. I had meetings scheduled and an office to run. Pulling out my phone, I e-mailed my assistant and asked her to push my schedule by a week.

I wanted to dump the whole damn thing and drop off the face of the earth with Bess, but somehow, I knew that wasn't an option for either of us.

Walking back into the small house, I smelled coffee brewing.

"Bess, want me to feed Brooks?" I called out.

"Sure! I'll be right out. I just want to brush my teeth," she called back.

I definitely want to drop off the face of the earth with her.

I hunted around the kitchen until I found the dog food, then scooped some into the bowl on the floor, filled the other with water, and patted the big dog on the head as he ran by me to his meal.

Then I searched through the cabinets until I found some mugs, and poured us each a steaming cup of coffee and went looking for Bess. I found her standing in her room, staring at herself in the mirror, fingering the heart necklace now around her neck.

After setting the mugs on the dresser in front of her, I wrapped my arms around her, pulling her back into my embrace. Feeling her wiggle her ass up against my semi almost tempted me to take us back to bed. But this wasn't about making love or fucking or anything more than the way my heart beat in sync with hers.

Sliding my other hand along her collarbone, up her neck, and pushing her hair back, I whispered in her ear. "Looks perfect, but could be a little bigger."

She bumped her hip back into mine. "No way, it's already too much."

"Well, I like seeing it on you, its rightful owner."

"I don't think I can even wear this to work," she said with a frown, staring at my reflection in the mirror.

"About that, I'm sorry you had to get someone to cover for you. I decided I'm going to stay a week now, so maybe you can get a few more days off," I said with puppy-dog eyes.

She turned in my arms and lifted a hand to my beard. "I like this, by the way. A lot," she said with a wink.

Leaning forward, I rubbed my face over her cheek, letting the tiny hairs tickle her skin.

Her gaze pinned to my chest, she said softly, "But I can't miss a whole week of work, Lane."

"If it's the money—"

"No, it's not that."

"I have more money than I know what to do with, Bess. And if we're gonna make a go of this, which I assume is where we're heading, you have to learn to accept things from me," I said firmly, knowing it was probably not going to win me any brownie points.

But Bess went somewhere I never thought of. She continued to amaze me.

Raising her big brown eyes to meet mine, she said, "Listen, I'm sure I won't always be comfortable with letting you do so much for me, but work is something more to me. It keeps my mind and hands busy, because too much idle time is bad for me. Work is part of my coping mechanism with my past, and maybe for you too."

She was wrapped tightly in my arms at this point, and her revelation shook me to the core. Kissing the top of her head, I let my mouth linger before responding. "You may be right. Thank you for explaining how you feel about work to me. I can't say that I don't want you to call off work for forever and be with me, but I get it."

Her stiff posture relaxing somewhat, Bess brought her arms up around my neck and kissed me. We tangled tongues and lips, allowing our actions to speak our feelings.

Breaking free, she said, "I'm going to take a few days off, and then I have to go back. But you can stay however long, for forever if you want. I want as much as I can get of you."

Without thinking, I said, "I can't be here for forever," ruining the moment.

"I know, but a girl can dream," my girl said, halting any more conversation.

Then we ended up back in bed. For the day.

After a few days of bliss, Bess told me she was going in early the next morning for work, but she would be home around two o'clock. Figuring I could use the time to catch up on e-mails and calls, I begrudgingly told her that would be fine.

When she got home, we spent the afternoon taking a walk in Cooke Forest with Brooks by our side, his tail wagging madly. With every step we took together, holding hands, my fears and anxiety drained further from my bones.

Yes, I still craved my life in Florida. The office, the hours, the job . . . they were indeed my coping mechanisms. But I was facing my demons here in the chilly air with the leaves turning all around me, and began to feel a glimmer of hope that everything might turn out okay for us.

Bess had packed lunch and we stopped for a picnic, sitting on rocks next to a stream bubbling beside us. We warmed our bodies with coffee she'd packed in a thermos, and while rubbing all over each other in a mad kiss on the mountain.

When we got back from our adventure, she told me about work before making dinner. That was when the air changed, and I wasn't sure why. Bess was busy destroying a salad she was making, taking out some unknown tension on the poor lettuce when I asked, "What's up," placing my hands over hers, stilling her jerky movements.

"I just feel like a bad person . . . girlfriend . . . or whatever I am," she said in a tight voice, jolting my heart.

Bad?

Turning her to face me, I said, "Why would you think that?"

Her eyes wide with emotion, they brimmed with tears until they began to overflow.

"Bess, what the hell?"

"B-because I'm here making dinner after a beautiful day together and I don't have any beer or wine to offer you." She sniffed, reaching up a hand to wipe at her nose as she said, "I don't think it bothered me that you have a cocktail when we've been out in the past, but I just don't think I'm good with keeping any of that around, here in my house."

At that, her shoulders heaved and she began to wail.

I was at a loss, but did my best to find the right words. "Bess, I don't need beer or wine. I'm fine. You don't need to keep any of that stuff for me, and I can clear my house out. This moment is perfect, baby. No substances needed to make it any better."

"Are you sure?" she asked, sniffing back tears. "I just feel like if this were a real relationship, you'd be having a cocktail while I made dinner."

"This is a real relationship, Bess."

"But it—"

I dug deep inside me, thinking fast for a solution. "Bess, I've been here for four days, and you haven't been to a meeting. I don't know much about all that, but I know you go and it's important that you do. Maybe you need to do that tonight?"

Averting her eyes, she said, "I didn't want you to see that part of my life."

Frustrated, I tipped her chin up so she could see me. "Bess, did you hear me? This *is* a real relationship. I know we're both avoiding talking about the geographic difference between where we live, but this is real. I told you the truth about all my secrets, and you accepted me. I want all of you, accept all of you, love every bit of you . . . meetings and all."

"Are you sure?" she whispered, her eyes red and her lower lip trembling.

I walked over to the oven and flicked it off. "Is there a meeting? Soon?"

She nodded.

"Come on," I said, grabbing the car keys.

CHAPTER FORTY-FIVE

lane

I DIDN'T know what to expect or hoped to gain from the whole suggestion, but it was clear Bess was hurting and needed something more than I could give her. After all, I was a fixer despite the fact that I needed repairing myself.

We hustled into the small town in Bess's Jeep. I'd rented a car, but liked that Bess enjoyed me driving her little SUV. It made this whole thing feel even more real.

Although, driving to an AA meeting smacked with reality.

Bess is an ex-addict. The woman I love is an alcoholic and a junkie.

This was something I couldn't ignore. Not now, not ever—even when I walked away from it almost five years ago at the gym.

"Make a right up there," Bess said, interrupting my thoughts.

For most of the ride she'd been silent, looking out the window and leaving me to my own thoughts, when I should have been attentive to her. Because that was Bess. She thought she was selfish, but she was the most selfless person I knew.

As we pulled into a church parking lot, Bess turned to me. "I have to go in alone. We don't allow visitors unless they're pre-approved, and I know you'd be confidential and all, but it's just the rules."

I nodded. "No worries, I understand. I can wait here?" I posed it as a question, sensing that Bess needed to be in charge of the decision-making regarding this. After six months of intensive therapy on the heels of being in and out of it for a half a decade, I was almost a shrink myself.

"Do you mind?" she asked.

"Of course not. I'll be right here. Take your time."

She got out of the car without another word and ran toward the door in her Air Force Ones, her lithe body wrapped in a sweater coat, her long brown hair blowing in the wind.

As I waited, I fidgeted with nervous energy, hoping her support group didn't encourage her to cut ties with me.

They wouldn't. Would they?

A while later a group of people exited the building. I got out of the car and waited, leaning against the passenger door as I huddled in my down parka, facing the mismatched crew heading my way.

They were all so different—tall, short, fat, black, and white—yet while they all struggled from similar addictions, they persevered. Unlike Jake and myself. We were identical in appearance, but carried different emotional burdens. And neither of us seemed to be able to get a hold on them very well.

But I would die trying for Bess.

She was walking out with another woman, talking as they held on to each other's hands, bundled against the wind. Deciding I wanted to meet her friend, I headed their way, rubbing my hand along my beard as I walked before stopping dead in my tracks about ten feet away. The sky could have parted and dumped an avalanche of snow on me, and I wouldn't have moved. My feet were glued to the concrete as if it weren't dry and they were sinking into its wetness.

Miss Shirley. I wasn't sure if I said it aloud or in my head, but my initial thoughts were confirmed when she lifted her head.

"Lane."

"Miss Shirley." She was older, not as skinny as she used to be, and a lot shorter than I remembered. Or maybe I was just a lot taller.

We stood frozen in our spots, confined to our corners as Bess looked between us in confusion. This was no happy reunion where we went running into each other's arms. At one point in time, this woman brought only a smile to my face. Now all I saw was blackness surrounding her form.

Sorrow swirled in and around me like the ravaging wind. Wracked with emotion, I was afraid I was going to fall, blown over by either the sorrow or the wind, or both.

CHAPTER
FORTY-SIX

bess

L ANE stood there, his eyes no longer caressing me but stealing my resolve, sucking all my strength right out from under my skin. He'd turned deathly pale, his eyes widening as his jaw went rigid, just like the rest of his body.

"Lane, are you okay?" I separated myself from Shirley and walked over to him, sliding my arm around his back.

We'd had a good meeting. I'd shared, asked for help when it came to being in a relationship, and had spoken my fears aloud. I felt a lot better just from that alone.

Shirley had been particularly quiet as I'd shared with the group, eyeing me with a curious expression. I hadn't seen her in a week or more, and chalked it up to us not seeing each other. But now I wasn't certain.

"Shirley, what are you doing here?" Lane said through gritted teeth.

Taking a wary step toward him, Shirley said, "I live here now." She'd clenched her hands, but I could still see them shaking.

"How?" he wheezed out.

When he balled his fists at his sides, I slid my hand over one of his and pried his fingers open, slipping mine in between.

Shirley pressed her lips together, obviously trying and failing to keep them from trembling. "I came here years ago, cleaned up, got married. I work in the diner now. Not a day goes by that I don't think of you and Jake."

Shocked, I struggled to keep my mouth shut as my gaze pinged between them. *Think of you? And Jake?*

"Come again?" Lane responded, his brow pinched tight.

"I think of you two all the time, how I was wrong and I'm an awful person." She shifted nervously from one foot to the other, then licked her lips before saying, "It plagues me, but then Bess met you. When I heard how successful you'd become, I was so proud of you. And I thought I'd be able to watch you succeed more through Bess."

"Through Bess?" he said through gritted teeth. "My Bess? Successful? Shirley, I have nightmares like a prison inmate, ones where I lash out and hurt people, like Bess. Thanks so much for tampering with my life once again, but no thanks."

Grabbing my arm, Lane turned and dragged me to the car. Once inside, he locked the doors and turned to me. "Did you know she knew me? Did you?" he yelled.

I wasn't afraid. Lane's bark was bigger than his bite, but I did back up against the window at the cruelty of his accusations.

"Know? How would I know? Know like you knew I was a drug addict and nearly OD'd in yoga? That kind of know?"

He buried his face in his hands, running his hands through his thoroughly mussed hair as he let out a loud, "Fuck. This is so fucked up."

"I didn't know anything, Lane. You have to believe me. I met Shirley after I met you, at the morning meeting because I was avoiding AJ. She took care of me, but she did encourage me to pursue you," I admitted, wanting to be transparent.

Still unsure of how Shirley was woven into the very tangled web we'd already spun, I sat quietly.

"Shirley was our sitter. Mine and Jake's when he fooled around with the car. The one who told us to not tell anyone," he said in a whisper.

Gasping for air at this news, I jumped in my seat when Lane yelled, "Shit!" He banged his hand against the steering wheel. "Jake mentioned something about Shirley when we were fighting, and I completely ignored him."

"Jake? I've never introduced the two of them . . ."

Lane cupped his head back in his hands, leaning into the seat as he sighed.

"Ugh!" Again he slammed his hand against the steering wheel. "We saw her, when we were leaving AJ's when we got the necklace. The woman in the Buick, I knew she looked familiar. Jake must have pursued it. Little asshole."

Leaning forward, I turned and put my hand on Lane's chest, resting it above his heart. I felt the pounding beat, coming strong and fast through his jacket. "Lane, I didn't know. You have to know that. I would never do anything to trick you," I said, sensing he needed to know that, especially after the scam Shirley had pulled on them. They were kids, for God's sake. They wouldn't have gone go to jail.

But she would have.

My world spun as my emotions unraveled. Self-loathing filled me at the thought that Lane had tried to do something right for me, and it ended up crumbling at his feet. I hated myself for ever trusting Shirley, and at the moment, I despised Jake for not filling me in.

But I loved Lane, so I said, "Why don't we call Jake? Maybe he can fill in the blanks."

Later that night, after making coffee and sitting around the fire with Lane and Jake hashing out the present muck they waded in, I crawled into bed next to Lane. He was on the left side, his arms behind his head, his chest bare, and I crawled into the crook of his arm and shoulder, running my hand along his stomach.

As Lane had assumed, Jake had recognized Shirley leaving AJ's and took it upon himself to find her. A few of the times I'd seen him over the last few months, he'd really been up in Ligonier scoping her out, confronting her and not being able to appropriately put her in her place. He'd wanted to tell Lane in Miami, but Lane had become wholly focused on getting back to me.

I made slow circle eights on Lane's abs while I thought about how painful his and Jake's childhood must have been, and now another scab had been ripped off. Abruptly.

Shirley had never mentioned any of this to me. She'd probably thought that being able to watch Lane through my eyes—to see him succeed and fall in love—would ease her conscience. Jake had tried to tell her that was bullshit, but she wouldn't hear it.

As we lay quietly in bed, sneaking soft touches while we listened to Brooks snoring on the dog bed, I came to terms with losing the second person crucial to my staying sober. Who would be my rock now? I wasn't strong enough to do it on my own.

"I'm there for you now, Bess. And you're a lot stronger than you think," Lane said, turning to face me as he threaded his hand through mine.

"Did I say that out loud or are you a mind reader?"

"The latter. This evening started out about me supporting you, and ended with you taking care of me . . . again. I just want you to know that I'm right by your side, no matter what," he said before kissing me.

"I said it out loud."

He chuckled. "Yeah."

I ran my hand through his dark hair falling on his forehead. Seeing him with his head on my pale pink pillowcase, exposed and vulnerable, did something to my heart. I fell more in love.

"I love you, Mr. Wrigley."

"Lane," he said with a wry smile, reminding me of when we first met.

"Why me?"

"We were always meant to be, Bess. You were the bright yellow in my colorless, bland life."

And then he kissed me again, this time not stopping. With his hand traveling south, his fingers found me.

"Don't stop," I said, my breath coming in small pants as he stroked me.

He put another finger inside me as his thumb teased my sensitive spot, and I concentrated on pulling air in and out of my lungs.

"I believe you like calling me Mr. Wrigley," he teased, then nibbled on my neck.

My fingers dug into his back, scratching their way down to his ass as I called out his name with my orgasm.

The second his fingers left my body, I wanted something to replace them. Reaching down, I wrapped my hand around his erection, stroking up and down its length, my thumb smoothly grazing over the tip.

"Bess," he growled.

I didn't answer; instead I straddled his legs and guided him inside me. Exhaling a low moan, I sank all the way down.

"Come here," Lane demanded once I was seated on him. When I leaned forward, he took my mouth, sliding his tongue inside while his hand went to my hip, setting the pace at which he wanted me to move.

It was slow and languid. I pulled up and slid back down with the grace of a ballerina until Lane's hand held on for better purchase, encouraging me to go faster. With his hand bruising my side, I rode him like a stripper in Vegas.

Racing to the finish, not concerned when we would make love again because we knew we would—hoped that we would—we both hit our climax quickly, crying out into the night, squeezing out every last emotion of the day from each other.

As Lane spooned me, I let out a little sigh and said, "I've got to go back to work tomorrow, you know."

"Okay," he said easily as he slid his hand down my back, coming around from behind to tease my clit. "Are you sure I can't convince you otherwise?"

CHAPTER FORTY-SEVEN

bess
One month later

It was freezing. Snow whirled everywhere, the sky an angry gray landscape as I waited for Lane to get to my place. He'd just flown in that afternoon, and I almost couldn't breathe with want.

And worry.

And anticipation.

And lust.

Finally he'd walked through my door, bundled in his leather jacket and jeans with a wool scarf wound around his neck just so—not from the thrift shop, but Burberry. Although I loved teasing him about his expensive "country" wardrobe, I couldn't stop staring, or wishing I could rip them off right away. But we had a plan.

Over the phone last week, he'd agreed with some convincing to go to Pittsburgh on the Friday after Thanksgiving to see Jake. We'd even made a plan to meet my dad for coffee. My dad and I talked more often now, our more regular contact a salve for ancient but still-healing wounds.

But it was Jake I was most concerned about. He'd planned to be alone for Thanksgiving, insisting he didn't want to intrude on our first holiday together. I desperately wanted Jake to join us at May's place for the holiday dinner, but he was licking his wounds. With his past mistakes ripped wide open and oozing into everything in his life, he probably just needed for them to scab over. I hoped for his sake it was soon.

The clincher on Lane's giving in to seeing his brother was my agreeing to get a Christmas tree. Since we couldn't pick it up on the day after Thanksgiving, he was adamant about going the day before.

Which was why now, instead of getting naked and warm in the sheets, we were cruising down the mountain in my Jeep on a frigid Wednesday night. The church was having a fundraiser, selling trees and wreaths, and it seemed appropriate we go there. The night sky spread out above us as Lane navigated the winding mountain road, the moon low and full with a halo glowing around it. More snow was on the way.

A meeting was letting out as we parked the car. Stepping out into the night air, Lane squeezed my hand and then went rigid. I looked up to see what was wrong, and saw a small figure with a mass of red hair underneath a hat leaving the building.

"Come on, we'll come back," I said into Lane's shoulder.

"No, it's fine. I'm not letting her take away any more of my life," he said, pulling me toward the trees on display.

Scolding myself for wanting to turn around and see if she saw us, I kept walking. Sadly, I couldn't find compassion in my heart for Shirley, and neither could Lane. Maybe one day.

Life was better. I'd been going to morning meetings and only working the lunch shift—another change at Lane's insistence. He'd made sure I was enjoying myself, finding hobbies, volunteering at the rehab center.

But I loved this church; it would always have a special place in my heart for giving me sanctuary when I needed it most. And Shirley was part of that for a while, so it hurt when I thought about not being able to forgive her.

Lane stopped me and pulled me in for a hug. "Let it go. This is our time, and I'm not having her ruin it."

He truly was a mind reader.

I kissed him and whispered, "Love you," into his shoulder. Then spent the next half hour debating with him over which was the perfect tree.

Getting the tree home was a pain in the ass, but Lane insisted on tying it to the top of the car and lugging it in on his own. I helped drag it to the corner I'd cleared for it, and set about hanging all kinds of ornaments that had arrived via courier a few days before.

There were so many of them—shiny metallic lemons, fake dog bones with ribbons twisted around them, Labradors wearing Santa hats, plastic palm trees, and a billion sparkly balls of all shapes and sizes and colors.

CHAPTER FORTY-EIGHT

bess
Two weeks later

S NOW was coming down heavy again, sticking to any surface it found. Drifts of it had piled up on my porch, nearly blocking my front door, so I had to dig a passage for Brooks to get down to the yard so he could do his business. It was even deeper in the yard and he loved it, his tail wagging, brown eyes shining as he jumped and bounced through the drifts.

My man, Brooks Bailey. His life would be changing after the New Year. We were moving for a few months to Florida, a decision I'd made the Sunday after Thanksgiving, but still needed to get used to. It wasn't final, I wasn't selling my place, just trying out something new for a while. With Lane.

I wondered how Brooks would like the sand and warmth and constant sunshine, not to mention the noise and crowds. It was quite different from what he was used to here. It would be a big adjustment for him, and if I were honest, for me too.

Huddled on my porch with a scarf wrapped tightly around my neck, the wind blowing wet snow on my cheeks, I called for Brooks.

He was whooping it up, his paws cutting through the fluffy powder, throwing it high in the air until it came fluttering down on his head.

"Brooks, come on, baby," I yelled, and he came padding back to me. We walked through the door, and being the good boy he was, he shook off the snow while standing right on the towel I had laid out. And then he went and drank from the bottom of the Christmas tree.

We'd never had one before in this house. My dad and I always had a cheap artificial tree when I was growing up—typically a tiny thing on the table with gaudy white tinsel and lights that never worked quite right.

But there was nothing insignificant about the one that I had now. It stood regally in the corner by the window, holding its star up high, shimmering in all its glory. *Thanks to Lane.* Now those silver and red balls were shaking and shimmering in the light as Brooks turned around, his tail swishing against the tree.

Shivering, I put on the tea kettle just as my phone rang.

"Hello?" I said, not recognizing the number.

"Bess, it's James. How you doing, doll face?"

"Hey, James! Happy holidays!" I said, leaning my hip into the counter.

"Same to you, my love."

"So, what's up?" I said, waiting for the water to boil.

"Just checking in, saying hi. Are you all ready for the move?"

"James . . . spill!"

We'd become close since my last visit to Miami. Lane and I had gone to a Halloween party at the Dylan—I was trying to venture out—except it was way too wild and crazy for me. We left early, and James grabbed us a quiet table in the back of the restaurant where we shared coffee and dessert. When we were waiting for the car, James came to check on me, and I learned that he was in the program. He noticed my apprehension at being around all the craziness and nonstop partygoers, and recognized my nervousness for what it was.

The next day, I had a few hours while Lane went to the office, so I met James for a coffee at the News Café. Sitting outside, watching all the beach babes work out in the sand, we shared stories. A few days later, he took me to a local meeting and introduced me to a few others in recovery in the area. And we had stayed in touch, chatting about my move.

His newfound warmness toward me did not go unnoticed by Mr. Wrigley, but they set down their swords when it came to me.

James came clean, his voice interrupting my thoughts. "Ugh, love. Lane told me to check in on you while he's back in Madrid with the time difference."

I laughed as I pulled the whistling teakettle off the heat and filled a mug with steaming water. "Of course he did. I'm fine. The snow is coming down and I'm making tea."

"Life in the fast lane. So, what happened over Thanksgiving? You never told me. Did Lane and that hunk of a brother mend fences? How was your dad?"

I let out a sigh as I rubbed a hand across my temple, massaging away the headache about to come on. "Jake and Lane weren't great. They're at odds over the best way to leave everything in the past. Jake wants a sit-down with Shirley; he wants to hear her voice out loud her regret and guilt. Lane doesn't want to see her ever again. As for my dad, he and I are in an okay place. He feels bad about my childhood and is open to trying to reconnect slowly. And he understands it has to be on my terms."

"That's good," James said. "And you know Lane is nuts when it comes to you. That's why he has me checking on you . . . duh! He'll follow your lead with Jake, my love, you just watch. More important than all of that, are you ready to escape that shitty snow and come and live by me? Sand and surf twenty-four/seven?"

"I don't know. I'm sure I'll love the weather, but I'll miss my house . . . and work. I still don't know what I'm going to do down there, and it's worrying me. Do *not* repeat that to Lane," I warned him as I dipped my tea bag in my mug, letting the cranberry color seep out into the hot water.

"Well, that's the other reason why I'm calling. Lacey left, she's the other girl who helped at the desk, and since you have hotel hospitality experience and a marketing degree, doll, I recommended you. And management went for it."

Walking away from my tea, I began to pace my small kitchen with the phone tucked into the crook of my neck. "James! This reeks of Lane's doing!"

"Maybe a little," he said with a hint of a whine. "He did mention that you needed something. He knew you were obsessing over working, but this was all me. Think of how much fun we'll have, making fun of people the way I used to make fun of Lane!"

I couldn't help but laugh out loud. James did give Lane a healthy dose of banter, especially now that Lane had apparently settled down. It should bother me more—that playboy past—but I figured I got the real Lane. All of him, and that was way better.

As for the job, other than Camper and Jake, I didn't have many friends my age. Now I had James, and I could truly be myself around him. It was the perfect opportunity, and even though I was sure Lane had way more to do it with than James had let on, I said, "Okay! What do I need to do?"

Later that night I woke to something tickling my cheek. My breath caught in my throat as I was about to scream when I heard, "Shh, Bess, it's me," in the gravelly voice I loved.

I sat up in bed, my heart racing despite realizing Lane was the intruder. No wonder Brooks didn't bark.

"Hey," I said, swiping the hair off my face.

The bed dipped as he sat down next to me in the darkness, kissing his way up my cheek to my ear, where he nibbled on the lobe. "Hey, I missed you," he whispered.

"What are you doing here?" I reached around to his back, pinching him, making sure I wasn't dreaming.

"Ouch! I finished early and jumped on a flight."

His breath lingered over my lips. He was waiting to see if I needed to say anything else before he kissed me.

I didn't.

Pulling him down the rest of the way, I grabbed his hair and kissed the hell out of Lane Wrigley.

He didn't let me stay in control for long. After a toe-curling kiss, he stood up and quickly got rid of his clothes, his erection springing to life in front of me.

"Why, hello there," I joked from the bed, and started to pull my tank off and shimmy out of my boy shorts.

"Have some mercy," Lane said, setting a knee down on the bed. "I just flew back on an international flight and then drove another ninety minutes in the snow and sleet with a raging hard-on."

"Did you now?" I teased as he crawled over to me, whipping the blanket off me in one swoop.

"Lane! I'm cold," I said, laughing through my words.

"Not for long, love," was all he said before his face was between my legs, his tongue running a familiar path. And then he went back to teasing me, planting a path of kisses along my inner thigh, his breath barely coasting over where I wanted his mouth.

"Please," I pleaded.

He didn't make me beg. His tongue homed in on that special place, his finger dipped deep inside me, and I came apart. My body burst into flames, my heart beating too fast. Love and contentment ran through my veins, emotions I never thought I would feel like a normal woman, but I was.

"Want inside you," he said, bringing me out of my orgasm-induced haze.

"Mmm, me too," I murmured.

And then he was. To the hilt, before he pulled all the way out and slid back in again. He tortured both of us like this for a while. In and out, long and languid, his dick hitting every single nerve along my walls, our mouths staying together while our hips did a sensual dance.

"More," I whispered.

"More what," he asked as he slid all the way out, torturing me.

"You. Deep. Faster. Please, Lane," I said, giving in, saying what I wanted and couldn't wait for.

"Okay, baby." And he gave me everything I asked for.

EPILOGUE

lane
One year later

STEERING down our long driveway, snow and gravel crunching under the large tires, I maneuvered my enormous SUV through the dark. After five days abroad, I was fucking thrilled to be home.

As I pulled the car around the back of the house, I frowned as I took in the multitude of twinkling white lights covering the wraparound porch and knew who was inside waiting for me—all the way in quiet and quaint Ligonier.

Shit. I couldn't get away from that dapper little shit.

Slamming the truck into park in front of the garages, I jumped out in a hurry. There was someone I needed to get my arms around, and it wasn't him. Stepping into ankle-deep snow, my Prada boots sinking into the wet white slush, I made a mental note to move the garages to the top of the renovation list.

After unlocking the front door, I stomped my feet on the throw rug just inside the foyer, opening my mouth to yell, "I'm home," when I was greeted with a firm, "Hush!"

Narrowing my eyes, I turned to the man behind the bossy words . . . and glared.

But with Brooks nearly toppling over the small stack of Nikes at the door, panting and begging for me to pet him, I obeyed. I didn't dare make a sound. Not because of the jerk who told me to be quiet, but the only reason I ever needed to shut my mouth. And I wasn't happy about it.

Lowering my voice to a whisper, I said, "Hello, James. I see you've taken over my entire house."

Taking in his rumpled shirt and jeans, I gathered he'd been at it a while. Moving my sights to the roaring fire, hearing the Christmas music playing softly in the background, I shrugged my coat off and tossed it over the banister.

James brought his hands together in a quiet clap. "I know, aren't the lights outside fabulous? And the way they bounce off the snow? They're real beauts!" he said in an excited whisper.

A very quiet, "Yes. Fabulous," came out of my mouth as I feigned excitement. If I didn't compliment the man, I might never be able to move on to the real "beaut" of the house.

"Where's my girl?" I asked in a low voice.

"Which one?" he asked, softly chuckling.

"James," I hissed in a warning tone, losing my patience.

"Okay, okay. Bess is taking a bath, relaxing. I insisted she take some time for herself as soon as Madison went to sleep."

"Damn," I whispered, my suspicions confirmed. I wanted to hold my baby for just one minute when I got home.

James threw his arm around me. "Think of it this way—you get your wife all to yourself. Seriously, Bess tried to keep Mad awake as long as she could, but the little princess needed her beauty sleep." He winked and added, "You think those birth control pills are gonna work this time?"

"Enough," I growled, heading straight to the stairs.

"What? I was there, her only friend, working side-by-side with her. Who else was she going to call from the bathroom floor while she waited to drop the bomb on you?" he said, pretending to be coy.

Rolling my eyes, I brushed past him, pausing a moment to point at the dog and tell him to stay on the first floor. But the memory of that day was still burned in my mind.

"Bess?" I'd called as I came in from the garage, greeted only by the air-conditioning slapping me in the face. I'd called her name again as I headed down the hallway and up the stairs.

When I searched the upstairs, becoming more frantic the longer I searched, I breathed out a sigh of relief when I finally found her sitting on our bathroom floor.

"Hey, babe," I said, entering with caution. Her eyes were red and swollen, and her hair was a holy mess. Wearing only a tank top and boy shorts, with her sad tattoo on display, she was the picture of dejection.

"I'm sorry," she whispered, her eyes huge as she gazed up at me.

"For what?" Taking in the scene, it was pretty obvious, but who knew what was going through Bess's head.

"I'm p-pregnant," she stammered. "It's yours."

"Well, I should hope so." I sat down on the floor with her, settling right next to her as my suit pants wrinkled, but I didn't care.

"You're not upset?" she asked, flinging one of the sticks she'd peed on toward the wastebasket, but missing it.

"Whoa, why would you think that?"

Curious, I reached over to pick up the little pee stick and noted the pink plus. When I saw it, my heart swelled to what felt like twice its normal size. An intense sense of completion swept over me, a feeling of rightness that I never thought I'd experience. And it was all because of her.

She let out a little whimper. "Because you went from playboy to playing house with me, and now this—"

"Bess, stop."

With a practiced move, I reached out and took her hand, then guided it to my pocket. She knew the drill already and reached her hand inside when I said, "Take it out." When she slid her hand out, holding the ring, I took it from her and moved to one knee.

"Bess, will you marry me?"

That day was nearly a year ago. When I opened the door to our French country master bath tonight, floral-scented steam swirling around the large room, I was whisked back to the present—where my gorgeous wife lay naked in the tub in front of me. Her dark eyelashes fanned out over her cheeks as her head laid back against a small spa pillow—compliments of the WildFlower—and her arm was draped over the side of the tub.

On her hand was the ring I'd given her that day. The four-carat yellow diamond set in platinum was out of place in the middle of the wilderness where we currently lived, but Bess didn't care.

"I never want to forget this day," she'd told me that night after she got up off the bathroom floor. We'd had Chinese takeout outside by the pool, my hand resting on her still-flat belly. Looking at her hand, she'd said softly, "It's too much, but so, so, so pretty. Every time I look down, I'm going to think of kissing you for the first time . . . I don't know why, I just am. Maybe because that's when I gave you my heart."

As for hearts, Bess had owned mine since the day she seated me for breakfast and I realized she was still alive. Maybe even since she stank like holy hell and collapsed on me in yoga. I might have found redemption with Bess, but I also found life. Amazing how two people, both stuck in despair, could come together and emerge stronger from the darkest of times. But we did.

Thank fucking God I'd picked that exact day to propose marriage, otherwise Bess would have never gone for it. She would have been completely convinced I'd asked her to marry me because of the baby, and would have driven me fucking crazy with arguments and questions.

Since there were as many wedding planners as muscle heads in South Beach, we tied the knot that week; there was no reason to wait. We said "I do" on the tiny patio of the Dylan with our hammock swinging in the background and Bess's hair blowing in the ocean breeze. James was our only witness.

Seeing her currently naked, wet, and luscious in front of me, did I feel shortchanged in my time alone with Bess?

Of course.

Did I love anyone more than my daughter, Madison Jake Wrigley?

Absolutely not.

We named our daughter for Bess's former supervisor, Maddie, who had helped bring us together by insisting she meet me for dinner. And of course for my brother, who had forced us to reconnect when I'd given up, whether I liked it or not.

With a full head of soft, curly brown hair, perfect little hands, and blue eyes just like Jake and me, Madison stole my breath—and my heart—from the moment I first saw her image on the 3-D ultrasound.

"Hey, babe," Bess called to me, turning her head to the side and taking in my presence. Her voice was throaty and sultry.

Magnificent.

I sat on the edge of the tub in my suit, unbuttoning my shirt and pulling it off before I dipped my hands in the warm water and touched my wife.

"Hey." Thoroughly engrossed, I scooped up some bubbles, then slid them along her arm, over her side cleavage, and around her taut nipple.

"How was the trip?" she asked, leaning her head back, her eyes closing as I circled her nipple again.

"Good, closed the deal. So, James?"

She opened one eye. "Yeah, he didn't have anywhere to go for the holidays, so I invited him. And then the snow was coming, so he caught an earlier flight. He was just so excited . . . you know James."

I just nodded with a smirk. The guy had been torturing me for over a year, why should he stop now? What he wasn't going to do was stop me from making love to my wife.

Little prick—let him continue to decorate my house.

"Plus, he misses us," she added. "And he hasn't seen the house since we moved in and the kitchen was finished."

"I know," I grumbled, then leaned in and kissed her, the water sloshing on my pants.

"Want to come in? Mad is fast asleep after a big day of James and snow . . . and oatmeal cereal."

When she reached out and beckoned me, my gaze fell to her tattoo. It now had an added teardrop, and our initials in script inside each droplet. She said the eye was now "crying tears of happiness."

"Thought you'd never ask," I said while whipping off my pants and tossing them on the floor. The heated floor.

I might have bought a big old farmhouse, but I wasn't moving my family in until it had been updated. Bess liked living in Florida okay and all. But between the baby on the way and the party scene, it wasn't the best place for her.

For the first few months, she worked with James, fed her growing belly, and I continued to work with my therapist. Eventually I came to the decision to take Bess back north. She had a few friends up there and loved the quiet comfort of the woods. I was making peace with my past and thought it might be a good idea to be close to Jake, who was working hard at getting his shit together.

Once I was naked I slid in behind my wife, stretching my legs around her small frame, and she lay back against my chest and sighed.

"Ah, amazing." I relaxed and inhaled, breathing in my life. I felt like gasping for more and taking huge gulps; it would never be enough. Seeing Bess as a mom, watching her take pride in her new purpose—raising our daughter—made my heart beat and skip at the same time.

"The best," Bess said in a breathy voice.

I looked around at the high ceiling and the large frosted glass windows they put in during the remodel. The place was growing on me. The house didn't have the sleek modern comfort of Florida, but it had history, and its warmth seeped through your bones like hot chocolate on a cold day. I'd bought it back in early May, when Bess was getting close. She didn't know, but AJ's foreman, Jax, had put me in touch with a contractor who was able to rush the renovation for us, making it possible for us to move in right after the baby was born in July.

Watching a newborn Madison sleep on her momma's chest inside the cabin, I knew I'd made the better choice. Both my girls deserved peace and quiet to live. And the little country town was benefitting too with Bess as a regular speaker at the same rehab place she'd gone to.

She was so strong, the stronger of the two of us, and I wanted our daughter to have all of that strength in its fullness. Not clouded by the bright lights and plastic smiles of the beach.

Like the rumpled piles of shoes by the door and the goofy dog with a big wagging tail, this place was a crazy, wild home. It wasn't completely controlled and sterile, but I liked it more and more. My dad would have loved it here.

As my hair fell toward my face, reminding me of him, I smiled inside.

As for AJ, that fucker was still messed up and confused, but who the hell wasn't? Anyway, I was fine with him as long as he kept his distance. He'd called me after getting down to North Carolina to apologize.

I'd answered the phone with a hurried hello, and he'd said, "I know you know the program by now, so I gotta ask you for your forgiveness. Sorry, my man."

I didn't want to give it to him, but I knew Bess would be upset if I didn't. AJ deserved to stay clean and sober just like anyone else.

"Yeah, I got you," I said reluctantly. "Just do what you need to do."

"I loved her, man. I'm getting over it, but I want to know she's happy."

At this, I blew out a loud breath. "She's happy, having my baby."

"Shit . . ." he breathed out. And then he hung up.

"I missed you, Lane," Bess said, drawing me way out of my ill-timed and worthless thoughts of AJ.

Leaning in, I kissed her neck. "I know. I missed you and Mad. I have to go to California after the New Year, maybe you two will come?" I slid my hand down her side, under the water, and right to her center. She squirmed as I teased her, tickling her inner thigh, trying to get my hand where she wanted it.

"I like the beard, glad to see it's back," she said. I'd started to grow it before I left, but it had filled out while I was gone.

"I know you do. Want to feel it between your legs, babe?"

"Yes," she said as she jolted from my touch landing right on her clit. "Can we get out?"

"Why?" I taunted her.

"You know why. I want that."

"What?"

"Your beard in between my thighs, Lane," she barely rasped out, hoisting herself up and throwing her leg over the side of the tub, not bothering to wrap herself in a robe.

By the time I stood up, she was standing there impatiently with a towel, waiting for me to get out.

I quickly dried off and picked my wife up, carrying her to the king-sized sleigh bed. A moment later, we heard a crash of some sort on the first floor and both said, "James!" before ignoring it and going back to what we were doing.

And Bess got my beard in between her thighs. Tickling her in all the right places.

jake
Meanwhile . . . a few days later

The metal door clanked shut, the sound of its lock slamming into place echoed off the cold wall I currently leaned up against. As I pressed my back against the coarse cinderblock, reality hit me smack in the chest like a bullet train barreling through my heart.

Christ. Look at where I fucking landed after a whole goddamn year of trying to get my life in order, to heal past wounds and move forward.

Shit.

Did they hold mass in the slammer? Not that I was religious, but I would need someone like God on my side, because there was no way in hell Lane was coming to get me. Actually, for the first time ever, I told myself I wasn't calling him. I'd leaned on my twin brother for two decades too long. I'd only deserve whatever wrath he served up if I called him from the clink.

Again.

Forget it being fucking Christmas, he'd finally gotten his life together. He had a gorgeous wife, cute little baby daughter, a big house in the country, huge career, and lots of cash. He deserved to be left alone.

Me, I deserved this. I'd get to make one phone call, and it looked like it was going to be to that little wench—the same woman who landed me behind bars.

My frayed jeans tightened around my thick thighs as I slumped to the floor. I tilted my head back against the wall, rolling my neck. Taking a long breath, I noticed the guy opposite me—he was big, tattooed, hairy, and snarling at me.

I could fucking take him. Let him just try to approach me. *I own a gym, for Chrissake.*

"Jake Wrigley?" the guard yelled as he approached the holding cell. "Which one of you fools is Jake?" he asked as he shoved his key in the keyhole, eyeing me up and down. Nothing like a big-as-fuck black dude with his biceps bulging through his polyester uniform looking at me like he was thoroughly pissed.

Who shit in his eggnog?

I stood. "That's me." I ran my hand along my buzz cut and smoothed out my beard. "Time for my phone call?"

"Nah, man. DA's here to see you."

"Oh, good. Maybe he wants to go home to his family, and I'm gonna get out of here in time for the holidays," I said, then chuckled to myself.

"I wouldn't hold your breath, my man," the guard said, shoving me toward the next set of locked doors.

"Thanks, Paul, I got it from here," a soft feminine voice called out from behind us.

Sweet . . . a female guard.

"That's okay, Ms. Road. I'll make sure he gets to the interview room. This one here's a live wire," he said, keeping his hand on my arm as he escorted me forward, not allowing me to turn around.

To be continued . . .

Read more of Jake's story in:
Absolution Road
Coming late fall, 2015

EXCERPT

Read more of Rachel Blaufeld in *Electrified*, Book One in the
Electric Tunnel Series.

electrified

CARSON GRAHAM shifted into fourth gear as he hightailed it away
from the club toward his hotel. Why did he keep coming back to
Vegas? Who the hell knew. If there was one thing he didn't have any
trouble finding or getting, it was willing women.

He knew women weren't really "things." They were interesting,
often complicated creatures, and he both appreciated and respected
them. He just happened to like women in his bed who came with no
strings. It was the twenty-first century, after all, and there were plenty
of women who liked that kind of deal.

He had never settled down, and he sure as hell wasn't about
to start now. At closer to forty years old than thirty-five, he felt
the bachelor life suited him just fine. Or maybe it was that he only
deserved the single life. His particular circumstances hadn't exactly
set him up for success in the relationship department.

Picking up a little speed, he changed course and steered toward
the mountains, needing more time to clear his head.

It would be great to be on his motorcycle right now, to be able to
lean into the steep and winding curves, but it was back in his garage

on the East Coast, grounded—just like his life at the moment. The sports car he'd rented here in Vegas would have to do.

As he shifted the engine into fifth gear the car jetted forward, allowing the tension to bleed from him with the increased RPMs. He was trying to drive away from the pull as fast as he could; the pull coming from an insanely gorgeous stripper he was lusting after in a big way.

There was something magnetic about Sienna Flower, dragging him in deeper and deeper. More than her sleek, toned body and her sensual moves when she wrapped herself around the pole, there was a draw deeper than the physical. Carson wasn't a hard-up kind of guy. He never got like this over a woman. Ever.

Growing up without a mom, he was fairly certain there was nothing lasting about "love." If a mother could actually up and leave her child without any notice, like his did, there was no such thing as forever. His dad had done the best he could to be everything to Carson, but the fact remained: When a six-year-old's mother left and never came back, that fucked with a kid.

It fucked with a grown man too. As a result, Carson never considered love an option.

Lust, a few cocktails, dinner out, and then a good roll in Egyptian cotton sheets—that was Carson's modus operandi. He definitely didn't have any delusions of long-term love.

In reality, his thoughts on the subject of love didn't really matter. His lifestyle and career didn't allow for love; at least, that was what he told himself. After joining the FBI, he traveled all the time, leaving at a moment's notice on any number of classified assignments. He was wise enough to know the FBI lifestyle didn't lend itself to successful relationships, so he never pursued them. If he were honest with himself, he might admit maybe that was why he originally chose to take the FBI job, but who wanted to look that closely at their own motives?

He certainly couldn't be hunting down a suspect in a different time zone while pretending to be at a sales conference in Orlando when he called home in the wee hours of the night . . . or morning, depending on where he was.

Eventually all the lies, fibs, or whatever you wanted to call them caught up in a field agent's relationship. As a man who avoided conflict in his personal life for fear of being deserted, he knew the lying would eat away at him.

After cracking a high-profile missing person's case at the FBI a few years ago, Carson had struck out on his own. Going solo, he built his own firm, still traveling and having a grand fucking time doing what he did best, which was remaining uninterested in a long-term relationship. Now he was an independent private investigator, making his own rules, and it suited him just fine. His reputation followed him and he took the cases he wanted—except for this current bitch of a case—which allowed him to have a good time living life.

To most people, he introduced himself as a bounty hunter or some shit like that. No need to have every Tom, Dick, and Harry asking him to take this or that heartbreaking case. Carson worked, traveled, and enjoyed the finer things life offered. He liked getting paid too much to take on pro-bono cases.

Although his recent case was starting to feel like one . . . that and a big, annoying crock of shit.

A vibration in his pocket partially dragged him out of his funk. Holding the wheel steady with his knee, Carson pulled the phone out of his pocket and hit ignore. Speak of the devil who got him involved in this crap. His best friend, Alex. He should have answered; the guy's family had practically raised him. He owed him that but he wasn't in the mood, since it was Alex's fault that he'd taken this damned case.

Guilt overtook him as he traveled the long, dark desert road, and Carson dialed his friend back.

"Hey man, what's up?" He focused on the open road ahead of him, the mountains bleeding into the skyline, the moon lighting his way.

"Not much. Just checking in. Making sure my oldest friend is still alive and causing trouble wherever he may be at the moment."

"Yeah, yeah. All good here. Kicking around out west, trying to solve that shit case you sent me. Taking a much-needed break in

Vegas as we speak." He pushed his speed a little more, feeling the car purr.

"Way to make me jealous. I'm stuck at home watching the baby while my wife is out on a girls' night out, and you're probably on your way to getting laid. What's wrong with this picture?"

"Nah, Alex. You go be with your baby and let your wife have a good time. You're not missing anything. Except for a few strippers." He laughed out loud.

A small chuckle came from the other end. "I'm gonna get you for that one. Have some fun for me, will ya? Keep me updated on the case. I know I can't be much help, but if you need anything, let me know."

Carson chuckled. "I wish you could help with the case. It's turning into one hell of an adventure. I'm trying my best to help out your relative's friends, but for the first time I just don't know. Hell, listen to me rambling like I'm a spoiled bitch. Forget it, man. Go love your baby."

"Okay, but stay in touch, Carson. Don't go MIA so often."

"I hear ya."

As he disconnected, he thought about Alex's comment. Going MIA, doing his own thing, was part of who he was.

His current personal life lined up with his new career perfectly. He had a few women around the country who knew the 411 when it came to him. Lavish times with no commitment; that was how he rolled. Period.

Now here he was, rushing back to Vegas every weekend. Why? What the hell was the draw? Carson sighed because he knew damn well.

Sienna Flower, adult entertainer with moves that would ignite a dead man, and eyes like a virgin, making him feel like a young kid all over again.

Christ, he had a problem.

The case he was currently working was burning him up and playing with his mind, besides displacing him to the West Coast. Although the job was lining his bank account—even at his lowest rate—it was taking much longer than he expected. He needed it to be over.

Am I losing my touch already?

He sighed and turned the car back toward the Strip while something nagged at his gut over this assignment. There was something odd, some piece of the puzzle missing, which was why the case was taking longer than expected.

What was wrong with him that he couldn't find it? What was he missing?

It was a first for him, and he didn't like it. Not. One. Fucking. Bit. Which was why he found himself running off to Sin City every weekend.

He needed to let off steam, and where better to do so than Las Vegas? It was an occupational hazard of his . . . letting loose. Going back to his FBI days, Carson always needed a little fun, a tiny walk on the wild side to let go of the stress of the job. Otherwise, he lived and breathed his cases, working late into the night to solve them.

He needed a good time to release the pressure, which he currently was finding at the Electric Tunnel, but the pressure only mounted more after visiting the club. What originally started out as a method to clear his head and make way for him to solve the case, was clouding his judgment even more.

Sienna Flower had happened . . . that was what.

His latest client—or *clients*, since it was a married couple—was able to pay him. Yeah, they were making good on his rates, but their friends raised the funds, not them. They were willing to keep transferring money to him, yet he didn't like the eerie feeling that had begun to dog him. They were lying to him. Withholding information, at the very least.

For the first time ever, Carson was considering giving up the case. The only thing that stopped him was the worry that nagged him over the missing person he was hunting down.

Shit, I'm going soft.

He was turning into an emotional cream puff, which was a bigger occupational hazard than having a grand time in Vegas.

Originally, he'd needed a respite from the bone-deep worry that something was terribly wrong with the case, so he started heading to Sin City for the weekends. Now, his gut was messed up from the case *and* his head was fucked up from a stripper.

The family who had hired him was pretty certain their missing relative had fled out west or thereabouts. Why were they so convinced of that theory? Carson had been stuck scouring small towns for the last month and a half. He didn't like small towns with strange people all up in each other's business. Almost as little as he liked the case.

He was starting to need his weekly adventure to Vegas by Tuesday of each week. It was a place where he could disappear and enjoy himself for forty-eight hours. After all, he was still a man with baser needs.

The problem all began when he went to check out the infamous Sienna Flower the first night he got to Vegas. He hadn't been able to tear himself away from her image, nor enjoy himself at all since that night. He couldn't figure it out. He'd had many women over the years—gorgeous, seductive, exotic women when he was traveling—and now he was stuck on some Vegas showgirl. No, not a showgirl. Exotic dancer.

Carson downshifted the car as the lights of the Vegas Strip came into view, rolling around what little he knew about her in his head. Nothing about her made sense. She'd arrived on the scene a few years back, and before long became the biggest thing Vegas had seen in years. She didn't do private rooms or parties. Ever. Asher Peterson, king of the adult dance club world, pulled her from lap dancing after only a year of dancing at the Tunnel. Now all she did was grace billboards, shake her ass onstage, and bring millions of dollars into the club.

He knew all this from Google. Fuck, after the first night seeing her, he couldn't get her tits, firm ass cheeks, and electrifying eyes out of his mind. He'd Googled her like a horny teenager, and decided she must have been a local Asher had taken a liking to.

Were they romantically involved? Was Asher tapping that?

And why was he even thinking about Sienna's potential bed

partners? He was fairly certain that wasn't a role even he could fill.

Do I want to?

Unfortunately, Carson had developed a nasty habit of heading to the Tunnel every Thursday through Saturday nights for the last month. Tonight was no different. He went to see Sienna dance. Then he left to go back to his hotel to either pick up someone in the hotel bar or jack off. Lately, his preference was to stroke himself to recent memories, those of a striking, gorgeous, naturally curvy woman with a heady combination of innocence and salacious moves.

He might as well have been in high school all over again, lusting after the prom queen, not knowing what to do about it other than rub one out.

This evening was different, though, because he had felt Sienna lock gazes with him. She looked right out at him as her act ended. She was smiling, but he could see right into her eyes. She was examining him back as though she wanted to know more about him.

It was disturbing on so many levels. He was a private eye. He should be able to read people. Yet she seemed to be reading *him*, looking deep within him.

He couldn't begin to figure out Sienna Flower, and now she was trying to figure him out? The thought made him harder than he normally was when he exited the club. Tonight he was practically limping as he walked out.

He needed to get laid, stop coming back to Vegas, and leave his thoughts of Sienna Flower at the door.

Of course, he knew he'd be back at the same place tomorrow night with his eyes homed in on one stripper, his dick standing at attention. Weeks ago, he'd paid the concierge at his hotel extremely well to keep him on the weekend list for the Tunnel. Open ended. No need to waste that.

Leaving his rental sports car at the front of his hotel with the valet, Carson bypassed the gaming tables and slot machines and went straight to his favorite bar for a drink. He grabbed a seat at the far end of the bar and nodded at the bartender, Victor, who now viewed him as a regular and brought him a drink without his even needing to order. Top-shelf scotch on the rocks.

Fuck, he was officially a Vegas groupie. The valets knew him, the bartender knew his drink and had it ready as soon as he stepped foot in the lounge, the front desk gave him the same room each weekend, and he was lusting after a woman who starred in Lord only knew how many other men's fantasies.

If his FBI buddies caught wind of this, they'd never let him live it down. Most of them were settling down, either resolving themselves to living double lives, or trading in their FBI badges for white-collar jobs. Not Carson, he was living the dream. Fast cars, motorcycles, big money, booze, high-end escorts—or dancers, depending on how you looked at it—and his current bullshit case.

He needed to relax and get a handle on all this shit. Carson caught Victor's eye and then lifted his chin, smiling when Victor made his way over to him.

"Hey, Vic, how's it shaking? You got any cigars back behind the bar, or do I have to move my ass to a special bar to smoke one?"

Victor chuckled as he wiped his hands on a bar rag. "You're in luck, buddy, this is Vegas, where anything goes. I just happen to have a few select ones in a humidor under the bar. Let me grab it and you can pick your poison."

Moments later Carson inhaled deeply, scotch in one hand, a fresh cigar in the other, his view on the casino floor. Actually, he was relaxing for the first time all week, coming down from his dark mood, and found himself not wanting another woman. He wasn't even sure if he wanted to take care of himself either, which was new.

Surprised at that revelation, Carson decided he was content to only finish his drink and cigar before heading upstairs to go straight to sleep.

There was always the promise of tomorrow night, and Sienna locking eyes with him again.

ACKNOWLEDGMENTS

My acknowledgments could be a very, very long novella on their own. I hate leaving anyone out, and there are so many people I need to thank—thoroughly.

Let's start with my editor.

To Pam Berehulke – Love, adore, and need you all day, every day, 24/7 to clean up my über-lyrical purple prose. But I love the color purple, and italics, and ellipsis marks . . . and you.

On a much more serious note, Pam, you know what your virtual red pen means to me, and I couldn't do any of this without you. Nothing makes me happier than a little praise from you in tracked comments or our late-night chats about whatever is on our mind. Here's to many, many more.

To Sarah Hansen – Best words I ever spoke to you—"DO NOT LISTEN TO ME!" Thank you for taking me on and being way more creative than I am.

To my betas on this project –

Robin B. – Your colorful commentary and daily texts make writing a book worth it. I meant it when I said we met through the most uncomfortable circumstances, yet you became irreplaceable.

Stacey P. – When you don't like something, I ax it . . . and then you send cupcakes. This equals perfection.

Debra D. – Your need for perfection rivals mine. Having you

as a part of this project was phenomenal. One day we will have our much-needed phone call.

Jennifer W. – When you read, I hold my breath for hours waiting for a message. But it works and in the end, you're always right.

And Queen V. – I cannot do anything without your smiling face, sweet words, and encouragement. You rule my world!

As for all of you, you outdid yourselves and really pushed me to put my best story forward. For that, I am forever indebted to you in coffee, wine, and pictures of hot men. Thank you so very much.

To my family – All of you—immediate, extended, not even blood-related—thank you for sticking by me, believing in me, and buying my books. And even reading them.

To my kids – Can you throw your dirty clothes down the laundry chute? Thanks. And do not read this.

To my author friends – Debra Doxer, Nicole Jacquelyn, Heidi McLaughlin, Ilsa Madden-Mills, S.L. Scott, Joanne Schwehm, and Madeline Sheehan – Thanks so much for all your author/writing/general bullshit support.

To Fabiola Francisco and Christy Pastore – Without all the virtual cocktails, late-night chats, and endless ramblings on manly muses, where would I be?

To Susan Ward – Thanks for talking me down off the mountain and your endless stream of stats and algorithms. Are you sure you're not my mom?

To Becca Manuel – You're like a little angel who came into my life. Thank you for taking the story in my head and making it a movie.

To Emily Tippetts – You rock. Especially at three a.m. while I'm uploading my book.

To the bloggers – There are so many wonderful bloggers who take hours out of every day to share covers, blurbs, and reviews. You make teasers, run contests, and support the independent community for very little in return. Thank you. Special thanks to Heather Maven, *Love Affair with Books*, *Love N. Books*, *Twin Sisters Rockin' Book Reviews*, Maryse, Gitte and Jenny of *Totally Booked*, *Under the Covers*, *Fresh Fiction*, Michelle Kannan of *All Romance Reviews*, *Lovely Ladies & Naughty Books*, *Smutty Book Friends*, *Romance at Random*, Jennifer of *The Starlets*, *Southern Belle Book Blog*, and *Kris and Vik Book Therapy Cafe*. XOXOXO

To Chas of *Rockstar Lit* – I fucking adore you.

To Stef, for the donut deliveries and cocktails; to the Hummus Hustler, for Greek Gourmet Buffalo Hummus; and to The Coffee Tree Roasters, for providing me with a quiet corner when I desperately needed it. To Lisa, for reminding me to breathe deeply.

And to YOU, the readers – Thank you so much for all the messages and kind words. Getting a little e-mail or message from you makes my day. Seriously, you should see how I start jumping around!

So if you liked this book, feel free to leave a review where you bought it or on Goodreads. Send me e-mail when you do, and I will thank you personally!

Please connect with me on:
www.rachelblaufeld.com
www.facebook.com/rachelblaufeldtheauthor
twitter.com/rachelblaufeld

ABOUT THE AUTHOR

Rachel Blaufeld is a social worker/entrepreneur/blogger turned author. Fearless about sharing her opinion, Rachel captured the ear of stay-at-home and working moms on her blog, *BacknGrooveMom*, chronicling her adventures in parenting tweens and inventing a product, often at the same time. She has also blogged for *The Huffington Post*, *Modern Mom*, and *StartupNation*.

Turning her focus on her sometimes wild-and-crazy creative side, it only took Rachel two decades to do exactly what she wanted to do—write a fiction novel. Now she spends way too many hours in local coffee shops plotting her ideas. Her tales may all come with a side of angst and naughtiness, but end lusciously.

Rachel lives around the corner from her childhood home in Pennsylvania with her family and two dogs. Her obsessions include running, coffee, icing-filled doughnuts, antiheroes, and mighty fine epilogues.

9 780991 592852